Lightning
in the
Blood

Lightning in the Blood

Gregory S. Fallis

St. Martin's Press
New York

Design by Diane Stevenson/SNAP·HAUS GRAPHICS

Library of Congress Cataloging-in-Publication Data

Fallis, Greg.
   Lightning in the blood / Gregory Fallis.
      p.   cm.
   ISBN 0-312-09340-3
   I. Title.
   PS3556.A39L5   1993
   813'.54—dc20   93-15047
                                           CIP

First Edition: June 1993

10 9 8 7 6 5 4 3 2 1

To Ruth Greenberg and Mona Danner
an stiúir agus crann

Lightning
in the
Blood

K e v i n   S w e e n e y

Thursday Morning

When the telephone rang at three A.M., it was Mary Margaret
who vaulted from the bed and rushed to the kitchen to answer
it, clutching at her fuzzy robe and whispering bits of prayer as
she went. I heard her muffled voice, then the sound of the
receiver chunking down on the kitchen counter, and then she
came whisking back to the bedroom.

I put the pillow over my head.

"It's Joop," she said, getting back into bed.

I peeked out from under the pillow. "What's he want?"

"God only knows," she said. "I didn't ask."

I forced myself out of bed, grabbed the robe, and stumbled into the kitchen. I shielded my eyes against the glare of
the twenty-five-watt bulb and cursed Joop. While I was at it,
I cursed Mary Margaret too, for thinking a telephone in the
bedroom is an extravagance.

"Joop," I said, "this had better be good."

"Well, I don't know if it's what you'd call *good*," Joop
said. He has one of those Southern accents where you're
never really sure when he's serious. "But it's *interesting*.
Anka Stiffel has got herself arrested."

I nearly asked who Anka Stiffel was. But I was just awake
enough to know that if I asked, Joop would tell me, and the
truth was I really didn't want to know who she was, let alone
why she'd been arrested. At that hour I wouldn't have cared
if the British Army had kicked in the rectory door and dragged
away poor Father Hannan, and him eighty years old.

"I just got a call from Kath O'Mara," Joop said. "She just
got a call from a woman who says she's a friend of Anka
Stiffel, and this woman says *she* just got a call from Anka her

own self, who is at the police station. Did that make sense?"

"Woman got arrested, she called a friend, who then called Kathleen, who called you," I said. "And now you're calling me."

"That's right. Nothing gets by you, does it, Kevin."

"At three in the morning, you're calling me."

"Is that what time it is?"

"That's what time it is here."

"Oh. Did I wake you up?"

I closed my eyes. "Joop, why are you calling?"

"Well, Kath, being the good lawyer she is, is heading down to the station to make sure Stiffel doesn't say anything stupid. And she thought maybe she ought to have an investigator along. You know, just in case."

"Then go with her," I said.

"I'm going to. I just thought maybe you'd like to tag along too. It being Anka Stiffel and all."

I struggled against my curiosity, knowing all along I was going to give in. It's the detective's curse: I had to ask the question. "Who is Anka Stiffel?"

"Anka Stiffel," he said. "You know, the poet."

"The poet?"

"A person who writes poetry."

"I know what a poet is," I said. "What I don't know is why I should care if this particular poet gets arrested."

"My, you get a tad cranky at three A.M., don't you, Kevin."

"I do when I'm called from my warm bed and asked to go to the police station to see a poet I've never heard of."

"Well, when you put it like that," Joop said.

"What's so special about Anna—what was her name?"

"Anka Stiffel. She's a famous lesbian poet."

"A famous lesbian poet."

"Well, maybe not exactly *famous*."

"Not exactly?"

"Kath said she's pretty well known," Joop said. "In the poetry world. Whatever that is. I think Kath said she had something published in *The New Yorker* a while back."

"I've never in my life read *The New Yorker*," I said.

"Ah. That accounts for your attitude. I don't read a lot of lesbian poetry my ownself. Or any other kind. But I thought you might know her. Since you read a lot of poetry, I mean."

"Joop," I said, "I've never heard of a poet named Anka Stiffel, lesbian or otherwise. And Joop? I don't want to hear any more about her. And Joop? There's nowhere on earth I want to go right now except back to bed. And Joop? Even if I wanted to go somewhere right now, I guarantee you it wouldn't be the police station."

"Kevin Sweeney, I declare you must be jaded something terrible," Joop laughed. "We're talking caged lesbian poets here. Which isn't the sort of thing a Southern boy happens across very often."

I smiled, but tried not to let it show in my voice. "Joop, I'm going back to bed now."

"You sure?"

"Good night, Joop."

"Okay," he said. "I'll just go ahead on with Kath. I'll see you at the office in the morning and let you know what happened."

"You do that, Joop."

"Sorry I woke you up."

"It's okay."

"Say good night to Mary Margaret for me," he said.

I promised I would and hung up. The clock over the stove read three-ten. I found some iced tea in the refrigerator and drank it straight out of the pitcher, which I can only do when Mary Margaret isn't watching. She says it isn't sanitary. I've asked her to explain how drinking from the pitcher is less sanitary than some of the other ways we swap bodily fluids, but she says it's not the same. And who can argue with that?

I switched off the light, found my way back to bed, and spooned up against Mary Margaret.

"What did Joop want?" she asked, sleepily.

"Some poet has been arrested."

"Really? Who?"

"Woman named Anka Stiffel."

"Stiffel? What kind of name is that?"

"Lesbian."

"What did she do?" Mary Margaret asked. "To get arrested."

"I didn't ask." I gave her a good-night-again kiss on the shoulder and another on the neck. She rolled over and kissed me back. Then gave me a second, more careful kiss.

"You've been drinking tea out of the pitcher again, haven't you, Kevin Sweeney," she said.

I kept quiet. You do enough criminal-defense work, you learn never to admit to anything.

Joop Wheeler

Thursday Morning

I dearly love my work. Name me another job where you get paid—*paid,* mind you—to talk to lesbian poets at police stations at a quarter to four in the morning and I'll buy you a hat.

Of course, I've never much cared for police stations, never mind the hour. Too many guys with short hair wearing uniforms and carrying weapons. Though at least at three forty-five in the A.M. all the bureaucrats are home asleep. So I didn't have to dick around very long. Which is what I usually have to do at police stations.

After examining my detective's license like a Third World customs agent, a tired-eyed cop led me down a drab hallway to an interview room. Another cop with equally tired eyes sat outside the door, thumbing through yesterday's paper. I guess he was guarding the door. God only knows what he was supposed to be guarding it against.

Inside the room Anka Stiffel and Kath O'Mara were sitting at a stained and battered old table. Kath wore a pair of faded jeans and an old Boston University sweatshirt. She looked more like a student than a kick-ass criminal lawyer. Which is what she is. Her long black hair was pulled back in a loose bun that was either fashionable or messy, I couldn't tell which.

Anka Stiffel, on the other hand, was just plain messy. Her hair stuck up in funny places and her clothes looked like they'd been slept in. She smelled of stale sweat. Sort of a locker room–gym sock aroma.

I'd assumed Anka Stiffel was going to be about half scared and semi-dazed. Most folks are when they get themselves arrested. But this woman looked downright feral.

When I was a boy down in South Carolina, I'd go out some nights when my uncle Amos was running his coon hounds. That's how Anka Stiffel looked. Like a treed raccoon. Like she was right there on the ragged edge of madness. Turned out she was over the edge.

Kath gave me a grim smile and waved me into a chair. "Anka, this is Mr. Wheeler of G & H Investigations. He's one of the private detectives I told you about."

"No men," Anka said. "No men." She waved her hands in front of her. Like she was warding off mosquitoes or doing some sort of weird semaphore signal.

She had scars on her wrists. Lots of them. Most were thin, whitish lines crossing her wrists. But on each wrist she also had a jagged, lengthwise scar. The type you only see on folks who are seriously suicidal and know what they're doing. You really want to kill yourself, you don't cut crossways. You cut lengthwise down. Or up. Either direction will do the trick. Otherwise you have to saw your way through the muscle. It's like cutting steak across the grain.

Kath reached across the table and touched one scarred wrist. "Anka, listen to me," she said. "Listen to me. It doesn't matter if they're men. We have to have investigators. And I have to use somebody I can trust. I've worked with these men before and I trust them."

Anka pulled her arm away and covered her eyes.

I leaned back in my chair. You walk in on some pretty confusing scenes in this work. But this was a tad odd even for the police station at four in the morning. I looked a question at Kath. And she picked up on it right away.

"This is what we've got," she said to me. "Anka was brought in yesterday morning on a disturbing-the-peace charge. A few hours ago she was also charged with attempted murder. After they sort matters out, there will probably be more charges."

"What happened?" I asked.

"Anka's ex-lover . . ."

Anka made a protesting noise.

Kath shrugged. "Amanda Owen, the woman Anka lived with up to a week ago. She was found unconscious in her back yard yesterday morning by a neighbor. She'd apparently been beaten in the head. Looks like she might not make it."

"But I didn't do it," Anka said, looking up. She glanced in my direction for about half a second, then turned back to Kath. "I didn't. I'm sure I didn't. I wouldn't have left her like that, like a slab of meat. The cats would eat her." She looked in my direction, but focused on my shoulder. "We have four cats," she said. "Maya, Sweetie, Spud, and Grimalkin."

"They sound real nice." I smiled. I was beginning to smell an insanity defense cooking. "A cat's name is important."

Anka turned her eyes up to a corner of the ceiling. She moved her lips, frowned, and then said "No," the way a parent would say it to a child who willfully refused to obey.

Kath watched her for a moment, then took a deep breath and patted her on the hand. "Like I said, Anka and Amanda split up about a week ago. Last night they apparently got into an argument in a bar and, according to the cops, Anka threatened to kill Amanda." She looked at her notes. "Uh, 'I'll bash your head in,' or words to that effect."

I considered this for a moment. "Do you mean 'last night' last night? Or Tuesday night 'last night'?" It's easy to get confused at four A.M.

"Tuesday night."

I looked to Anka for confirmation or denial. She shifted her eyes from the ceiling to the palm of her hand. She pinched her hand very hard several times.

"They got anything else?" I asked.

"That's all I know so far," Kath said. "I'm certain they have more." She turned back to Anka. "I've been explaining to Anka that the police will be taking her to the Women's

House of Correction pretty soon. I'd like you to call her therapist." She scribbled a telephone number on a piece of paper
and handed it to me. "Her name is Dr. Leah Rifkin. Would
you call her and tell her what's going on? See if she'll agree
to meet with us tomorrow." She frowned and shook her head.
"Strike that. See if she'll meet with us later today."

"You want me to call her now?" I asked. "It's four in the
morning."

"Call her now," Anka said quietly. "Right now. Leah will
know what to do. I'm going to need something. It always gets
worse when I'm in trouble."

"What gets worse?" Kath asked.

Anka shook her head. "Call her now," she said.

Kath looked at me, then nodded.

"On my way," I said. The cop in the hall was drinking
coffee from a foam cup. He'd finished the newspaper and was
working his way through an old copy of *Sports Illustrated*. He
barely glanced at me as I stepped out the door.

"Excuse me," I said. "Is there a private phone I can
use?"

He looked up from the magazine, looked at me like he
was trying to decide if I was trying to trick him, then shouted,
"Marty!"

A man in a Red Sox jersey stepped out of an office down
the hall. "The hell are you shouting for?" he asked. He looked
like he might have played some college football—the broken-
nose style played by some of the littler schools.

"Man here wants to use a private phone," the cop said.

"Well, Jesus Christ, you don't have to wake the fuckin'
dead, do you?" The man frowned and waved for me to join
him. His office didn't have room for much more than him and
his desk. He stuck out his hand. "Marty Coyle," he said.

I shook his hand. "Joop Wheeler."

"You're the guy works with Kevin Sweeney? How's he
doin', Sweeney?"

"He's doing okay. Says he's starting to lose half a step, but I don't see it."

Coyle laughed. "If Sweeney's dropping half a step, it's so he can get behind somebody, kick 'em in the ass."

"That's the boy," I said.

"He was a good cop, Sweeney. And his father and his brother Emmett too, that got killed overseas. All of them, good cops."

"I'll tell him you said that. He'll appreciate it."

"What can I do for you?" Coyle asked. "You say your name is Joop?"

I nodded.

"The hell kind of name is that?"

"It's a dog's name, is what it is."

"No shit?"

"No shit. I used to have this dog when I was a kid," I said. "Nice dog. Bluetick hound. We went everywhere together, me and this dog. His name was Joop and whenever anybody would call him, I'd come too. It got so I started answering to the name even when the dog wasn't around. Folks took to calling me Joop. Which is a hell of a lot better than Wendell. Which is what my folks named me. Wendell Joseph Wheeler."

Coyle grinned and shook his head. "Well, what can I do for you, Joop?"

"I need a private phone to call our client's therapist."

"Somebody better be callin' somebody," he said. "She's pretty wacked out, that one. We're puttin' her on a suicide watch once we get her over to the House." He pointed at the telephone on his desk. "There you go. Don't be lookin' at nothin' on the desk and come see me soon's you're through." He left the office and closed the door behind him.

I stood there about half stunned that a cop—a detective, no less—would leave me alone in his office. With files on the desk. Had to be because of Sweeney. Friends in high places.

I pulled the phone across the desk and dialed the number. A calm, sleepy woman answered. I asked to speak with Dr. Rifkin and wasn't at all surprised to learn that I was. There was a lack of tension in her voice that told me she was used to getting phone calls at all hours. It's only folks with weird jobs that don't panic at early-morning phone calls.

"Dr. Rifkin, my name is Joop Wheeler. I'm sorry to wake you like this, but I'm a private detective working for Kathleen O'Mara. Ms. O'Mara is an attorney representing a woman who says she's a patient of yours. A woman named Anka Stiffel."

"Anka? Is she okay?"

"No ma'am, I'm afraid she's not." Would I be calling at this hour just to tell you she was okay? I asked myself. "She's at the police station. She's under arrest."

"Under arrest?" A note of distress entered her voice. "On what charge?"

"Attempted murder," I said.

"Attempted mur— Was it Amanda Owen?" she asked.

"Yes ma'am, it was." I couldn't see any reason not to confirm it. But I didn't ask how she knew. I didn't *think* the police would listen in on the conversation. But there's no point in being stupid.

"Is Amanda okay?" she asked.

"Well, ma'am, I don't know. But like I said, Ms. Stiffel has been charged with attempted murder. So I suspect Amanda's not okay." Dr. Rifkin might sound calm, but she obviously wasn't thinking too clearly. Not that many folks would at four in the morning. "Of course, that's just a guess."

"Do you know if Anka is hallucinating?" she asked. "Has she made any attempt to harm herself?"

"She hasn't tried to hurt herself that I know of," I said. "But I just got here. As far as hallucinating goes, who knows? I can tell you she keeps looking at the ceiling like there's somebody up there."

"You say you work for her?"

"For her attorney, yes ma'am."

"You're not a police officer?"

"No ma'am."

"May I come see her?"

"Probably wouldn't be much point right now," I said. "She's going to be transferred to the House of Correction pretty soon. That's what the folks here call the jail. You'll probably want to wait and see her there."

"Will you have them watch her closely?" she asked. "Anka could be dangerous to herself."

I told her the jail staff had already been alerted and Anka would be placed on a suicide watch.

"Good. I'll want to see her lawyer as soon as possible."

I assured her we'd like to speak with her as well. After giving her Kath's office number and apologizing again for waking her, I hung up and went to look for Detective Coyle.

He was down the hall in a small lounge area, drinking coffee and eating what looked like a banged-up cheese Danish. He offered me a cup of oily-looking coffee. I took it all the same. Never hurts to be polite, is what my old momma taught me.

"Get a hold of your shrink?" he asked.

I told him I had. I sipped the coffee. Which was only lukewarm, but stronger than rent.

He looked at me for a moment. Like he wanted to ask about the conversation, but knew I wouldn't answer. So he made a face at his coffee. Which deserved it.

"Now you're gonna try to sleaze some information out of me, right?" Coyle asked. "Like what we got, who we got it from, that sort of thing? Am I right?"

"That's the plan," I smiled.

Coyle frowned at his coffee again. Then he nodded and said "Right. What we got is this." He ticked the points off on his fingers. "We got one dyke what had her head caved in with some sort of statue thing, looking like she might croak any minute. We got the statue that did the cavin' in. We got your dyke"—he jerked his thumb in the direction of the interview room—"who we're told couldn't get her face 'tween the first dyke's legs no more. We also got your dyke hidin' out at the Roadhouse Motel under an assumed name and actin' so damn crazy that the manager has to call the cops, get her out. On top of that, we got a whole bar full of dykes who heard your dyke say she was gonna bash in the other dyke's head. So there you go."

"See how it works," I said. "And folks say it's tough to get a cop to talk."

Coyle made another face. "What the hell. Your lady lawyer would be gettin' it all eventually anyway, soon as we get the reports all typed up and over to the DA's office. No point in us tryin' to piss on each other."

"Sweeney says the whole process is a pissing match," I said.

"He ain't far from wrong, Sweeney." Coyle sipped his coffee. "Listen, I got a question."

Here it comes, I thought. Time to pay for the use of the office and the information. "Shoot," I said.

"What would you call a group of dykes? You know, like a pride of lions, a gaggle of geese. Like that." He seemed seriously puzzled. "Best I can come up with is a henhouse of dykes, which don't really work. You know what I mean?"

I swirled the coffee around in the foam cup and watched it. "Is this what happens to a person who works nights too long?" I asked.

Coyle grinned. "Hey, guy's got to do something to stay awake."

I fought off a yawn. "Why would you *want* to stay awake?" I asked.

"Hey, I figured you guys were used to this. Gettin' up early, followin' cheatin' husbands and all that."

I shook my head. "Anybody cheats this early in the morning isn't going to get caught by me," I said. "Husband or wife."

After a few minutes I thanked Coyle for the coffee and the information and headed back to the interview room. When I left, Coyle was just sitting there, staring at his coffee cup. Maybe thinking about the case. Maybe trying to figure out a collective term for lesbians.

Kath raised her eyebrows when I walked in. Anka didn't seem to notice I'd come back. She was standing in the corner of the interview room, softly slapping her hand against the wall.

"I spoke with Dr. Rifkin," I said to Anka. "She'll meet you later this morning. After you've been transferred to the jail."

"Good," Kath said. "While you were gone, Anka told me she might have an alibi witness."

"Yeah?" This was good news.

"A woman she spent the night with. Or part of the night."

"Great. What's her name?" I asked.

Kath made a face. "Anka doesn't seem to remember."

I nodded. I guess I've heard that line—or one just like it—about eighty million times. Give or take.

Kath turned back to Anka. "Anka, is there anything you can remember about this woman? Anything at all?"

Anka put her hands over her ears. "No," she said. "I won't do it."

"Won't do what?" I asked. When she didn't answer, I turned to Kath. Who looked back at me and shrugged.

Anka began to shake her head, her hands still held over her ears. "No, leave me alone. I won't do it. I won't."

I don't know who she was talking and listening to, but it sure wasn't us. It's a tad spooky, being in a room with a person who can see and hear things I can't.

I'd started to fill Kath in on my chat with Dr. Rifkin, including the fact that she'd guessed the name of the victim, when there was a knock on the door.

Marty Coyle peeked his head in. "Counselor, we're just about ready to go here, it's okay with you. You think maybe you could finish up?"

Kath nodded slowly. "I think we're done here," she said. She looked at me. "Is there anything else you want to ask?"

There was. But I just shook my head. I wanted to know who or what Anka was talking to. But I didn't even know how to frame the question.

Kath stood and touched Anka on the shoulder. She explained again that the officers were going to take her to the Women's House of Correction. She told Anka she should be polite and cooperative with the police, but should not answer any questions or discuss her case with anyone. Kath might as well have been talking to a stump.

Coyle nodded to somebody in the hall and a woman officer stepped in. She spoke gently to Anka for a few moments, then cuffed Anka's hands in front and led her out of the room. Coyle held the door and snuck a peek at Kath's ass as she walked out. He made a silent whistle and winked at me.

I followed him out of the room. "Coyle?"

"Yeah?"

"How about this? A rage of lesbians."

Coyle let his grin widen. "I like it," he said. "Your mother must have been Irish."

I walked Kath to her car. It was a perfect late-summer morning. The sky was beginning to lighten and turn that early-morning shade of blue. It's not really blue. Or purple. It's one of those colors that don't have a name. You see it more in New England than in South Carolina. If you ever get up that early.

I wanted to point out how pretty the sky was. But I knew

it would seem insensitive while Anka Stiffel was being hauled off to jail. I like to think I'm as sensitive as the next guy.

It was too bad, though. The sky was real pretty.

Kath put her briefcase on the hood of her car and leaned against it. I'd never seen her dressed in anything except a suit before. In casual clothes, with her hair escaping the bun and the sky getting light behind her, she seemed more approachable.

I leaned against the car beside her. "Woll," I said. "Now what?"

"I don't know," she said. "I'm almost too tired to think. I can't decide whether I should rush home and sleep for a couple of hours, or find a diner and eat breakfast."

"Go for the breakfast," I said. "I'll join you." A quiet, intimate breakfast with a lovely dark-haired, soft-voiced woman sounded like a fine idea.

"Breakfast is the most important meal of the day," I said. "That's what my dear old momma always said. And she wouldn't lie to me. At least, I don't think she would."

She looked at me and smiled. "Joop, you look exhausted."

"It's just the light," I said. "It's not very flattering."

Kath sighed and touched the back of her hand to her cheek. It liked to break my heart, that sigh. There was a lot of weight in it. I forget sometimes how much responsibility lawyers carry. I was there because I enjoy the weirdness. And to make a buck. Kath was there to fight for Anka Stiffel.

After a moment she nodded. "Breakfast it is," she smiled.

"I'll buy," I said.

Kath shook her head. "I'll buy, thanks. Business expense. While we eat, we can discuss the case."

"Oh." A business breakfast with a lawyer didn't sound half so nice as a quiet, intimate breakfast with a lovely dark-haired, soft-voiced woman.

But what the hell, she was buying.

Thursday Morning

Most mornings Joop will pull into the office about the time I've finished my morning tea and the *Globe*. But that morning the poor man was there when I arrived, asleep at the desk where our secretary used to sit, back when we had a secretary. He was making a soft sound—not a snore, but a whishing sound, like a puppy makes when it sleeps.

There are times I'm envious of Joop. He's from one of those Southern families that were impoverished during the Civil War, which Joop calls the War of Northern Aggression. He has an air of gentility about him—a faded gentility, but there it is and you can see it in him. He looks like he's made from fine, tough wire.

The sight of him makes me feel the thick Irishman. We're navvy stock, the Sweeneys—squat, solid men who look at home on the loading dock. There's not a jot of grace in any of us, nor much in the Sweeney women either, sorry to say, though my sisters are all blessed with pleasant features.

I went to the small room in back of the office and started the tea. While the ancient hot plate labored to produce a boil, I took the newspaper back to the reception area and sat in the good chair.

We keep two chairs in the reception area for clients, even though we don't get much walk-in business. They're fine chairs, both of them, but a couple years back Bernie the Sot pissed himself while sitting in the one. It was that same day our secretary quit, no surprise. We'd cleaned and kept the chair. But we never bothered to replace the secretary, who was a nasty, mean-spirited woman.

I riffled quietly through the newspaper until I found the short article on page seven.

LOCAL SCULPTOR ASSAULTED

POLICE HAVE ARRESTED FEMINIST POET ANKA STIFFEL AND CHARGED HER WITH THE ATTEMPTED MURDER OF AMANDA OWEN, HER FORMER LOVER. DISTRICT ATTORNEY STAN WERTZ STATED MS. STIFFEL REPEATEDLY STRUCK MS. OWEN IN THE HEAD WITH A STONE SCULPTURE. THE D.A.'S OFFICE IS PREPARED TO AMEND THE CHARGE TO MURDER IN THE EVENT MS. OWEN DIES.

MS. OWEN WAS ALLEGEDLY FOUND LYING IN A POOL OF BLOOD IN HER BACK YARD BY A NEIGHBOR. THERE WAS NO INDICATION OF ROBBERY OR FORCED ENTRANCE, ACCORDING TO POLICE ON THE SCENE.

BOTH MS. OWEN AND MS. STIFFEL HAVE BEEN ACTIVE IN THE LOCAL ARTS COMMUNITY. MS. OWEN'S SCULPTURE HAS BEEN EXHIBITED ON BOTH COASTS. MS. STIFFEL IS CONSIDERED TO BE A PRINCIPAL FIGURE IN MODERN POETRY. HER WORK HAS BEEN PUBLISHED IN SEVERAL LITERARY JOURNALS.

By the time I'd finished the article, the hot plate had worked up enough energy to generate a thin whistle from the old teapot. The noise was enough to wake Joop. He raised his head, blinked several times, stretched, and sneezed like a cat.

"Good morning," I said.

He nodded and fussed sleepily with his hair.

"Tea's on," I said. "Like a cup?"

"Yes, please, very much."

I went back to the kitchen area and filled mugs with tea. Joop takes his with honey, which he keeps in a squeezable plastic bear-shaped container given to him by one of his hundreds of aunts when he was a child.

I ferried the tea back to the reception area. Joop was making a face.

"You okay?" I asked.

He frowned. "Kevin, you didn't shit in my mouth while I was asleep, did you?"

"Yeah, I did." I nodded. "I probably shouldn't have."

Joop shook his head. "No, no, it's okay. My own fault. I just wanted to be sure. I knew that taste in my mouth couldn't be natural." He pulled the cap off the plastic bear and lugged in a sizable dollop of honey.

"Up all night, were you?" I asked.

He nodded and checked his watch. "Got back here a little after six. We got to get us a couch, Kevin. Sleeping at a desk sucks." He sipped some tea and sighed.

"Feeling bad, are you?" I asked.

"Rotten. How do I look?"

"Like week-old rotten."

He nodded. "Yeah, I thought so. It's even worse from the inside. . . . Met an old buddy of yours last night. Detective named Marty Coyle."

"He's a good man, Marty. He has the case?"

Joop nodded. "And I think he's got a jones for Kath."

I didn't ask what a jones was. I only understand Joop about half the time, which is usually enough and sometimes too much. "How's our Kathleen?" I asked.

Joop smiled. "Kevin, I could fall in love with that woman." He put his hand over his heart and made it flutter.

I made a rude noise. Joop falls in and out of love with the regularity of the tide.

"We had breakfast together," he said. "She had sausage and eggs. Fried, over easy. I like a woman who's not afraid of sausage and eggs. And real butter on her toast."

"She's a brave woman, our Kathleen. Did you find a moment to discuss the case? Or were you content to make mooncalf eyes over the eggs?"

"I was the only one making mooncalf eyes," Joop said. "Whatever those are. Kath was all business. She's a tough woman. I like a tough woman. What's that poem? The one about lightning in the blood?"

I smiled. "Oh, there was lightning in my blood / Red lightning lightened through my blood / My Dark Rosaleen." I didn't tell him the poet was referring to Ireland, not to an actual woman. Why spoil it for the poor boy?

He grinned and nodded. "That's it. Red lightning lightened through my blood. How is it you know so much poetry but never heard of Anka Stiffel?"

"I might have heard of her if her name had been O'Stiffel," I said. My mother, God keep her, used to read the Irish poets aloud to me when I was a child, and the habit took.

Joop nodded. He clearly had no idea what I was talking about, but was either too polite to ask for an explanation or too tired to care.

"Besides," I said, "You told me she was a lesbian poet."

Joop slapped his forehead. "Oh, that's right. She *is* a lesbian poet. I forgot. You have to show proof of gender and sexual preference in order to read her poetry. I'm such a goof. I don't know *what* I was thinking of."

I sipped my tea. "A little early for sarcasm, isn't it?"

Joop grinned. "Have I hurt your feelings?"

"You're a brute." I handed him the newspaper opened to the Anka Stiffel clip. "Take a look at this." I drank my tea and read the comics while Joop scanned the article. When he put the newspaper down I asked if it was accurate.

"As far as I know," he said. "And as far as it goes."

"Okay," I said. "Do you feel capable of work?"

"Sure."

"Then give me the book on Anka Stiffel."

With a great show of eye-rubbing and arm-stretching, Joop filled me in on his predawn rendezvous with Kathleen O'Mara and Anka Stiffel.

Anka Stiffel and Amanda Owen were, as Joop put it, your standard artsy lesbian couple. At least, they had been until a week ago, when Amanda gave Anka the boot.

"Four-plus years," Joop said. "And, boom, out the door."

"It happens."

"Yeah, I guess it does," he said. "How long have you and Mary Margaret been together?"

"Six years," I said. "Nearly so."

He shook his head. "It seems unnatural," he said. "How do you do it?"

I shrugged. "It's simple. We like it."

He nodded and finished his tea. "Well, I guess Amanda Owen didn't like it so much anymore."

"Do we know why they split up?" I asked. "Did something happen to rend the marital fabric?"

A grin spread over Joop's tired face. When we opened our agency one of our first jobs was a divorce case. Our client was a sixty-year-old woman who suspected her husband was unfaithful. We tailed him and learned that he'd spent two nights a week for the previous thirteen years paying a 230-pound black woman to masturbate him while he wore diapers. In court, our client's attorney said the husband's behavior "caused an irreparable rend in the marital fabric."

"Something pretty much did rend the marital fabric," Joop said. "Shredded the marital fabric all to hell, is what it did."

"What was it?"

"Anka went nuts again."

"Nuts?" I asked. "Again?"

"Nuts again. We're talking full-blown lunatic poet here. This woman, Kevin, she sees and hears stuff that isn't there. It's fascinating. The whole psycho works."

"Wonderful." Crazy people make me a little uncomfortable.

"Kath says she's been hospitalized maybe half a dozen

times. Anka, I mean. Not Kath. Kath is as sane as you or me."
He looked puzzled. "Or is that 'you or I'?"

"Me. I think." I waved it off before we got involved in a
debate over grammar. "Does this happen often, her going
nuts?"

"Often enough, I guess."

"Is it a phase-of-the-moon problem we're talking about?
Or something as simple as her refusing to take her medication?"

"I think the medicine."

I nodded. It's a common story, especially for poor people
with psychiatric problems. They start hallucinating and acting
strange and soon wind up on some psych ward, where it's
easier and cheaper to pump them full of drugs than to take
care of their real problems. The drugs stop the hallucinations,
and when the voices and the golden-winged creatures have
faded away, the poor bastards get discharged with a prescription but no supervision. The drugs make them feel dull and
lifeless, so they stop taking them and before long the winged
creatures are back, shrieking in their ears and ripping at their
flesh. Then it's only a matter of time before they're back on
the nut ward. A lot of the people you see roaming the streets
acting strange could tell you the same story.

"I guess Amanda got tired of living with a crazy woman,"
Joop said. "So she told her to pack her bags and scoot. Go be
crazy someplace else."

"So Anka cuffed her on the head with a stone sculpture?"

Joop shrugged. "The police say yes. Anka says no." Joop
pronounced it "*po*leece." Well, actually Anka says she doesn't
think she did it."

"Ah," I said. "She doesn't *think* she did it."

"Hey, the woman's crazy. It's asking an awful lot of a
crazy woman to remember whether or not she whacked her
lover upside the head with a work of art."

I told Joop he had a point.

"Did I mention the alibi?" Joop asked.

I shook my head. "She has an alibi?"

He made a noncommittal motion with his hand. "She told Kath she'd met some woman at a bar and spent the night with her at a motel."

I waited for a moment, then asked, "Where's the problem?" There's always a problem.

"The problem is this: Anka doesn't know the name of the woman. Or the name of the bar where they met. Or how we can find her."

"Why am I not surprised?"

Joop smiled. "I believe you've heard this song before."

"The lyrics are different," I said, "but the melody is the same. Do we know the name of the motel?"

Joop nodded. "The Roadhouse."

"I know the Roadhouse."

"Yeah, I bet. Sleazy place. That's where she was arrested, by the way."

"How did the police know where to find her?" I asked.

"They didn't. It was an unrelated arrest. Your buddy Marty Coyle said the manager of the Roadhouse called in a complaint."

"A complaint? At the Roadhouse?" They didn't even call in stabbings at the Roadhouse, unless a body was blocking the drive.

"Yeah. Apparently Anka was howling like a dog at the moon."

"Like a dog at the moon," I said, trying to picture it. "I take it we're planning an insanity defense."

"Kath says not yet. Not until we know more about what happened."

"Howling like a dog at the moon is not normal behavior," I said. "Even for the Roadhouse."

Joop shrugged. "Maybe she was having great sex."

"Was this other woman there when she was arrested?"

Joop shook his head. "Not when the police arrived, she wasn't. But all that proves is that howling like a dog at the moon may not be the best way to keep your sex partner around."

"So, is that it? How does Marty connect her to the assault?" I asked.

"They always look to the spouse or lover," he said. "You know that."

"I do know that. But I also know that just being the spouse or lover isn't enough to justify an arrest for assault."

"But they didn't pop her for the assault. At least not at first. They popped her for disturbing the peace. When the cops hauled her crazy ass to jail, they didn't know who she was. Let alone that she was wanted for questioning in an attempted murder. All they knew was that she was acting crazy. Kath said Anka was in the pokey for hours before some bright boy connected the howling motel lunatic with the missing poet lunatic."

"You haven't answered the question," I said. "How do they connect her with the assault?" Joop is a good friend and fine investigator, but he has a tendency to forget the point.

"They learned that Amanda and Anka had a fuss at some bar. And that Anka threatened to whack Amanda in the head. Which is what happened to her."

"That's enough for an arrest," I said.

"The police seem to think so."

"Who was the room registered to?" I asked.

Joop said he didn't know. "Your buddy Marty Coyle said Anka was registered at the Roadhouse under an assumed name. Which either means that he doesn't know about this woman Anka picked up—"

"Or that he knows the woman doesn't exist," I said. "Which seems more likely."

"You think the mystery alibi woman was a hallucination?" Joop asked. "Or that Anka is lying? Or any combination of the two?"

I said I wasn't sure it mattered to us, though it might to Kathleen. The mystery woman either existed or she didn't. If she did, then we could find her, and if she didn't, then the reason she didn't wasn't important. "How does Marty figure it?"

Joop picked up his mug and looked at me through the handle. "He thinks Anka checked into the Roadhouse after the fight with Amanda and got more and more pissed off. Or more and more crazy. At any rate, Coyle thinks she drove over to Amanda's house, did her head in, drove back, and commenced to howling."

"You don't buy that?" I asked.

"Doesn't make a whole hell of a lot of sense, does it?"

I shrugged. "You were the one pointed out the woman is crazy. She doesn't have to make sense."

Joop made a face. "I hate it when you're logical," he said.

"Did the motel clerk ID Anka?" I asked.

"Don't know."

"Anybody at the motel see her leave and come back?"

He shrugged.

"What about neighbors? Did they see Anka's car that night?"

He gave me the patient look a parent gives a child who has asked a silly question. "Well, Kevin, I just don't know. I suspect those are the things Kath has hired us to find out."

His snotty tone irritated me. "She's hired us, has she?" I asked. "Haven't I got anything to say about who hires us?"

Joop was taken aback. "Well, yeah."

"Am I not the 'H' in G & H Investigations?"

"You're the 'H,' " he said. "But why are you being so pissy about it? It's too early in the morning to fuss like this."

I swirled the remaining tea around in my mug. Joop was right. I was being pissy. The fact was, I was a little jealous.

Joop looked exhausted, true enough, but the red lightning that lightened through his blood wasn't just from his breakfast with Kathleen O'Mara. Joop was electrified because of the case.

I knew what he was feeling, the way your blood cooks when you've been up all night, caught up in a strange or desperate venture. And I knew that if I wasn't married, I'd have been thoro with him, talking to Iusane lesbian poets and eating fried eggs with a lovely dark-haired woman instead of sleeping.

I knew what he was feeling and it bothered me that I wanted to feel it. It bothered me because I was a man as happily married as any man I know, married to a marvelous wife, who is herself a lovely dark-haired woman and whom I love dearly. And still I was envious of somebody who looked dead exhausted and bleary-eyed.

There are times when I think there must be something terribly wrong with me.

"So?" Joop asked. "You want to tell me what the fuss is?"

I shook my head and smiled. "No fuss."

"You're not opposed to taking the case?"

I shook my head. "Couldn't disappoint our Kathleen."

Joop grinned. "Red lightning lightened through my veins," he said. "Kath's meeting with Anka's shrink sometime today. One of us should be there."

"I'll go. You go home and take a nap."

He stood up and held back a yawn. "I got a feeling about this one, Kevin. I got a feeling this one is going to be jazz."

J o o p   W h e e l e r

Thursday, Late Morning

I've known Kevin Sweeney for seven years. Or thereabouts. Seems like longer. I met him not long after I left South Carolina and moved to Hobsbawm, Massachusetts, to work as a reporter. I'd done some reporting down home, but like lots of Southern folk I wanted to make a name for myself up north.

Hobsbawm is a medium-sized seacoast town about half an hour north of Boston. It used to be a hardworking fishing town. Then it became something of an artists' community. Now it's turning into a Saab-infested zone of yuppies who want to live *near* Boston but not *in* Boston. They actually say that.

Hobsbawm is not the sort of place you'd expect to see fat white guys dressed up in sheets and shouting how much they hate niggers and Jews. Which was my first big reporting assignment, to cover a Ku Klux Klan rally. I guess the editor thought a Southern boy would be better able to get along with racists. Which is typical New England bigotry.

Sweeney was there, a uniformed cop doing crowd security. Which basically meant keeping the half-dozen zipper-headed Klansmen from getting beat up by a large crowd of angry anti-Klan protesters. Mostly white college kids.

Midway through the speeches, I found myself about half hoping some of the college kids would start tossing a few of the overripe tomatoes they'd been toting around. Anything to shut the Klan speakers up. They never did throw the tomatoes, though. Spoiled Yankee rich kids, is all they were.

Sweeney kept himself between the sheet-heads and the few demonstrators who looked like they might get rowdy. After the Klan ran out of stupid things to say, Sweeney hustled them off to a waiting Volvo station wagon and bundled them in. Real quick and no-nonsense. I've seen my old grammy do the same thing with a bunch of my unruly cousins. Get them loaded and on their way.

I followed along as he bundled them off, hoping the reporter's hope—that something would happen. Nothing did. Except this. I saw one of the Klansmen put his hand on Sweeney's shoulder and thank him for his help. Sweeney pushed the man's hand off his shoulder and said "You touch me with that hand again and I'll be tearing it off at the shoulder and beating you silly with it. Not that you could look much sillier."

The Klansman looked surprised and hurt. After he got in the Volvo and drove off with his chubby buddies, Sweeney noticed me watching. He moved toward me, rolling his head a little and hunching his shoulders. I figured he was going to take the standard tough-cop attitude toward reporters. So I put on my Freedom-of-the-Press face and waited for him.

Sweeney looked at me and shook his head. "Now tell me," he said. "What in the name of all-merciful God are those half-wits doing in a Volvo?"

I saw Sweeney fairly often after that, covering the crime beat. I used him as a source on occasion, but made certain I didn't abuse the privilege. Even when the story was something really important. We slowly got to be buddies. I was one of the few non-cops to get invited to the party when he got promoted to detective. He even used to invite me to Croker's Pub, his local boozer, as he calls it.

Croker's is an Irish bar, but it was the first place I felt at home since leaving South Carolina. Southerners have a lot in common with the Irish. We're both farming folks. We both love to talk and write. We both appreciate strong drink, and we're tolerant of its effects on our people. And we both tend to be sociable and hospitable, even to unwanted guests. So long as they're not part of an invading army. And both Irish and Southern folk share a romantic tradition of rebellion and a love of lost causes.

Probably the main reason Sweeney and I became such good friends, though, is because of Mary Margaret, his wife. She liked me right off. Only in part for my own charming self, I'm afraid. The other part was because I wasn't a cop. When I came to visit, Sweeney and I didn't spend the evening telling war stories while Mary Margaret did whatever it was cops' wives are supposed to do while the guys are bonding away like bastards.

And I liked her right off, too. Mary Margaret doesn't have a job, which is something I've always wanted not to have. But she doesn't spend her life taking care of the house. She keeps a garden big enough to feed a small army. Which is what she does with it—feed a small army. She gives most of the produce to the local homeless shelter and soup kitchen. And she does volunteer work for her parish—visiting old folks or supervising kids on trips. She also teaches an evening course in Gaelic at the community college. And she reads a lot. And in the summer, she follows baseball. The Red Sox. Which is an attractive quality in a woman.

Sweeney became disillusioned with police work about the same time I got fed up with journalism. So we decided to pool our talents and resources and started our own private investigation agency. G & H Investigations. A Grit and a Harp. I thought up the name.

So I know Sweeney pretty well by now. Well enough to know that when he gets pissy, it doesn't signify anything. He's just moody. And there's not much a person can do about it. Take a nap and hope it goes away while you're asleep. Which is a pretty good plan for any unpleasant situation.

So that's what I did. I went home and took a nap. Napped near on three hours. And dreamed about eating fresh shrimp.

Kevin Sweeney

Thursday Afternoon

I stood as Dr. Leah Rifkin entered Kathleen O'Mara's office, and not just because Joop's Southern manners were beginning to rub off on me. I also stood out of surprise. Dr. Rifkin was the homeliest woman I'd ever seen outside a medical journal.

A small dark woman, hunched over like a retired hod carrier. I guessed she was in her mid-forties, though it's hard to tell with extremely homely people because you don't want to stare at them. Her hair was thick and absolutely black, and it could have been attractive if it hadn't been so badly cut. It looked like one of her more deeply disturbed patients had taken pinking shears to it.

She seemed to have dressed in the dark, pulling clothes at random out of the closet and putting them on as well as she could. Though her clothes were obviously expensive, nothing matched. And her skirt was on crooked.

Before she walked in, I'd been quietly reading Kathleen's notes from the night before. Although she was clearly tired, Kathleen was working on a motion to get Anka Stiffel transferred from the jail to a secure ward at the psychiatric hospital. She'd called in some favors and had arranged a hearing on the motion for that afternoon. She wanted me to do the interview with Dr. Rifkin while she listened and continued to work on the motion.

Kathleen did the introductions. When Dr. Rifkin spoke, everything changed. Her voice was soft and deep and melodic, with an assumed intimacy in it and obvious compassion. It was seductive and made a person forget how homely she was. I was charmed, in the oldest sense of the term.

She said she was pleased to meet me, and I believed her.

I cleared my throat and asked if she'd had a chance yet to see Anka.

"I've just come from the jail," she said.

"And how is she?"

"Not good," she said. "Better than I'd expected, but I'd prefer she was in a setting more conducive to treatment."

Kathleen told her about the motion hearing.

"Good," Dr. Rifkin said. "We've been through this before, you know. Not the jail and criminal charges, but the emotional crisis. It happens when she stops taking her anti-psychotic medication."

I nodded and gave myself a pat on the back. Just like I'd predicted. "Was she coherent when you spoke with her?" I asked.

She gave a tiny shrug. "It will take a few days before the new dosage reaches therapeutic levels and begins to mute her psychotic symptoms. I suspect her condition will continue to deteriorate for the next few days."

"You think she'll be competent to stand trial?" I asked.

"Well—"

"Assume she will," Kathleen interrupted. "That's something I'll deal with later. I just want you to focus on the facts, such as they are."

"Right, then. The facts." I turned back to Dr. Rifkin. "Did you discuss the incident with Anka?"

"The incident," she said, and shook her head. "Such a polite term. No, we didn't discuss the incident. For the most part, I simply tried to reassure her and keep her calm. It didn't seem like the appropriate time or place for a session."

"Probably best," I said. "Do you think it would okay for me to ask her some questions later today?"

She smiled, a crooked, ugly smile that somehow made her attractive. It went with her voice, the smile. "I don't think it will profit you to ask Anka questions at the moment," she said. "If she responds to you at all, she'll probably be delusional."

"You've known her a long time?" I asked.

She had. She'd been the admitting physician five years earlier when Anka put in one of her periodic appearances at the psych ward. She'd been assigned the case and continued to treat Anka as an outpatient after her discharge. During that five-year period, Anka had been hospitalized three other times.

"What's wrong with her?" I asked.

"Anka is usually diagnosed as a schizophrenic of the undifferentiated type," she said.

"Which means what, exactly?"

"Exactly?"

"Not too exactly," I said. "Easy on the technical stuff."

She smiled her twisted smile again. "In simple terms, it means Anka suffers from a psychosis that doesn't meet the diagnostic criteria for other schizophrenic disorders."

"Ah," I said. "Maybe we should avoid simple terms and use terms for boneheads."

In bonehead terms, Anka Stiffel was crazy as a loon, but her symptoms weren't consistent with more typical forms of psychosis. For as long as Anka could recall, she had heard a woman's whispered voice coming over her right shoulder. The voice didn't sound like anybody Anka knew and, for the most part, all it did was describe or comment on the things Anka saw or did.

But as Anka got older, the voice began to turn mean. It became demanding and critical. Sometimes it ordered her to do things that would humiliate her, like urinating and defecating in her pants during a high school basketball game, or exposing herself at a family barbecue.

"She ever refuse to do what the voice said?" I asked.

"Oh, yes. But that only made matters worse." Dr. Rifkin said that when the demands were refused the voice would become relentless, tormenting Anka day and night, calling her names, telling her how worthless she was. "And then," Dr. Rifkin said, "it would deny Anka the thing she wanted more than anything else in the world."

"And that is?" I asked, just as she wanted me to.

"Poetry."

At times the voice would speak to Anka with great passion, and Anka would be allowed to see the world with startling precision. These weren't hallucinations, according to Dr. Rifkin; Anka experienced only what actually existed, but with dazzling intensity. She became powerfully aware of everything—the texture of her clothing, the sound she made walking on the grass, the bright taste of an apple.

"Anka said it was as if she saw the world through gauze most of the time," Dr. Rifkin said. "Then the voice would lift the gauze and for a while she'd be allowed to actually see. Colors and shapes, the singularity of everything. And the voice would talk to her about what she saw."

Kathleen stopped writing and listened.

Dr. Rifkin leaned forward in her chair, her eyes excited. "Anka wrote down what she'd seen and what the voice had said. Not for others, but for herself, to remind her of what she'd been given, to help her experience the feeling again."

"The poetry?" Kathleen asked.

Dr. Rifkin nodded. "The poetry."

"Is it the same voice?" I asked. "The one that does the poetry, is it the same voice that made her wet her pants in school?"

"Anka says it's the same," she said. "I tend to think of them as different voices, but Anka says it's the same one."

"She'd be the one to know," I said.

"The terrible thing," Dr. Rifkin said, "the truly terrible thing is that the voice always extracts a price. For every glimpse she gets into that bright world, she has to pay. And pay dearly."

"The humiliation?"

She nodded.

"Poor kid," Kathleen said.

Dr. Rifkin shrugged. "In some ways."

I asked what she meant. She put her elbows on the arms of her chair and put her hands together, as if she were praying. "Anka certainly pays a high price for—for her gift. But she is also able to see things we ordinary people cannot even begin to imagine. While we live out our dull daily lives, Anka is living a life of almost indescribable passion."

"Sounds like a painful bargain," I said.

Dr. Rifkin looked down at her fingernails and nodded. "For you or me it would be. Anka seems to think it a fair bargain," she said. "Most of the time."

"And what about the other times?" I asked.

"The other times, Mr. Sweeney, Anka tries to kill herself."

I nodded and said, "Ah," like I knew it all along. And I guess I did.

"She does not want to live without the poetry voice," Dr. Rifkin said. "At the same time, she's not a masochist. She does not enjoy the pain or humiliation. She simply feels her options are severely limited. Suicide or medication, which for her is the emotional equivalent to being blinded. Or . . ."

"Or?"

For the first time Dr. Rifkin looked uncomfortable. "Or she can try to find a balance. Something that will give her the strength to refuse the command hallucinations—the orders to hurt or humiliate herself—but still allow her to hear at least a muted version of the poetry."

"You're talking about drugs," I said. "Something that would keep her sane enough not to hurt herself and yet crazy enough to write her poetry. Like being in a controlled chemical skid?"

"I suppose you could put it that way," she said.

"And that's what you did?" Kathleen said, laying down her legal pad. "You tried to help her find that balance? Is that right?"

"Yes."

"By giving Anka a less than therapeutic dosage? Is that correct?"

Dr. Rifkin shook her head, making her chopped hair fly about. "No, I gave her a therapeutic dose. My idea of therapy is different from that of other doctors. They tried to silence what she most wanted to hear. I've tried to help her control it, to let her carve out a life in which she could still write poetry without having to pay so high a price."

Dr. Rifkin, it seemed, supplied the air support for Anka's low-intensity war on reality. "When the voice tells her to do something, hurt herself or whatever, is she aware of what she's doing?" I asked. "Or is she in something like a trance?"

She frowned and startled me. I'd become so engaged by her voice and her story that I'd forgotten how truly homely she was. The frown turned her into a gargoyle. A charming gargoyle.

"You must remember that Anka hears the voice often. It's a frequent companion, but it doesn't usually interfere with her interaction with the real world. I think it must be similar to the way we feel when a persistent song runs through our minds. It's distracting, but not overwhelming."

"I know the feeling," I said. "Last week I kept hearing the theme to *The Beverly Hillbillies.*"

"Oh, you poor man," she said.

"So she's aware of her own actions? Aware and in control?"

Dr. Rifkin nodded, effectively shooting down any hope of an insanity defense. Regardless of how crazy your behavior might be, the law says you're sane if you can understand the difference between right and wrong and you can control your actions.

But there was a warped sort of logic to her madness. "I guess if Anka *didn't* know what she was doing when she peed her pants in the gym, she wouldn't feel humiliated. And that's the point, isn't it?"

Dr. Rifkin raised her eyebrows. "Why, yes, that's exactly right. It would not be punishment if she were unaware of the humiliation."

Kathleen picked up her tablet. "So she knows what she's doing, even when she's under the influence of this voice?" she asked. Despite what she'd said about assuming Anka would be found competent to stand trial, Kathleen was clearly still hoping she could fall back on the insanity angle. It wouldn't help the case if Anka's own psychiatrist said Anka probably knew what she was doing when she hit her lover in the head with a stone sculpture.

Dr. Rifkin frowned. "She's aware, but with an extremely narrow focus. The experience of the poetry voice, as I understand it, is almost too intense. She can't see *everything* clearly—that would lead to sensory overload. She sees a few things very exactly. Anka has a poem called 'Shoes,' which is about just that. People's shoes. For two days she was lost in the poetry voice, sitting on a doorstep, and apparently never saw anything other than the feet of the people who walked by her."

"Two days?" I asked.

She nodded. "When she returned home, she had no notion of the amount of time that had passed. Amanda said she was a mess. She hadn't eaten, hadn't bathed. She'd urinated and defecated in her clothing. And she refused to wash or eat until she'd written the poem."

"And I bet she didn't call to say she'd be late for dinner," I said, thinking that would be the first thing Mary Margaret would say to me if I'd been gone for two days. Not that she wouldn't have worried about me, but she'd put all her anger and worry into that one issue.

"No, she didn't. That's a very perceptive observation, Mr. Sweeney. It was one of the things Amanda found hardest to cope with. Periodically Anka would simply disappear. Amanda would have no idea where Anka was or where to look for her, or even if she was safe. It was very distressing for her."

"Tough all around," I said. "Tough to be crazy, tough to care for someone who's crazy."

"Very tough indeed," Dr. Rifkin said. "But Amanda Owen is a very tough woman."

"Tell us about Amanda Owen," I said.

"Amanda," she said, smiling. There was a lot of affection in that smile. "Amanda would have been just another upper-middle-class housewife if it weren't for her sculpture. And her sculpture would have been just another upper-middle-class housewife's hobby if it weren't for Anka."

Amanda Owen was unhappily married when she met Anka at an art exhibit. Anka was in a stable period at the time, and was attracted to Amanda. When she discovered that Amanda was an amateur sculptor, she coaxed Amanda into taking her home to see her work.

"I think Anka was more interested in seducing Amanda than in seeing her work," Dr. Rifkin said. "She was surprised to find that Amanda actually had talent."

They began to spend time together. Anka encouraged Amanda to take her sculpture seriously, something her husband hadn't done. Anka did something else Amanda's husband hadn't done: she excited Amanda sexually. They became lovers. Six months later Amanda's husband moved out of their home and Anka moved in.

"How did he take it, the husband?" I asked.

"Ex-husband, I should think," Kathleen said, without looking up from her legal pad.

"Actually, they're still married," Dr. Rifkin said.

"A tolerant man, her husband," I said.

"Not so tolerant," she said. "Greedy. Mercenary."

"How so?"

When Amanda announced that she was a lesbian, her family refused to accept it. They thought it might be a symptom of a mental disorder and tried to get her to see a psychiatrist. She refused.

"But she's seeing you," I said.

Dr. Rifkin shook her head. "I'm treating Anka. I do see Amanda, but only in connection to her relationship with Anka. And certainly not to 'treat' her for being a lesbian."

"Got it," I said. "But what does this have to do with Amanda staying married?"

Dr. Rifkin held up a hand for me to be patient. Amanda's parents, she said, continued to hope Amanda might eventually "come to her senses" and return to her husband. In order to be ready for that day, they offered to supplement the husband's income in exchange for his agreement not to file for divorce.

"He's in it for the cash, then?" I asked.

She waffled. "Perhaps that's a little harsh. But he is aware of the business opportunities her family can provide. In fact, her family helped him start his architecture firm. After they were married, of course. A wedding gift, you might say."

"They're rich, her family?"

Dr. Rifkin waved a hand. "Moderately wealthy."

That means rich. "And Amanda hasn't filed for divorce?"

Dr. Rifkin shook her head. "No. Her parents have made a similar arrangement with her. If she gets a divorce, they threaten to cut her off financially. And while Amanda is a gifted sculptor, it's not easy to support oneself through art."

"Nice little package for everybody," I said.

"Amanda's parents are apparently very traditional," Dr. Rifkin said. "They had, and still have, very traditional hopes for their daughter."

"And how long have Anka and Amanda been lovers?"

She waved a hand. "Approximately five years."

"And Amanda's family still hasn't twigged to the idea that Amanda isn't a traditional daughter?" I asked.

Dr. Rifkin wrinkled her forehead. "I've the impression Amanda's mother has accepted it," she said. "But her father apparently refuses to accede to reality."

It didn't sound like anybody in that boat was pulling with all oars. I decided to go back to basics. "Why did they split up, Amanda and Anka?"

"I don't know," she said. "Anka skipped her last two appointments. I haven't seen her for three weeks. I knew they were having difficulties, but I wasn't aware they'd separated until I received the call from your Mr. Wheeler this morning. Anything I say would be pure speculation."

"I'd appreciate your speculation, then," I said. "You know them both. All I want is your opinion. I won't hold you to it."

She considered a moment before answering. "I suspect Anka began to decompensate again, at which point Amanda's emotional stamina probably failed."

"Anka began to what? Decompensate?"

Dr. Rifkin frowned and searched for a bonehead term. "She began to, uh, go nuts," she said.

"Ah. Got it."

"If I had to hazard a guess—and I'm only doing so at your insistence, you understand—I'd guess some incident sparked the actual separation," she continued. "But it had been coming for quite some time. As you may have surmised, Anka could be difficult to live with."

"Yes." I smiled at the understatement. "I can see that."

Dr. Rifkin spoke very seriously. "Amanda has been extremely patient for an extremely long time. She took very good care of Anka, or at least she tried to. She tried to make sure Anka took her medication, and during those times when Anka was under the influence of the poetry voice, Amanda tried to keep track of her, to see she ate properly and kept herself clean."

"She sounds like a saint," I said.

"I suppose she could be seen that way. She was certainly Anka's anchor to reality. How she put up with Anka's behavior for four years . . ." She shrugged. "I cannot help but feel that Amanda has an aberrant need to be needed. Perhaps even a need to suffer." She screwed up her face in another smile. "It's not uncommon, I believe, for saints to seek martyrdom."

"Maybe she was just in love," I said.

Her smile softened and she inclined her head. "I've always wanted to credit it to love."

I was very much taken by her lopsided smile and the sentiment that spawned it. "But love for Anka?" I asked. "Or for her poetry?"

"Why, for Anka, of course." She looked surprised. "As much as I admire Anka's poetry, I cannot imagine anybody would endure her behavior merely for the sake of poetry."

It was my turn to smile. "Dr. Rifkin, I'm Irish. I come from a people who celebrate mad poets and honor the ones who support them. That sort of patience makes sense to me."

She touched me softly on the forearm with the tips of her fingers. Although her fingers were stubby and her nails bitten short, I found the gesture oddly moving. "I don't think Amanda is Irish," she said, "but there is no disputing her patience."

"At least up to a week ago," I said. I turned to Kathleen. "Do we know where our client was staying after she left Amanda Owen's house?"

She didn't look up from her yellow pad. "Woman named Stephanie Gibbs."

"Stevie," Dr. Rifkin said. "Everybody calls her Stevie."

"You know her?" I asked.

"I know who she is. Anka often spoke of her."

"Do you know where she lives?"

Kathleen spoke again. "Already got her address."

I gave her a thumbs-up and turned back to Dr. Rifkin. "Were they, uh . . ." I waggled my hand.

"Lovers?" Dr. Rifkin smiled. "No, I don't think so."

"Did either Anka or Amanda fool around?"

Dr. Rifkin frowned and examined her hands.

"Dr. Rifkin," I said, "I only ask because I have to. The answers won't go beyond this room."

She nodded, then spoke carefully. "Anka often suspected Amanda was having affairs. But I must say I think that was simply projection on her part."

"Projection?"

"Yes. I believe Anka was seeing a trait in Amanda that actually existed in herself."

"Ah. So Amanda didn't trash around, but Anka did."

She nodded. "I've no knowledge that Amanda saw anybody outside the relationship, though it's certainly possible. In regard to Anka . . ." She held up her hands. "Anka is a poet. Poets have always considered themselves above the rules."

"Just women?" I asked. "Or did she sleep with men too?"

"Primarily women."

"Lots of them?"

"I don't know what you consider a lot," she said, "but Anka certainly had episodes of promiscuity."

"And yet she was jealous of Amanda?"

She smiled her homely smile. "Poets are seldom burdened by consistency, Mr. Sweeney."

"No," I said. "I suppose not. How do you think Anka would react to getting the boot?"

"The boot?"

"I'm sorry. Being asked to leave Amanda's house."

"Again, I really don't know."

"Take a guess," I said. "Please."

"Very well." Again, she considered the question carefully before responding. "It would, of course, depend on her level of disintegration. I suspect Anka would be hurt. Probably angry and resentful and almost certainly jealous."

"Jealous enough to attack Amanda?" I asked.

"You don't need to answer that," Kathleen interrupted. "Unless you think your answer will be in Anka's best legal interests." It was a lawyer's subtle way of saying "Don't tell me anything I don't want to hear."

Dr. Rifkin twisted her face into a grimace and looked at her watch. "I'm afraid I must be going," she said. "I've an early-afternoon appointment." A psychiatrist's subtle way of saying "You're damn right I think she could be that jealous."

I walked Dr. Rifkin to the door, hoping to find some way to make her smile her gargoyle smile again and touch me on the arm. And me a happily married man.

When I returned, Kathleen said, "So, what do you think?"

"The woman's got a great voice," I said.

"Yeah, yeah. But what about the case?"

I shrugged. "I think Anka probably caved in her lover's head. I think the good doctor feels the same. What do you think?"

Kathleen slumped in her chair. "I think we'd better get this resolved as soon as possible. If our client isn't too crazy to make a plea agreement."

"Why?" The standard defense strategy is to stall, hoping witnesses will disappear or forget what they saw.

"Because the evidence sucks," she said. "And because the cops are saying there is a good chance Amanda Owen will die. If this goes to court, I'd rather lose an assault case than a murder case." She stood and walked over to the window.

"How much time has Amanda got?"

Kathleen shrugged. "I got the impression she'll either be

dead or beginning a long, slow recovery in two, maybe three weeks."

"We won't even have the police reports for two or three weeks."

She nodded. "Joop says the detective in charge is an old buddy of yours."

"Marty Coyle? I know him, but he's hardly a buddy."

"Try to make him your buddy," she said. "It's all we've got."

J o o p   W h e e l e r

Thursday Late Afternoon

There must have been something in the air. A rupture in the ozone layer, maybe. Something that allowed my poor country brain to be bombarded by Gazooney Rays from outer space. Because for the second time in twenty-four hours red lightning lightened through my blood.

It wasn't for a Dark Rosaleen this time, but for a curly-haired semi-redhead in painter's pants. Stephanie Gibbs. The woman Anka stayed with after she'd been kicked out of Amanda Owen's home.

Sweeney called me at home after he'd finished with Anka's shrink. And took huge pleasure from waking me up from my nap, the spiteful bastard. He filled me in on what the shrink had said and gave me Stephanie Gibbs's address.

"I'll go chat with her tomorrow morning," I said.

"This afternoon would be better," he said. When he decides to take a case, he likes to get it done.

So I brushed my teeth and went back to work.

Stephanie Gibbs had a loft apartment in the Moose Creek district of Hobsbawm. Years back, I'm told, Moose Creek was mostly Portuguese and Greek—folks who worked the fishing boats. By the time I came north, the fishing industry had just about shut down and those Portuguese and Greeks who could afford it had moved to the 'burbs. Moose Creek became the land of vagrants, rummies, and derelicts whose brains were hard-wired to receive radio waves from Venusians and the CIA.

Then the artists moved in. Attracted by the cheap rent and huge apartments, I suspect. In the last couple of years Moose Creek had become fashionable, a neighborhood for folks who like to hang around with artists and maybe pretend they're artists too.

One of the things I like about this work is that when you knock on a door, you never know who's going to open it. Stephanie Gibbs might be a frail old churchgoing lady. Or a biker dyke. Or an aerobics junkie.

What I saw when she opened her door, though, was the curly-haired semi-redhead in painter's pants I mentioned earlier. She favored Celia Kendall, who used to live just down the road from my uncle Altus. I had a fevered passion for Celia when I was about fourteen. I guess I never really got over it. Both Celia and Stephanie Gibbs had a faint—and I mean *faint*—spray of freckles running across the nose.

And when she asked could she help me, she asked it with a Southern accent. Which still does it for me. A lot of folks— by which I mostly mean a lot of Northern folks—think all Southern accents are alike. Which is just nonsense. If you bother to listen—which Yankees don't very often—you can tell working-class upper Alabama from cultured Charleston from dirt-poor East Texas. Stephanie had a nice lilt in her voice. Tennessee horse country, maybe.

It was the happy combination of the freckles, the hair, the accent, and the resemblance to my young love Celia Kendall that jump-started the red lightning. Wasn't a damn thing I could do about it. Just fight against it, and try not to let it interfere with the work, and hope it would eventually go away.

After I told her who I was and what I was doing, she invited me in and sat me on an uncomfortable futon sofa thing. I rooted around for a moment trying to find the least uncomfortable position. She started right in asking questions. Which I should have resented on account of that's *my* job, but which I didn't resent on account of the freckles and all.

"Is Anka okay?" she asked. "What's going to happen to her?"

I didn't know the answer to either of those questions. So I asked her, "What do you mean by 'okay'?"

"Has she hurt herself?"

I could answer that one. "Nope. At least she hadn't as of early this morning."

"Is she in touch with reality?"

That one was tougher. Normally I don't discuss a client's status, mental or otherwise, with a witness. Regardless of the quality and quantity of the witness's freckles. On the other hand, I was going to need this woman's help. So I hedged.

"Well, anybody who gets arrested and charged with a serious crime usually has their sense of reality jarred," I said. "It's the sort of experience that tends to disturb the senses."

"Mr. Wheeler . . ."

"Please, call me Joop," I said.

She wasn't about to be jollied. "Mr. Wheeler, I know Anka. I've known her for years. She's a dear friend and I'm worried about her. I also know she's schizophrenic. So will you please just tell me what's going on with her?"

She was obviously sincere. And I'm a sucker for sincere. I might have given in and told her, even if she hadn't favored young Celia. "Right now her lawyer, Kath O'Mara, is trying to get her transferred from the jail to a psychiatric hospital."

She shook her head. "I should have seen it coming," she said. "I knew she was acting crazy, but I didn't think it was that bad. I should have seen it."

I shrugged. "I don't know. When I saw her last night she seemed a tad out there, but she wasn't raving or barking at the moon or anything. I don't think you can, or ought to, blame yourself." It's always good practice to make witnesses feel better about their role in the problem.

"I'm sure it must have been an accident," she said. "I cannot believe Anka really meant to hurt Amanda. Anka is the gentlest of women."

"You're assuming she did it," I said.

"Didn't she?" Her eyebrows went up.

I shrugged again. "I don't know."

"The police seemed to think she did it."

"You've already talked to the police?"

She said she had. Apparently the police had learned from one of Amanda Owen's neighbors that Anka had moved into the Gibbs apartment. When they came looking to interview Anka, Stephanie had told them she hadn't come home that night. That made them suspicious. Then she told them about the fight at the bar. And that got them hot.

"I feel like it's all my fault," she said. "When the police came, they only wanted to talk to Anka. By the time they left, I think they'd decided she was a suspect."

"Probably so," I said.

"What did Anka tell them?" she asked.

I shook my head. "I've bent the rules of confidentiality totally out of shape," I said. "I'm not going to break them into bitsy pieces."

"Oh, I'm sorry," she said. And she sounded like she meant it. She gestured like she was going to touch me on the hand. Which I would have allowed, being a polite person. "I *am* sorry," she said again. "It was thoughtless of me to ask."

I waved it off and smiled.

She inclined her head. "Now, tell me what I can do to help Anka. I feel responsible for all this."

Helping Anka Stiffel seemed like an awfully tall order for one person. But since she sounded sincere, I told her what she could do. "You can tell me all about Anka," I said. Which was why I was there, after all.

"What is it you want to know?"

"I don't exactly know just yet," I said. "Why don't you just tell me about everything you can think of. We can sort out what's important later."

"Everything?"

I nodded. "Every little thing. Just start at the beginning

and talk ahead on. If I have any questions or need more details, I'll interrupt you."

She nodded slowly, then looked upset. "I'm afraid I've completely forgotten my manners," she said. "Would you care for something to drink? Coffee? Or a soft drink? Or iced tea?"

I told her iced tea would be very nice, and she went to the kitchen to fetch it. Freckles and good manners. The red lightning sizzled through my Southern veins. Of course, I reminded myself, she could be stalling for time. Trying to decide what she ought to tell me and what she ought to leave out. Having a circulatory system on fire with red lightning is fine and dandy, but there's no reason to let it make you stupid.

She returned with the iced tea, and there was a sprig of mint in each of the glasses. Which liked to make my heart curl up. But I steeled myself against it. I was made of sterner stuff, I told myself. I would not be seduced by a sprig of mint.

She sat cross-legged in an overstuffed chair. "Now then, where were we?"

"You were just about to tell me everything you know about Anka," I said.

Southern folk, if they're raised right, learn a tone of voice that's both intimate and formal at the same time. It's a trick we use when we speak to strangers, welcome or not. For example, if you hear a Southerner say "Next time y'all are in town, you just stop in with us, stay as long as you like, we'd be glad to have you," you have to understand we don't really mean it. At least not entirely. We're just being polite. Which is how folks are *supposed* to behave.

She used that voice on me. Which put me in my place and at the same time let me know I was welcome in her home because I was trying to help a friend of hers.

"I've known Anka for about six years," she said. "Maybe longer. Certainly I knew her before she and Amanda became involved."

They'd met at the university, where they both taught evening classes—Stephanie Gibbs taught something to do with women's mythology and Anka taught writing. They became friends and often took dinner together after their classes let out.

Anka must have been in a stable period. Or Stephanie Gibbs was being circumspect, which was not a good sign. She claimed she didn't notice anything unusual about Anka for months. When she did begin to notice a certain oddness in Anka's behavior, she simply put it down to artistic eccentricity.

Then one day they went to a brunch sponsored by the university women's association and Anka stabbed a salad fork into her own wrist.

Stephanie toyed with her iced-tea glass as she told me about it. "It wasn't a dramatic gesture," she said. She kept her eyes on the glass, but spoke with soft intensity, as if she wanted to be certain I understood what she was saying. *Truly* understood, not just accepted.

"I should say it wasn't *intended* to be a dramatic gesture," she said. "It certainly wasn't done dramatically. She did it as if stabbing a salad fork into your wrist were perfectly normal table etiquette. She very calmly took the fork into her right hand, then tried to drive it through her left wrist. Like this." She placidly drove an imaginary salad fork into the underside of her wrist.

"Must have been scary," I said.

She frowned and shook her head. "It's strange, but it wasn't. Not *scary*, exactly. 'Unsettling' would be more accurate. She was so matter-of-fact about it that I knew she was very . . ." she searched for a word.

"Disturbed?" I offered. Then I bit my tongue. It's not good form to put words into the mouth of a witness. It's something I have to fight against. But sometimes folks seem to think so slow.

"Yes, exactly. Disturbed."

"Then what?"

"Why, I took her to the hospital," she said.

"Did you ask her why she did it?"

She shook her head. "It didn't seem important at the time," she said. "I was more concerned with getting her to the hospital. And later it didn't seem polite."

She said "polite" and my heart went all woolly on me again. A crazy woman tries to skewer her wrist to the table and her lunch partner's trying to be polite about it.

I asked how the salad-fork affair affected their friendship.

"In some ways we became more close," she said. "I knew she was troubled—'tetched,' my grandmother would have said. I tried to let her know I wasn't repelled or frightened by her illness, and that seemed to seal our friendship."

Which brought up a delicate issue. Up to that point I hadn't considered just how close they might be. I hadn't thought that Stevie might be a lesbian. I was hugely attracted to her and so just assumed she was as hetero as I was. Could a lesbian spark red lightning like that? In a man, I mean. In me?

Maybe so. Maybe she was. She obviously consorted with lesbians. And she said she was a member of some sort of women's group. And she was active in a women's studies program at the university.

But so what? Most of those things also applied to Kath O'Mara, and Kath wasn't a lesbian. Was she? I didn't think she was. How the hell is a person supposed to know these things?

I decided to ask. "I know this is an impertinent question," I said. "But were you and Anka, uh . . . were you two physically, uh, *intimate* is the word I'm looking for, I guess."

"Were we lovers?" she asked for me. "No, we weren't. Just good friends."

I nodded. Perfect.

"Is there anything else you'd like to know?" she asked.

I sipped the tea and gave myself up to the mint. Was there anything I wanted to know? Lordy yes. I wanted to know if she was in love with anybody at the moment. And, if not, if she was taking applications. I wanted to know what it would take to set red lightning racing through her blood. I wanted to know a lot of things, all of them totally improper and unprofessional.

I sighed and tried to get businesslike. "I'd like to know how Anka came to stay with you after she and Amanda split up."

For the next half hour or so we ran on, interrupting each other, clarifying this point or that, getting the facts ironed out. Then a fine thing happened. She asked me if I would like another glass of iced tea.

Now this may not sound like a significant incident. But you have to remember that the standards of Southern courtesy had been met. Refreshments had been offered and accepted; she was under no social obligation to repeat the offer.

But she did. Which I took as a sign of acceptance and, to some degree, of trust. I smiled and said, "Yes, I would very much like another glass of iced tea, Ms. Gibbs. It's so kind of you to ask."

"Call me Stevie."

"If you'll call me Joop."

She agreed and went to fetch the tea. While she was gone, I stood and wandered over to inspect her bookshelves. I keep hearing that a person's eyes are the windows of their souls. I don't know about that. Souls aren't really my area of expertise. Peeking in windows, though, is a thing I know something about. And I'm here to tell you that looking at a person's bookshelves is like peeking in that person's spiritual windows.

There was a passel of books on women's studies and

women's issues. Which wasn't at all surprising, considering her work and the folks she hung out with. But she also had shelves crammed with fiction. All sorts of fiction. Serious South American mystical, trashy airport, New York hip, prissy English smarm, depraved Southern drunk. Lots of it, all jumbled in haphazardly together.

I rubbed my finger on the spine of a beat-up old paperback copy of *The Chosen* and said, " 'For the first fifteen years of our lives, Danny and I lived within five blocks of each other and neither of us knew of the other's existence.' "

"Say that again." Stevie was standing behind me, holding the iced tea and looking at me like a dog that's just learned to shake with its paw.

I shook my head and could feel a blush beginning. Private detectives aren't supposed to get caught like that.

"I was just talking to myself," I said. "I have this weird habit. For some reason, I memorize the first lines of books."

She absently handed me one of the glasses and nodded at the bookshelves. "Pick a book," she said.

I took a moment, then pointed to *The Prisoner of Zenda*.

She smiled and said, " ' "I wonder when in the world you're going to do anything, Rudolph?" said my brother's wife.' "

Zing—red lightning.

"The second line is better," she said. " ' "My dear Rose," I answered, laying down my egg-spoon, "why in the world should I do anything?" ' "

It was all I could do to keep from grabbing her and dancing a fandango. Whatever that is. I desperately wished I had an egg-spoon to lay down. I knew I ought to be saying something clever, but couldn't think of anything. Total brain lock. So I turned back to the bookshelves and scanned the titles.

"I didn't know anybody else did it," Stevie grinned.

I saw maybe a dozen titles I recognized and knew the

first lines to. But I wanted to find the *right* title. Why waste such an opportunity?

I hesitated over *A Clockwork Orange*.

Stevie beat me to it. " 'What's it going to be then, heh?' "

And then I saw it. *Catch-22*. Nothing could have been more appropriate. I laid my finger on the spine of the book and said, " 'It was love at first sight.' "

And it was, oh my droogies, it was.

Kevin Sweeney

Thursday Evening

Joop stifled a yawn. "So it was like this," he said. "When things between Anka and Amanda began to go sour, Stevie told Anka she could sleep on her couch for a while."

"Nice of her," I said.

"What are friends for?" he asked. "They're for couches to sleep on when things go sour at home, is what they're for."

"Ni heaspa go dith carad," Mary Margaret said. Her parents had insisted she learn to speak Irish as a child, and she likes to show it off whenever she can. It's her only flaw.

"Gesundheit," Joop said.

Mary Margaret translated with a smile. " 'There's no need like the lack of a friend.' "

I nodded. "This Gibbs woman—"

"Stevie," Joop said. "She said to call her Stevie."

"Stevie, then. Did she know Anka was decompensating when she offered her the couch?"

"Decompensating?" Joop frowned. He turned to Mary Margaret. *"Decompensating?"*

Mary Margaret shrugged. "Who knows where he learns to talk like that?"

"Did she know Anka was going nuts again?" I asked.

"Ah." Joop nodded slowly. *"That* decompensating. Yeah, I think she sort of knew."

Mary Margaret whooped and began to bounce on the sofa and slap me on the shoulder. On the television Ellis Burks had just hit a double and it looked like the Red Sox might rally and beat the Yankees. The dog-ass Yankees, as Joop called them. Joop joined in the celebration, almost spilling his beer and nearly upsetting the guacamole.

I hadn't really expected to see Joop that evening. Mary Margaret had invited him over for dinner and baseball—they're big Red Sox fans, the pair of them—but I assumed he'd beg off. He'd been up most of the night at the police station and had worked into the evening interviewing the Gibbs woman. But he showed up, a six-pack in his hand and a smile on his face, ready to feed and cheer on the team.

After the uproar died down, I repeated the question. "Did the Gibbs woman know how crazy Anka was when she invited her to sleep on the couch?"

He nodded. "Stevie knew Anka was generally crazier than owl shit. But she didn't think Anka's behavior was much stranger than normal. In fact, she said Anka seemed a lot less stressed out than she expected. She didn't feel any need to hide the salad forks. If you know what I mean."

"She know Anka was hearing voices?" I asked.

"Nope." Joop shook his head. He frowned, then added, "Well, she knew Anka *had* heard voices in the past. But she didn't know Anka was listening to them when she moved in. At least that's what she told me."

"She hear Anka make any threats toward Amanda?"

He shook his head. "None she was willing to tell me about."

That was the second time Joop had qualified his statements. "You think the woman was less than honest with you?" I asked.

He made a face. "Naw. Not really. I'm just trying to be objective, is all." He looked at his beer bottle. "I got to tell you though, being objective is tough. I could about half fall in love with that woman. If she wasn't a witness, that is. And if I wasn't the sober professional that I am."

"Jesus Christ, Joop," I said, for which Mary Margaret thumped me on the shoulder.

"Lord's name," she said. She's from a religious family, Mary Margaret, with a brother that took the collar and two sisters that took the veil. The one sister runs a day-care center in Central America, the other bakes bread in a convent back in County Donegal, where Mary Margaret was conceived though not born, her parents emigrating to Boston before she arrived. The brother works on his golf at a wealthy parish in Phoenix.

"Sorry, but Joop is always falling in love," I said.

"Not always," Joop said. "Hardly ever, in fact. Mary Margaret, you can't believe the word of a man who takes the Lord's name in vain."

"It's true, though," she said. "You're weak around the women, Joop, and you know it yourself. If you'd only let me introduce you to a nice girl."

Joop laughed. "A nice girl? What would I want with a *nice* girl? And a *girl?* I'd get arrested. Now if you offered to introduce me to a woman who wasn't so nice . . ."

"You're an evil-minded man, Wendell Joseph Wheeler," she said. "And you don't deserve a nice girl. Nor a nice woman neither."

I smiled. "It was only this morning Joop was infatuated with a nice girl," I said. A nice girl, to Mary Margaret, is an Irish Catholic woman. "Kathleen O'Mara."

"Her that's the lawyer?" she asked. She turned and gave Joop a look—a raised eyebrow and a tilt of the head—that was congratulatory, questioning, and chiding all at the same time.

"Ah, don't look at me like that," Joop said. "My momma used to look at me like that."

"And a poor long-suffering woman she is, I'm sure," Mary Margaret said.

"What would your poor old mother say if she knew you were fawning over a lesbian?" I grinned.

Joop raised his eyebrows. "You mean Stevie? She's not a lesbian."

"Oh? I had the impression she was. How do you know she's not?"

"I asked her," Joop said.

"You never did," Mary Margaret said, aghast.

"Well," Joop said. "Maybe not exactly in those words."

"In what words?" I asked. "Exactly."

"I don't recollect exactly. What I asked was if she and Anka were sleeping together. And she said no, they were just friends." He smiled as if to say "So *there*."

"That doesn't make her heterosexual," I said. "It just makes her selective. Maybe she doesn't like crazy women. Maybe didn't find Anka attractive."

Mary Margaret whooped and bounced again. Mike Greenwell had singled, moving Burks to third.

"Back to the Gibbs woman," I said.

"With pleasure." Joop smiled.

"Tell me about her."

Joop has an unorthodox way of interviewing, but he does get a lot of information. Stevie Gibbs, he'd learned, taught in the women's studies program at the university—courses in history and mythology from a feminist perspective. She was also a well-known authority on Goddess worship.

"What in the name of God's holy trousers does that mean, 'Goddess worship'?" Mary Margaret asked. "It has a pagan sound to it, if you ask me."

"Goddess worship," Joop recited, "was the predominant religion in Western Europe until approximately 2500 B.C." He broke into a grin. "At least that's what Stevie said. I don't have any reason to doubt her."

"Small wonder these people go about bashing each other's heads in with stones and such. They're all pagans."

"Well, we don't know that the folks involved in the actual bashing were pagans," Joop said. "And even if they were, it doesn't mean that being a pagan leads inevitably to bashing in heads with stones."

"This is all fascinating, Joop," I said. "The pagans and all. But what about the case? Surely you found time to discuss the case?"

"Oh, sure," he said.

"Did you learn anything about the fight Anka and Amanda had in the bar?"

"Sure did."

"Well?"

"Okay. It was like this. They had dinner at La Roma. The two of them, Stevie and Anka."

"La Roma? Is that the Italian place over to Woodmont?" Mary Margaret asked.

"That's the one."

"I hear good things about that restaurant," she said. "Why don't you ever take me there, Kevin? You know I love Italian food."

"It's hard to get in," I said, "because of the crowds of lesbian poets and their companions." I turned back to Joop. "I thought the fight took place at a gay bar."

Joop nodded. "That's right, it did. I'm just trying to give you a picture of their entire evening. The events that led up to the fuss at the bar. I'm trying to give you what they call the big picture."

"The big picture," I said. I grabbed my beer and leaned back on the couch. There's no point in trying to rush Joop when he's talking. Mary Margaret smiled at me and patted my knee.

"After they left La Roma," Joop said, "Stevie wanted to go home. But Anka wasn't ready. They argued for a bit, then Stevie agreed to have a drink at Laurel's."

Mary Margaret leaned against my shoulder. "Laurel's is the women's club down to Parkins Ave.," she informed me. "Right across from that shop where they sell the boat fittings. They don't allow the men, you see."

I nodded. I knew Laurel's, though I'd never been inside.

It was a private club for professional women—lawyers and doctors and the like—but it wasn't a gay bar. "Is that where they had the fight?"

Joop shook his head. "Nope. They had a drink there and chatted with some friends. Stevie said she'd arrange for me to meet the friends." He grinned. "I'll get to meet them right there at Laurel's."

That's Joop—trying to get himself into a women-only club. He'll work twice as hard as necessary in order to get someplace he isn't supposed to be. "So what's the story on the fight?" I asked.

Joop made a "Be patient" gesture. "Stevie was hoping one drink would satisfy Anka and they'd be able to go home. But no. Anka had two or three drinks and wanted to keep going. To the Loading Zone."

I nodded and felt we were finally getting someplace. The Zone is a gay and lesbian piano bar. Not the sort of place that has a lot of fights, but at least it was a step in the right direction.

"Anka was getting herself whacked," Joop said. "We're talking commode-hugging drunk. And that's when Stevie began to think Anka might be looking for trouble. Maybe looking for Amanda."

"Wonderful." This wasn't going to help Kathleen's defense.

"She tried to talk Anka into going back to the apartment, but Anka wasn't buying it. Stevie thought it was better to go along to the Loading Zone and try to keep her out of trouble."

"The sober voice of reason," Mary Margaret said.

"Exactly." Joop nodded. "So off they went to the Zone. They met some more friends, had a couple more drinks. You get the picture."

"This Stevie, she was drinking as well?" I asked.

"She says not. Said she was drinking tonic." Joop

shrugged his shoulders. "Anyway, she's also going to set up a meeting with the women they saw at the Zone."

"Very nice of her, setting up all these meetings," I said.

"She's a nice woman." Joop grinned. "Besides, she feels guilty for having told everything to the cops."

I sipped my beer and waved for him to continue.

"Okay, so they have a couple of drinks at the Loading Zone, then they head for a place called Schotzie's."

"I don't know Schotzie's."

"Me either," Joop said. "I'd never even heard of it until this afternoon. I guess it's a lesbian dive. And *that's* where the fight happened."

Finally. "Tell me about it."

Joop laughed a little. "Talk about bad luck. First thing Stevie and Anka see when they walk into the bar is our own Amanda Owen. Slow-dancing with another woman."

"Ah. The fight."

"The fight." Joop nodded. "Stevie said Anka went bright red and rushed onto the dance floor. She shoved Amanda and called her a rotten cunt."

"Not a pleasant name to be calling anybody," Mary Margaret said. "Especially somebody you're supposed to be in love with."

"Not very poetic either," I said. "I'd have expected better from a poet."

"Cut her a little slack," Joop said. "The poor woman was drunk. And probably hallucinating like a fiend. Not the best conditions for poetic insults."

"Okay," I said. "She shoved Amanda and called her a rotten cunt. Then what happened?"

Mary Margaret punched my shoulder. "Your language."

"My language? Why are you hitting me? I only repeated what Joop said."

"Joop was only reporting what it was he heard," she said. "It didn't need repeating a second time."

Joop grinned, the bastard.

"Go on with your story, Joop," Mary Margaret said. "And when you've finished, I've made a lovely cheesecake."

"Cheesecake?" he said. "You know, I can eat and talk at the same time. In fact, when I was a boy my folks had to beat me with a switch to keep me from talking at the dinner table."

"Joop," I said, "if you don't get on with the story, I'm going to get a switch and make you wish for your father's gentle touch."

"Okay." He nodded. "Later with the cheesecake. Okay, Anka shoves Amanda and calls her a rotten cunt." He grinned, knowing he could get away with it. "Amanda pushes back. Anka slaps Amanda. Then, according to Stevie, the whole thing deteriorates into general face-slapping, hair-pulling, and name-calling. At some point Anka lands a solid blow and puts Amanda on her butt. Then Anka shouts—and I'm quoting Stevie here—she shouts, 'I ought to smash your fucking head in.'"

"How they talk, these lesbians," Mary Margaret said. "She's not a Catholic girl, I take it."

"Anka? I think she's Jewish."

"Ah." Mary Margaret nodded. "There it is then."

"What does that mean?" I asked. "Are you saying Jewish women talk dirtier than Catholic women?" Mary Margaret has acquired some very odd ideas from her parents. They're decent people and hard workers, the both of them, or were when they were healthy. But they're ignorant and intolerant. As Mary Margaret would say, they weren't much for the learning.

"Yes, I do mean that," she said. "Of course they talk dirtier. They don't have to go to confession, do they, the Jews. No, nor your Protestants or pagans neither. They wouldn't be using such language if they knew they'd have to be telling Father Hannan about it in the confessional come the morning."

"Tough guy, this Father Hannan?" Joop asked.

"Oh, is he tough," Mary Margaret said. "Eighty years old, bless him. He's not so harsh on the impure thoughts, Father Hannan, but for some reason he's the very devil on the vulgar language."

I shook my head and tried to get back to the subject. "What happened then?" I asked. "At the bar."

"Stevie and some other women at the bar got between Anka and Amanda and Anka backed off. Stevie checked to see if Amanda was okay and helped her to her feet. When she turned around, poof, Anka was gone."

"Poof?" I asked.

Joop grinned. "Poof. Just like that. Stevie looked around the bar for her, but no luck."

"She ask anybody where Anka had gone?"

Joop nodded. "Yep. A few people said she'd run out of the bar. Stevie looked, but Anka had just disappeared."

"Into thin air."

"That's what folks usually disappear into."

"Poof," I said.

"Took the car, too," Joop said. Apparently they'd been using Anka's car, but after the first couple of bars, Stevie had insisted on driving and carrying the keys. She hadn't trusted Anka to drive.

"I guess Anka had a second set of keys," Joop said. "Stevie eventually gave up and went home, hoping Anka might have gone back to the apartment. She hadn't, though."

I sat quietly for a moment, looking at the television and thinking. The Yankees were up to bat. Mary Margaret, who had shifted her attention back to the game, cleared her throat. "Excuse me," she said. "Is there a particular goddess you're talking about here?"

Joop and I exchanged confused looks. Mary Margaret looked at us as if we were simple-minded.

"Not five minutes ago," she said to Joop, "you were

talking about Goddess worship. What I'm asking is which particular goddess were you talking about?"

Joop shrugged. "I don't know. *The* Goddess, I guess. I didn't know there was more than one. There can't be that many goddesses, can there? I mean, they're not like Shriners."

"But she must have had a name," Mary Margaret insisted. "You don't worship somebody who doesn't have a name, now do you?"

"No idea." Joop shrugged. "It was a long time ago. Twenty-five hundred B.C. is what Stevie said. That was what, forty-five centuries ago? I'm not even sure people *had* names back then. Probably just grunts and whistles."

"Could have been a tribal thing," I suggested. "Different tribes all worshipping the same goddess under different names."

Joop shrugged again. "Makes sense to me. Why do you ask?"

"I've been thinking about it," she said. "And I think it's probably true, what you said. About it being the chief religion of all Europe."

Joop didn't seem to know what to say. He just nodded.

"And you, Kevin Sweeney," Mary Margaret continued, "you ought to be ashamed of yourself for forgetting your own heritage. Have you forgotten the Tuatha De Danaan, that ruled Ireland in the olden times?"

"The what?" Joop asked.

"The Tuatha De Danaan. The followers of the goddess Dana," she explained. "Goddess worship in ancient Ireland."

I gave the woman a smile and a kiss. It's when she pulls stuff like that out of thin air that I love her most. She chatters sometimes, but she never stops thinking.

"Didn't somebody mention cheesecake?" Joop asked. "I distinctly heard the word *cheesecake* used."

And Mary Margaret went all over wifely, a thing she

does only as a joke sometimes when Joop is over, or when the mood strikes her. She refused our offers of help, went to the kitchen, and returned with great slabs of cheesecake.

While we ate, Joop and I sorted out assignments. I'd see what I could get from Marty Coyle, then I'd concentrate on Amanda—her family, the neighbors, the medical people, and the staff at the motel where Anka was arrested. Joop would work the lesbian angle—interview the witnesses at all the bars Stevie and Anka visited and try to learn if Anka had, in fact, met some woman and spent the night in a cheap hotel making the beast with two backs.

The Red Sox took the game by a single run. Despite the excitement and Mary Margaret's whooping, Joop was stifling yawns throughout the last anxious inning. He left as soon as his Southern manners would allow.

Mary Margaret gave him a large plate of leftovers and a shingle-sized chunk of cheesecake to take home. She refuses to accept that Joop is a competent cook and perfectly capable of taking care of himself. And Joop eats it up.

At the door Mary Margaret gave him a kiss on the cheek. "Slan abhaile," she said. "Safe home."

Joop frowned for a moment, searching for the words I taught him. He grinned like a lord's bastard when he came up with them. "Slan agut, a Mharie," he said.

And she kissed him again.

"What are we going to do with the lad?" she asked after he was gone.

"We're not going to do anything with him," I said. "And he's not a lad. He's only a couple years younger than us."

Mary Margaret wrapped her arms around one of mine and kissed me on the shoulder she'd been punching all night. "Ah, us, we're an old married couple, us. Now Joop, he's ready to be married."

"Wouldn't he be a better judge of that?" I asked.

She gave me an affectionate look and told me I was an idjit.

Later, in bed, Mary Margaret looked up from her book. "Now tell me this," she said. "Do you think lesbian couples trouble themselves over their unattached friends? And do they try to fix them up with nice girls? And do you suppose they sit up in bed late in the night, asking each other the same questions we do?"

"I suppose so," I said.

She looked back at her book. "How old is your client, her that's the lesbian?"

"Mid-thirties," I said. "About our age."

"It must be a terrible thing to be thrown out of your home by your lover, and then thrown in jail. And her being a poet. They're sensitive, poets. And jails are such dreadful places. Or so my da says, and he should know."

Mary Margaret's father had been interned by the British in the 1940s for being an Irish rebel. Or so he says. If all the men who claimed to have struck a blow for Old Ireland had really done so, the Brits would have been gone a long time past.

"Does the poor woman have friends to visit her at the jail?" she asked.

"She's probably not in jail," I said. "She's probably been shipped off to a psychiatric hospital by now."

"Ah, that's as bad or worse. And you haven't answered my question, have you. Does she have friends to visit her?"

"I don't know.

Mary Margaret shook her head. "It's a terrible hard world for a woman," she said. "Terrible hard."

J o o p   W h e e l e r

Thursday Night

I was jazzed. Mentally, at least. Physically, I wasn't worth a popcorn fart, as my old daddy used to say. I'd had far too little sleep. I like my eight hours. Nine, if I can get them. And maybe a nap in the afternoon.

But mentally, I was jazzed. A good case will do that. Sort of set your mind to racing. Looking at possibilities, searching for a new angle, trying to get a grasp on the facts. A good case intrudes on your thoughts.

And this case looked to be a good one. It had everything. Folks with a way of life totally different from my own. Bars and clubs I'd never been in—some I'd never even heard of. Places I'd never get to see outside of a case. It had a client who'd hit the outer boundaries of reality, and maybe stepped on past them a few times. And it had a wonderful, terrifying urgency. The type that makes every step and every decision seem critical.

The urgency, of course, was a problem. You're not supposed to be jazzed when there's a woman lying in a hospital bed with her skull bashed all in. A woman who was maybe about to die. A woman who'd probably been put in that hospital bed by her lover, who was our own lunatic client.

That wasn't a very pleasant thought. So I thought about something else. I thought about Stevie Gibbs. And what I thought was that it was a damn shame she was involved in the case. And it was a double damn shame I hadn't had the chance to meet her under more agreeable circumstances. Of course, I probably wouldn't have met her under agreeable circumstances.

I was maybe halfway home when I decided for about the

thirtieth time that Stevie probably wasn't a lesbian. Would I feel red lightning arcing through my blood if she was? Any woman who could grin like she'd grinned when she heard me doing the line from *Catch-22* had to have her sexual identity on straight.

Didn't she?

Then again, there was no reason she couldn't have her sexual identity on straight and still be a lesbian.

Was there?

It was all too confusing. So I decided to think about something else. Like Kath O'Mara.

A smart woman, Kath. And tough. What she lacked in freckles and Southernness, she made up for in smart and tough and attitude. And most definitely in heterosexuality. Probably.

But could I ask her out? I didn't think I could. Surely not while we were working together on this case. Not that the case would last forever. Depending on Amanda Owen.

Which was the same uncomfortable thought. So I decided to think about something else. Except that all of a sudden I was home.

My apartment seemed awfully small and empty when I walked in. It almost always does when I come back from an evening with the Sweeneys. It makes me think about my life. Which also seems a little small and empty when I come back from the Sweeneys'. Not that I spend a lot of time thinking about my life.

But sometimes I do.

What I was thinking was that I wanted what Sweeney and Mary Margaret have. Which is love. You can see those two really love each other. You can tell by the way they touch. It's not like they're clinging to each other all the time. At least not when I'm there. But they'll be sitting around and Sweeney will reach over and take Mary Margaret's hand and hold it awhile. It's not even like he's *thinking* about it. It just sort of happens, like it was a natural instinct. Like when a newborn animal takes to its momma's tit. And Mary Margaret, she does it too.

One of the reasons I like spending time with the Sweeneys, aside from the fact that I just plain like them both, is that they let some of their affection splash over onto me. Which is a great thing when I'm there. But not such a great thing when I get back to my place.

I don't even think of my place as *home*. I think of it as my *place*. It's a great apartment, as far as apartments go. Which isn't very far. It's easy to take care of, and comfortable, and full of things I like. But it's not a home.

Which was also a thing I decided I wanted. What I really wanted was to be in love. To be in love with somebody who was in love with me.

What I had instead was a caseload. A lunatic poet and her next-to-dead ex-lover. Which is just not the same.

I turned on the television as soon as I walked in the door. Noise helps create the illusion that the place isn't so empty. I'd thought about getting a dog. For the company. But you can't keep a decent-sized dog in an apartment. And I hate apartment-sized dogs. I'd as soon have a cat as an apartment-sized dog. And I hate cats.

As tired as I was, I knew my mind was too active for me to go to sleep. So I poured myself a couple of fingers of Glenmorangie Scotch and flipped through the television channels until I found a fishing show. I took off my shoes, lay down on the couch, propped the Scotch on my chest, and fell dead asleep.

Kevin Sweeney

Friday Morning

The Roadhouse Motel & Café was a piece of work. On the old highway, it was a long cinderblock building that had been painted white at some point in the distant past. It had probably been a decent family motel back when the paint was fresh and people still traveled the old highway. But after the interstate was built, nobody drove the old highway, and the neighborhood deteriorated. Like the other businesses in the neighborhood, the Roadhouse fell on hard times. Now it had adult movies piped in, and waterbeds under mirrored ceilings, and I doubt it saw many travelers.

I'd decided to check out the motel before calling Marty Coyle. I knew Marty from when I was a cop, although I'd never worked with him. My brother, God keep him, had gone through the academy with Marty and had worked with him in uniformed patrol. Mary Margaret knew his wife, who went to mass twice a week at St. Aloysius, where Mary Margaret did her volunteer work.

So I knew Marty, but not well enough to ask a favor. On top of that, I didn't want to take advantage of the relationship I had with Marty, thin as it was. But if we waited until Kathleen had done all the legal maneuvering required to get the police reports, Amanda Owen might be dead and our client looking at murder charges.

I didn't want to call Marty and ask the favor, but I knew I had to. I also knew I was using the Roadhouse as an excuse to avoid calling him. At least it was a valid excuse.

A hollow-cheeked woman stood behind the reception counter, drawing hard on an unfiltered Camel and watching a soap opera on the television. She had the bony look of a junkie and wore the loose, mismatched clothing of the really poor. But it seemed unlikely she was a junkie; you don't hire junkies as desk clerks. Not even at the Roadhouse.

I showed her my license while I smiled and introduced myself. She said her name was Gigi, which was probably a lie.

"I understand you had a bit of a fuss here last Wednesday."

"Wednesday?" She thought it over. "Oh, yeah. You mean the guy with the dwarf girl?" she asked. "Or you mean the crazy woman?"

"The crazy woman," I said. "Though it sounds like the guy with the dwarf is the better story."

"People do some weird shit," she said.

I had to admit they did.

"A dwarf," she said. "I never saw anything like that before, a guy wanting to do it with a dwarf." She made a face, which I suppose was intended to look like a dwarf's face.

"I suppose a man with a dwarf could be weird," I said.

"Unless he's a dwarf too," she said. "And maybe even then."

"About the crazy woman," I said.

"What about her? Is she in trouble?"

"She is, yes."

"We didn't want her to get in trouble," she said. "We just wanted to get her out of the unit. We don't—what's the word? We don't want to prosecute her or nothing."

"She's in trouble over something else," I said. "Something that had nothing to do with your motel."

"Oh. Okay then." She didn't care what the problem was, so long as she wasn't a part of it. "What did you want to know?"

I asked if I could see the registration card.

She hesitated. "I don't know," she said. "I don't think I'm supposed to be giving out that sort of information."

I put a twenty-dollar bill on the counter. Without looking

at the money, I said, "This is important. I'd really appreciate it." I turned and looked out the front window. When I turned back, the twenty was gone.

"What the hell." She pulled out a recipe box and shuffled through the cards. "Let's see. We're talking about Wednesday?"

I nodded. "Late Tuesday night or real early Wednesday morning."

After a moment she held up a card and flicked it with a dirty fingernail. "Early Wednesday. Just before two. Unit twenty-seven."

I held out my hand and, after hesitating for a moment, she handed me the registration card. It showed that unit 27 had been let to an Amanda Standish at 1:55 A.M. for thirty-five dollars in cash. It also noted two occupants. Finally, there was an obviously fake license-plate number. I knew it was fake because Massachusetts doesn't have license tags that begin with that prefix. The advantages of being an ex-cop.

Amanda Standish. The name was probably too similar to Amanda Owen to be a coincidence. And Amanda Standish had the same initials as Anka Stiffel.

I tapped the card on the counter. "Were you on duty when this person checked in?"

"Nope. I work mornings. You'd have to talk with Ed."

"Ed. He have a last name?"

"Harriman. Ed Harriman."

"Where can I find Ed?"

"Right here. Comes on at eleven at night, stays till seven in the morning, Tuesday through Saturday."

"You know where Ed lives?"

She shook her head. "Somewheres around here. But I don't know where."

"Are you the person who called in the complaint about the crazy woman?"

She nodded and lit another cigarette. "Yeah, that was

me. Woman was howling like a goddamn dog. Like one of those women on the news."

"On the news?"

"Yeah, you know. Like in Israel or one of them other Arab countries. When their sons get themselves killed planting bombs or whatever it is they do over there. They howl, those women, at the funerals. And that's what"—she consulted the registration card—"this Amanda Standish woman that's what she was doing. Howling like an Arab at a funeral."

"You ask her to stop?"

"Goddamn right I did. I didn't just ask her. I damn well *told* her to stop. 'Knock that shit off,' I says, 'we got people trying to sleep here.'"

The idea of somebody trying to sleep at the Roadhouse was new to me. "You tell her this in person or over the phone?" I was hoping for a description.

"Over the phone. Called her up and told her to knock that shit off before I called the cops."

"But she didn't," I said. "Knock it off, I mean."

"Nope, not for long. Maybe for a few minutes, she did. I must have called her back, told her maybe four, five times. Then I said fuck it, and called the cops. I figured, let them deal with her."

"What time did this happen?"

"Christ, must have been eight-thirty. Maybe nine. Something like that. I didn't call the cops till like ten-thirty. I had to. Can't afford to scare off the lunch crowd, you know."

I nodded and smiled. "Got to take care of business."

"That's right."

"Tell me, how often do the rooms get cleaned?"

"Well, they're supposed to be cleaned after every guest leaves," she said with a smile.

"Does it always get done?"

She shook her head. "Between you and me? Sometimes

the sheets don't even get changed." She grinned. "Unless they're real nasty and messy."

"You mind if I look at the room?"

She shook her head and continued to grin. "I don't. But the people using it might not like it so much."

I looked at my watch. Ten-fifteen A.M. "They'll be checking out soon, won't they?"

"Honey, they only checked in an hour ago."

I smiled. "How long you think they'll be?"

"One o'clock," she said. "Usually. They're regulars, them two. Every other Friday, nine to one. Been going on for months like that."

I looked at my watch. "I can't wait until one," I said.

She shrugged. "If you can talk your way in there now, it's okay with me."

I thought about it. "Can't do any harm to try, can it?"

"You'd know that better than me," she said. "Last unit on the left."

Most of the cars in the lot were parked at the end of the building. Nobody staying at the Roadhouse wanted their car recognized from the street.

As I walked down the sidewalk, a very young, very effeminate black man walked out of unit 19, wearing a bright yellow rain slicker although it was a sunny day. He gave me a shy smile and a little wave as he strolled away. I started to wonder what was going on in unit 19, then decided I didn't really want to know. I probably wouldn't understand it anyhow.

I knocked on the door of unit 27. A moment later I heard the sound of bare feet pad toward the door. I stood directly in front of the peephole so I could be seen clearly and tried to look as trustworthy as the pope.

"Who is it?" a man asked.

"My name is Kevin Sweeney."

"What do you want?"

It was a good question. What the hell *did* I want? "I need to look in your room," I said. "A client of mine may have left something in it."

"A client?"

"Yes sir."

"Jesus Christ." There was more whispering. "What is it?"

"What is what?"

"What got left in the fucking room?"

"Oh. I'm, uh, I'm not sure."

"You're what? What do you mean, not sure?"

"Look, it'll take a long time to explain. But the sooner you let me in the room, the sooner I can find it and the sooner I'll leave you alone."

Still more whispering. I heard the man say, "He looks okay. What the fuck, I'm going to let him in."

I couldn't make out the muffled reply.

"Hey, I'm letting him in," the man whispered loudly. "You want to wait in the bathroom? What? Jesus, Tammy, just wait in the fucking bathroom, why don't you. Just till I can get rid of the guy. Well, you don't have to if you don't want to. But at least get under the sheet, huh? Cover yourself up. Jesus fucking Christ."

The chain came off the door and it opened. The man, a hairy guy about ten pounds too heavy and beginning to go bald, had a bedspread wrapped around his waist.

I thanked him and stepped into the room. A mousy red-haired woman was in the waterbed, with the sheet pulled up around her chin.

"Sorry to bother you like this," I said. "I appreciate you letting me in."

"Yeah, well, do what you got to do," the man said. He closed the door behind me.

I glanced around the room. "I'm going to be straight with you people," I said. "Here's my problem. I'm working for a woman who's been charged with a serious crime—attempted murder. She says she stayed in this room a couple nights ago, and maybe was here when the crime was being committed. What I'm looking for is anything she might have left behind."

"What're you, a lawyer?" the man asked.

"No, sir, I'm a private investigator," I said. I showed him my license. "I didn't want to say that when I was outside. I didn't think you'd let me in."

"Too fucking right," the man said, without bothering to look at the license. "Shit, you're not working for my old lady, are you?"

I shook my head. "No, sir. I'm not."

"Are you really a private eye?" the woman asked.

I nodded and showed her my license.

"Oh, wow, Bertie. He really is." She let the sheet inch down to her shoulders. She had freckles on her shoulders. "Is there anything we can do to help?"

"Well, you can help me look through the drawers and closets and bathroom. See if there's anything you didn't bring in with you, anything that looks like it might not belong here."

"Bertie'll have to help you," the woman said with a smile. "I'm naked under here." She raised the sheet and looked down at herself. "Sorry."

"Jesus, Tammy," the man said. "Advertise it, why don't you." He walked into the bathroom.

I started on the dresser. Aside from some cheap stationery and a few envelopes, all of which were blank and empty, the drawers were bare. The closet was just a cubbyhole and, except for Bertie's ugly sport coat, it was empty. There was some clothing—both men's and women's—strewn across a chair.

"There's nothing in here except for a Bible." I turned and saw Tammy stretched out across the bed, only her hips hidden under the sheet. She was looking at me over her shoulder, holding a green Gideon Bible. "Sorry," she said.

"Uh, that's fine."

She made no effort to crawl back under the covers, but continued to look at me over her freckled shoulder. Her feet wiggled playfully under the sheet. I turned and searched the empty closet again.

"There's nothing in the bathroom." Bertie stood in the bathroom doorway, staring at Tammy. "Jesus," he said A tent began to form under the bedspread, and a wild smile spread over his face.

"I'll just take a quick look," I said. "To be sure."

Tammy giggled. "I think you already had a quick look." Bertie waved me into the bathroom without taking his eyes off her.

The bathroom was almost as empty as the closet and took only a moment to search. When I came out of the bathroom, Bertie was sitting on the side of the bed. Tammy was back under the sheet.

"I, uh, I should probably look under the bed," I said.

Tammy smiled. "Oh, go right ahead."

I knelt beside the bed and looked. It was a platform bed; there was no "under" to it.

"Well, I guess that's it," I said, standing. "I appreciate your help. Sorry to bother you."

"Wait a minute," Tammy said. "Hand me my purse." She pointed to a woven bag hanging from the back of a chair.

I gave her the bag and she rummaged through it. She pulled out a shiny green matchbook. "Here," she said, holding it out to me. "This was in the ashtray when I got here."

I took the matchbook. It was from a bar called Jenever in Truro, on Cape Cod. Nothing was written on the inside cover.

"Does it help?" Tammy asked.

I shrugged. "I don't know. It might." I put the matchbook in my shirt pocket. "Well, thanks again."

"Wait a minute," Tammy said again. "You sure you have

to go?" She dropped the sheet to her waist and touched her breast. "We could have some fun."

I looked at her, then at Bertie. Then back at her.

"You could help me with a fantasy," she said. "Bertie says I give good head."

"*Great* head," Bertie agreed. "I got to tell you, buddy, this girl, she could suck the chrome off a trailer hitch."

I cleared my throat. "I've got an appointment," I said. I pointed to my watch.

Tammy ran her hand from her breast down under the sheet, between her legs. She didn't look mousy anymore. "You sure you wouldn't rather stick around?"

"Uh, I would. But I can't."

"Well, we're here every other Friday," she said. "Same time. Drop in again sometime."

I promised her I'd think about it.

J o o p W h e e l e r

Friday Evening

I'd never been to the Loading Zone before. Mainly because
it's a gay and lesbian bar and I don't fit into either of those
categories. I *could* have gone there, I suppose. If I'd wanted
to. You don't *have* to be gay to hang out there. I spend some
time at a little Palestinian coffee shop, after all, and I'm about
as Palestinian as I am gay.

Anyway, I'd never been to the Zone and so I was eager
to go there. I hadn't been to Laurel's, either, but that was
diffcrent. Laurel's was respectable. Even politicians went to
Laurel's. Women politicians, that is. After all, it was a
women's club.

That was the only attraction to Laurel's, far as I could
see. Men were barred from all but one room. A windowless
little twelve-by-twelve room stuck right off the entryway, so
you didn't even have a chance to snoop around. Wasn't hardly
big enough to hold two chairs and a table to put your beer
mug on.

It was about half frustrating, is what it was. Being confined to that little room, knowing there was a whole building
full of women doing whatever it is women do when men
aren't around. I tried to work up a sense of outrage at being
treated like a second-class citizen. Couldn't do it, though. I'd
been a white male too long.

Except for that one twist, Laurel's turned out to be a
yawn. Well, it wasn't that bad. I got to sit in that little room,
talking with one woman after another. Which is always nice.
And each time I'd finish with one, Stevie would wander off
and fetch me back another. If it hadn't been for the fact that
I was confined to that single room, I'd have enjoyed it.

Of course, I didn't learn a damn thing at Laurel's. Only that Stevie and Anka had, in fact, been there. And that a lot of folks thought Anka seemed irritable and distracted. And that a few of them thought maybe she was looking for Amanda Owen. But we already knew that.

I kept tossing out the name Amanda Standish, the name Sweeney got from the Roadhouse Motel. But nobody recognized it. Not even Stevie.

At the Loading Zone, I didn't have to confine myself. At least not in the regular sense. The Zone wasn't like any other gay bar I'd ever been in. Not that I've been in that many, and only in the line of duty. There wasn't a lot of mirrors, or any loud music, or any aggressive cruising.

The Zone was a pleasant little jazz bar that catered to gay folks. At least, it catered to gay men. Now, I know only idiots say things like "I can spot one a mile away." But the guys at the Zone were mostly the sort you'd look at and be willing to bet your paycheck they were gay. I know that sounds stupid and bigoted, but you really *could* tell. Maybe not from a mile away, but from the other side of a dimly lit bar it wasn't that tough.

It was different with the women. There wasn't anything about the women that made you think they were lesbians. Assuming they were. For the most part, they just looked like all women. A few sort of fit the dyke stereotype, but that might have just been me responding to the Zone's reputation.

In general, the Loading Zone seemed like a nice little place where folks would go to listen to music and chat quietly. I decided maybe I'd come back sometime, when I wasn't working. Maybe bring a date. Maybe.

But probably not.

Stevie and I took a table in the back of the bar, where we could talk in semi-normal voices and still have some privacy.

A cadaverous, pasty-white woman was singing on the tiny stage, accompanied by an equally cadaverous, pasty-white guy on the piano. Both were dressed totally in black. Classic East Coast hip. Except the woman had a satiny red patch over her left eye. It was the only lick of color to either of them. They favored each other so much they could have been brother and sister. The Albino Family Singers.

The singer's name was Michelle, and she was one of the women we were there to see. She and two other women had tipped a few drinks with Anka and Stevie on the night of the fight. I wanted to find out what they remembered about that night.

We were a tad early. The other women hadn't arrived, and Michelle had to finish her set. So Stevie and I ordered drinks and chatted. Detailed, mindless conversation is a Southern idiosyncrasy I learned to repress when I moved to New England. Northern folks don't really chat. Or when they do, they don't do it very well. Some of them don't even talk. They actually take *pride* in their lack of conversation. Taciturn, they like to call it. I swear Sweeney can go for days without making a sound, except for a few barks and grunts when he gets hungry. It's not that he doesn't *like* to talk. He does. He's Irish. It's just that he doesn't find it *necessary*.

I was telling Stevie about the time my uncle Hoover, who was a highly cultured man for a teetotaler, had been given a sizable jug of moonshine by an old school buddy of his. After a few experimental sips—just out of politeness to his old buddy—Uncle Hoover was suddenly and irresistibly overwhelmed by the impulse to steal a bulldozer that some poor fool had left in the parking lot of the Ezekiel Baptist Church and drive it over to the house of Miss Lucy Baxter, his first true love. Miss Lucy had broken my poor uncle's heart when she'd refused his invitation to the cotillion some thirty years earlier. They'd both got married in the intervening years—not to each other, of course—and raised up families. But Uncle Hoover, he continued to moon over Miss Lucy.

I'd just reached the point in the story where Uncle

Hoover had lost control of the bulldozer while crossing the railroad tracks. He was traveling at what the police called a high rate of speed for a bulldozer, and he took out about forty yards of fence, allowing almost all of Clell Purcell's horses to escape their pasture and scatter over a good part of Georgetown County.

Then the other women arrived in the bar and I had to hush up. Stevie stood and waved them over.

I didn't know much about the women we were supposed to meet. The little bit of information I'd got from Stevie as we drove to the Loading Zone from Laurel's was interesting. But not truly helpful.

"Deirdre and Carol Anne have their own business," she'd told me. "They do plants."

"They do *what* to plants?"

"They take care of them." Deirdre and Carol Anne, she said, rented plants to office buildings and hotels and the like, then contracted to take care of them, make sure they looked nice and green and healthy. Nobody likes to walk into an office full of brown, dying plants. Doesn't inspire trust and confidence.

"Great scam," I said. "Anything else I should know about them?"

Stevie nodded. "Deirdre is a TS."

"Is that right?" I asked. I was glad we were driving. I was able to pretend I was concentrating on traffic while I tried to figure out just what the hell "TS" might stand for. Totally sexy? Tough stud? Tropical storm?

Stevie must have picked up on my confusion. "She's a transsexual," she said.

"Oh." I nodded. "A transsexual."

"She's still coming to grips with her lesbianism."

"Pardon?" I said. "She's a transsexual lesbian?"

Stevie nodded.

"You mean she's a man who had surgery to become a lesbian?"

She nodded again and watched me closely, waiting for me to say something stupid. Which I could have done very easily. In fact, I couldn't think of anything to say that wouldn't be stupid. So I just kept my mouth shut and kept on driving.

I suppose once you accept the idea that a guy can feel he's a woman trapped inside a man's body, and feel it so strongly he's willing to go under the knife to change it, then it's only a small leap to accept that he might also feel he's a *lesbian* trapped inside a man's body. It's not the strangest thing I've ever heard of.

Pretty damn close, though.

After she saw I wasn't going to say anything stupid, Stevie told me about Michelle, the singer with the scarlet eye patch. She didn't mention the scarlet eye patch, though. Maybe because she didn't think it was important. Or because it wasn't polite to discuss another person's disabilities. Or maybe because it was just a stage prop. Who knows?

What she did tell me was that Michelle had a long-term and severe crush on Amanda Owen. Like Amanda, Michelle was a sculptor. When she wasn't singing.

"They spend much time together?" I asked. I thought maybe sculptors hang out together, the same way lawyers or cops do.

Stevie nodded. "Some," she said.

"Did Amanda know Michelle had a crush on her?"

"Probably. Everybody else knew."

"Anka? Did she know?"

She nodded again. "It wasn't a secret."

"Did Amanda and Michelle ever . . ."

"Sleep together?" Stevie shook her head. "Not that I know. And I'd know."

"Any artistic jealousy?" One of the first rules of criminal-defense work is to find somebody else to pin the crime on. Michelle might be a good place to start.

Stevie must have figured out what I was doing. Or else she suddenly remembered who and what I was. At any rate, she became reluctant to discuss her friends' personal relationships.

I couldn't blame her. It can't be pleasant to discuss your friends with a person whose job is to dig dirt. And since I wanted Stevie to like me—or at least trust me—I steered the conversation to a less stressful topic. My poor old uncle Hoover.

That took us all the way to the parking lot of the Loading Zone, into the bar, back to the table, and up to the moment when the plant merchants arrived.

Both were dressed in your standard businesswoman's outfit: semi-conservative suit with skirt; large bag; and sneakers. As they approached I tried to pick out which was the transsexual.

The tall one, I decided. The one with the linebacker shoulders and the jaw that hinted at five o'clock shadow. The other woman was too small. She was what my momma would have called willowy.

They stood near the stage and watched Michelle of the eye patch finish her set. Then they all headed back for our table. Michelle was the tallest of the three, but easily the thinnest. She couldn't have weighed much more than a hundred pounds. Anorexia as a fashion statement.

Suddenly I was confronted with an etiquette crisis. To stand or not? Being raised by a proper Southern woman, I was trained from an early age in the anachronistic drill of the social graces. I was trained to the degree that my courtesy had nothing to do with courtesy. It was involuntary behavior. Like a dog that salivates at the dinner bell. It would have been easier for me to drop trou in church than to be rude to a guest.

But we live in an unruly age. Traditional good manners

can be bad politics. You open a door for a woman, she thinks you're saying she can't open it her ownself. Your reasons for opening the door don't matter. The sad fact is, I was trained to open doors for *everybody*, man, woman, and child. And I did it for the same reason a Marine always checks the chamber of a weapon, even one he *knows* is unloaded. Not because it's necessary, but because of good training.

It was the discovery that etiquette can be rude that actually taught me good manners. Eventually, I learned that sometimes it's good manners *not* to open a door. Good manners also means learning to hesitate before doing anything that might stink of etiquette. Being among the heathen Yankees cost me my etiquette, but taught me good manners.

However, nothing in my training had ever prepared me to know the appropriate behavior for gay and lesbian piano bars. My feet told me a gentleman always stands when receiving company, regardless of gender. But my head told me it might be seen as condescending. And condescension is bad manners. Always.

While I was trying to decide what to do, my feet just up and took over. Before I knew it, I found myself standing up. Betrayed by my rebel feet. And there wasn't a damn thing I could do about it.

Then Stevie stood up as well. Which made my instinctive gesture seem harmless and nonsexist. I glanced at her to see if she'd done it on purpose, to save me from my sexist feet. And she smiled at me.

Wham—red lightning lightened through my heart.

I managed to wrestle the red lightning to the ground and get through the introductions. As we shook hands, I peeked, trying to confirm my guess about the TS. Men tend to have larger hands than women. And regardless of what sort of surgical wonders had been performed elsewhere, I doubted there'd be any major modification of the hands.

The tall woman's hands were about average size. Stevie

introduced her as Carol Anne. So much for Joop Wheeler, private eye, sees all, knows all.

The willowy blonde was Deirdre, the lesbian TS. I tried not to stare at her. And I tried not to *not* stare at her. But the pure fact is I was fascinated by her. Not along red-lightning lines. But architecturally, I guess you'd call it.

A waitron arrived as we sat down and the others ordered drinks. I refused another glass of white wine with the lie that a second glass would go right to my head. Some people like to see the stereotype of the hard-drinking private detective affirmed. Others like to see it contradicted. These women, I thought, would probably prefer not to share a table with the traditional P.I.

Truth was that the wine tasted like kerosene. I'd have asked for a beer, but I was afraid it would seem too overtly male.

After we got comfortable, I explained who I was, who I worked for, and what I wanted. Which was to find out about the events that led up to the fight between Anka and Amanda.

Michelle of the eye patch spoke first. "Anka was fuckin' out there that night, wasn't she," she said, in a sort of mock British accent. "It was like she was on a long speed run, all excited and edgy, like."

Carol Anne shook her head. "No, I don't think she was edgy. Excited, yes. But not edgy. I thought she was, I don't know . . ." She searched for a word. "I thought she was more . . ."

"She was fuckin' *wired*," Michelle said. "She was bouncing around like . . . I don't like what."

"Like water on a hot skillet?" I suggested. It was a line my momma used to describe me when I was about eight years old.

She nodded. "Yeah, like that."

I asked if they thought Anka might have been doing drugs.

"No, not Anka," Carol Anne said. "Anka didn't need drugs. She had everything she needed inside her."

"What bullshit," Michelle said. "Nobody's got everything they need inside." She wrapped a leg underneath herself. I swear, I don't know how women bend like that. "Anka Stiffel was more fucked up than anybody I ever met. Including me."

I turned to Deirdre, who hadn't said a word. "What do you think?"

She hesitated before speaking. When she spoke, her voice was very soft. She didn't sound like a man at all. She sounded like a woman with a very sexy whiskey-and-cigarettes voice.

"I think Anka was really upset about something," she said. "She was—what's the word?—agitated. But I don't think it was because of drugs."

"Why, then?" I asked.

"She was pissed 'cause she got dumped," Michelle said. "It's obvious, isn't it? She didn't have anybody to take care of her anymore."

"Well, I agree Anka was upset," Carol Anne said. "And I agree that it was probably because she and Amanda split up. But I don't think Anka was only interested in having somebody to take care of her."

"Amanda paid the bills, bought the food, did the fuckin' laundry," Michelle said. "And Anka took advantage of it."

"Well . . ." Carol Anne began.

"She fuckin' used Amanda, and you know it." Michelle leaned forward and pointed angrily at Carol Anne. "She may be a fine poet and a good lay, but she's also a fuckin' leech."

"Please," I said. "I don't think there's any point in getting angry."

"There's a perfect fuckin' point in getting angry," Michelle said. "Amanda's lying in that damn hospital and the bitch that put her there is trying to pretend like nothing happened."

"Do you know Anka did it?" Stevie asked.

"Too right she did it," Michelle answered.

"But you don't *know* she . . ."

I held up a hand, interrupting Stevie. I didn't want to see any arguments getting started. And I didn't want to get booted out of the bar for making too much noise. But I guess loud, angry discussions must have been common at the Zone, because nobody seemed to be paying us any mind. Nobody even seemed to be listening. Which was good. Because most of all what I didn't want was to hear Michelle say that she did, in fact, *know* Anka did it. Not in front of witnesses.

"Look," I said. "Let's just stick to the things you saw and heard with your own eyes and ears. Did Anka say or do anything that night that made you think she was angry with or wanted to harm Amanda?" I pointed at Deirdre.

She thought about it for a moment, then shook her head. "She was upset. And she might have been angry. But I can't say who she was angry at. Or why." She gave Michelle an apologetic look.

I pointed to Carol Anne, who shook her head. "I can't recall anything she said or did that would show she was angry at Amanda. But I have to admit I think she was."

"Why?"

"Well, Amanda *had* kicked her out of the house. And Anka loved that house, though I couldn't tell you why—it's far too suburban to be believed." She looked at Michelle. "And I still think she loved—*loves*—Amanda. Even if she was angry at her."

"Angry enough to hurt her?" Stevie asked. Which wasn't a question I would have asked.

"Maybe," Carol Anne admitted.

"Okay." I pointed at Michelle. "Did Anka say to you or do anything that made you think she was angry at Amanda?"

She nodded.

"What?" I asked.

Michelle squinted her one eye. "Anka said she was looking for Amanda. She asked me if I'd seen her that night. She knew I was . . . that I was, well, interested in Amanda. And I guess she thought maybe we were sleeping together."

"Were you?" Stevie asked. Saving me from having to ask the awkward question.

Michelle shook her head. "No. No such luck. Besides . . ." She rattled the ice in her glass.

"Go on," I said.

"Look, I don't like Anka. I don't think that's any fuckin' secret. But I don't want to be a snitch, either."

"There's a difference between snitching and giving the facts," I lied.

Michelle focused on the ice in her glass. "Anka asked me if I'd seen Amanda and I said no, I hadn't, which was the truth. Then she got real close to me and sort of whispered to me. She said, 'If she's sleeping around on me, I'll cut her throat. And the bitch she's sleeping with.' I just sort of looked at her, you know? I couldn't believe she was threatening me like that."

Her anorexic male clone dragged himself over to our table with a sigh of exertion. He tapped his watch and raised his eyebrows. He looked bored and petulant at the same time.

"Hey, I'll be there in a minute," Michelle said. She looked at me. "Is there anything else you want to know?"

I decided there was. "It's sort of a personal question," I said. "Nothing to do with the case."

"What is it?"

"It's really none of my business," I said.

She made a face, but waved me on.

So I asked her. "The eye patch. You wear it for a reason? Or just for effect?" I almost winced as I asked it. Not because it was so rude. But because it *sounded* so rude.

She looked at me like I'd just urinated in her drink. "None of your fuckin' business."

I nodded. It really wasn't.

After she left, Carol Anne said, "You'll have to forgive her. She's been infatuated with Amanda for a long time. This has really hit her hard."

"It's okay," I said. "Look, Michelle said she and Amanda weren't sleeping together. But is it possible . . ."

Stevie shook her head. "I don't think so. I only asked the question so you wouldn't have to. I doubt she'd have answered you."

I felt the snap and spark of red lightning again.

Carol Anne agreed. "The lesbian community here is pretty tight-knit," she said. "We usually have a pretty good idea who's doing who."

"Must be a problem sometimes," I said.

"You have no idea," Carol Anne said into her glass.

We talked for another twenty minutes, but nothing much came of it. None of them had ever heard of Amanda Standish. Who I was beginning to think didn't really exist. Sweeney had suggested that possibility, because of the coincidence of the name Amanda and of the initials—Amanda Standish, Anka Stiffel.

While I settled the bill—I told them it was going on my expenses, which made it okay—Stevie slipped off to the head. I was standing near the bar, trying to figure out fifteen percent of eighteen dollars, when Deirdre the TS approached me.

"Mr. Wheeler?"

"Call me Joop," I said.

"Joop, then." She leaned her hip against the bar and stared at her hands while she made up her mind to talk. "Do you know a bar called Kozinsky's? Over on Belmont?"

I nodded. I must know most of the bars in the tri-state

area. I know bars the way salesmen know their routes. At least I know the heterosexual bars.

"Can you meet me there in half an hour?" she asked. "By yourself?"

"Why?" It seemed like a reasonable question to ask.

"I think there's something I ought to tell you," she said.

As I looked at her, trying to decide what she really wanted, she shrugged and adjusted her bra strap. She didn't think about it. She just did it. It made me realize Deirdre was a woman and comfortable with it. Regardless of what her DNA might say.

"You can't tell me here?" I asked.

She shook her head. "I'd rather not."

I thought about it for a moment, then decided why the hell not? If you're going to avoid bizarre and peculiar situations, what's the point of being a private investigator? One thing that makes the job interesting is the potential for serious weirdness.

So I grinned and said, "Okay. Kozinsky's. Half an hour."

I had a date with a transsexual lesbian.

I do love this work.

Kevin Sweeney

Friday Night

Marty Coyle and I sat in a booth in the front of Mick Croker's Public House, far enough from the music and the dart boards to have a conversation. Even though it was a Friday night and there was a band, the pub wasn't crowded. Mick's was never as busy as the more rabidly Irish bars because he refused to hire "popular" Irish bands, the ones that played the "fun" Irish songs. Mick hated fun Irish songs. I recall the night he had to be physically restrained from taking a fish-billy to a duo that started to sing "The Unicorn Song," complete with hand gestures.

Mick Croker used to be an attorney, and a good one. Joop and I had done work for him before he quit lawyering and became a publican. One day without warning he'd stopped taking new cases and closed his old ones. Then he disappeared for five or six months—to Ireland, he said, and it might have been true. When he returned, he opened the pub, and he never seemed to regret it. The pub was modestly popular among cops, firefighters, and lawyers.

Marty looked at me over the top of his beer mug. His eyes showed the same friendly wariness I'd seen earlier when I'd invited him to join me for a beer when he went off duty.

I couldn't blame him for being cautious and skeptical. He knew the invitation carried more weight than a simple after-work beer.

It had taken me a while to gather the nerve to go see Marty. But I knew I had to see him in the flesh. I was going to do a thing I'd said I would never do—use my status as an ex-cop to get special treatment. Worse, I was trying to get the special treatment from another cop. It wasn't the sort of favor I could ask over the telephone.

I'd hated it when I was a cop. There was always somebody who wanted something—a ticket fixed, a child talked to, a creditor appeased, a debtor found and maybe leaned on. A cop is a useful "friend." And now I was about to use a cop myself.

When we were sitting, I said, "I know it's a little out of bounds, what I'm about to ask you. So feel free to tell me to go fuck myself."

"I always felt free to tell that to your brother Emmett," he said. "I guess I can do the same for you."

I was glad he'd mentioned my oldest brother, God keep him. Emmett had been a cop before quitting to join the Marines. He was killed in Saigon during the last days of the war in Vietnam. He and Marty had gone through the police academy together. By bringing Emmett's name into it, Marty was reminding me of the reason he was at Mick Croker's. Not for me, but for Emmett.

"I figure you know what this is about," I said.

He nodded. "Yeah, I got an idea." He took a long pull at his beer and used the cocktail napkin to wipe his mouth. "I'm guessing you want the book on your dyke assault, the one you're workin' on with your pal that's named after a dog."

I nodded. "Joop."

"Joop," he said, grinning. "That a true story, about the dog? Or is that just something that he runs on people, to get them interested?"

"True story."

Marty kept grinning and shook his head.

I cleared my voice and started in. "The reason we want the book on the Owen case is—"

"Is because you know the Owen woman is lookin' like she's probably gonna die, right?"

I nodded. "Right as rain."

"And she's probably gonna die pretty soon, which means if you wait until you get our reports through official channels, your dyke will be lookin' at a murder charge instead of the agg assault."

"There it is," I said.

"So you want me to unload everything now."

"Not everything," I said. "Just some of it."

"Some of it. Like what?"

"Like the results of your forensic boys, like—"

"Don't be callin' them 'boys.'" Marty grinned. "Maybe a quarter of them are girls now. I mean women. You call them boys *or* girls and you're lookin' at a lawsuit."

"Your forensic crew, I meant to say. And the name of the neighbor who found Owen. Maybe even a look in the house where it happened."

"Forget the house." Marty shook his head. "No way in hell you're gettin' in the house. Never happen."

"Fine," I said. That he specified the house was a good sign. Maybe he'd get in the car on the rest. "The house is forgotten. What about signs of forced entry or a struggle in the house?"

Marty picked up his glass and examined it. "This is just between you and me, right?"

"Right."

"I mean, you gotta understand this. I'm only tellin' you this because it don't make any real difference whether you get the information now or you get it in three weeks."

"I understand."

"And because you and your whole family was all cops. And Emmett was a good friend."

I nodded again.

"And it ain't like this is gonna get to be a habit, you lookin' for information from me."

I agreed with him.

"Okay then. No sign of forced entry," Marty said.

"Which is no surprise since your dyke had a key. And no sign of a struggle, so we figure the victim knew the person who whacked her." He grinned. "Sound like your client?"

"Probably just a coincidence," I said. "And the forensic stuff?"

Marty waved a hand. "No help. For you or me. The weapon was some sort of African-looking statue. Stone. Had some of the victim's skin and hair on it, but we couldn't lift any decent prints. Surface was too rough. Not that prints would prove much since your dyke lived there."

"Unless the prints didn't belong to either Anka Stiffel or Amanda Owen," I said.

Marty made a skeptical face. "Yeah. Well, we sent it down to the FBI," he said. "Let them do their high-tech magic on it. But I don't have no hopes for anything to come from it."

"This statue, did the Owen woman make it?"

Marty shrugged and made a dismissive gesture. "Who the fuck knows? What difference does it make, who made it? It's who whacked the victim with it that matters."

"Any chance of seeing the photos?" I asked without hope.

"None. Not until all the lawyer stuff is done."

"I didn't think so," I nodded. "How about the person who found the victim?"

"Neighbor named . . ." He squinted while he drew up the mental case file. "Named Callie Dobson. Lives directly next door to the victim."

"What's she like?" I asked.

"The Dobson woman? White bread. Uptight. A housewife, which is something you don't see much anymore, do you? Nosy neighbor. You know the type. Gave us a good statement, though. She's the one gave us the tip on your dyke."

"She knew about the fight in the bar?" I'd asked.

"Naw," Marty said. "I doubt she's ever been in a bar in her life, gay or straight. No, what she knew was that your dyke was crazy and that the victim had kicked her out. That was enough to make us want to ask her a few questions. We tracked your dyke down and found she was staying with a woman named . . ." His face screwed up again.

"Stephanie Gibbs," I said.

Marty cocked his head and grinned. "That's the name. You must be a detective. I ought to ask how you found that out."

"Learned it through good detective work," I said.

"Ah." He nodded. "Somebody told you."

"Right. How did *you* track her down?"

Marty waved a hand. "Nothing to it," he said. "Your dyke's new address and telephone number was stuck on the victim's refrigerator with a magnet." He began to laugh. "This magnet, Kevin, you should have seen it, it was shaped like a woman's pussy. You believe that? Robbins, that prick, tried to lift it. You remember Drew Robbins?"

I nodded. "What did you do?"

"Made him put it back. What are you gonna do? He's a prick, but that don't stop him from being a good detective."

"So you went looking for Anka Stiffel and found Stephanie Gibbs. She the one told you about the fight?" I asked.

"She's the one." Marty nodded. "Said they'd had a go at each other at some place called Shooter's or Shots or something."

"Schotzie's."

He nodded. "Jesus, and what a place that is. You been there yet?"

I shook my head. "Joop's handling that end of the stick."

"Better him than me. Some tough women there. But guess what else we found in this bar, this Schotzie's? What we found was a rage of lesbians who corroborated the Gibbs woman's story about the fight."

I sipped my beer. From our perspective, the case was looking about as healthy as Amanda Owen.

Marty Coyle critically examined the last of his beer, then drank it off and set down his glass with a grunt of satisfaction. "Kevin, I think your dyke is gonna go down over this." He looked up and smiled. "No pun intended."

It was far past visiting hours when I found myself walking up the steps of the Potterwood Memorial Hospital, looking for what was left of Amanda Owen. I hate hospitals, always have, the way they smell and the way they're always cold. And I hate the thought of what happens in hospitals and the way the people are treated.

As a cop and as a private detective, I've seen a lot of suffering and death, and I've become toughened to it. But hospitals are different. There is no passion in the suffering done in hospitals. Hospitals don't seem to bother Mary Margaret, who visits the sick members of the parish, but the very air of a hospital makes my skin crawl.

I should have been home with Mary Margaret, or taking her to that Italian restaurant she wanted to go to. There was no good reason for me to be wandering the dark halls looking for the intensive-care unit. It wasn't as though Amanda Owen would be able to answer my questions; the woman was comatose. And there wasn't anything I could learn simply by looking at her. But I felt obliged to see her. Must be a Catholic thing.

The halls were empty except for the housekeeping staff, who mopped and buffed the floors in a frenzy and left an obstacle course of little yellow signs warning that the floors were wet and slippery. At times the hum of the buffers was so loud I couldn't hear my footsteps and I had the feeling that my feet were barely touching the floor as I walked.

A thin, gray-haired nurse walked briskly down the hall. I almost asked her for directions to the ICU, but I was intimidated by her military bearing. Her dress was startlingly white and heavily starched, with a crease sharp enough to shave with. We traded nods as she passed and I could hear her white-nyloned thighs rustle against the stiff dress. It was a little erotic, and somehow a little spooky.

I thought about leaving and coming back during normal visiting hours, when the place would be less creepy. Maybe come back tomorrow. Or later in the week. Or maybe not coming back at all.

And that's what made me stay. I was afraid this might be my only chance to see her. Either her family or the hospital staff would keep me from seeing her during the day, and my nerves would prevent me from seeing her at night.

An orderly pushing a wobbly-wheeled gurney shot around the corner, startling me. There seemed to be an imprint of the last passenger on the gurney's thin black mattress.

That gurney mattress disturbed me. I had the feeling if I put my hand on it, I'd feel something of the last person to lie there. A warmth, maybe. Or a coldness. Something.

Eventually I reached the ICU. I tried to shake off the jitters before going in, but without much success. After the quiet of the halls, the noise and motion of the ICU was shocking. Heart monitors beeped, suction machines hummed, respirators chugged. Dials fluctuated, lights flashed, fluids dripped. Everything demanded attention, everything seemed active.

Everything except for the patients, who just lay there, pale and neuter. They were like extensions of the machines, as if flesh had to be attached to the machines in order for them to work properly. As if the machines were feeding off the patients.

The doctors and nurses moved around the room with an economy of motion that was almost graceful, going from machine to machine, adjusting this and arranging that. When they touched a patient, which they seemed to avoid doing, it was with brusque efficiency.

I'd brought along a recent photograph of Amanda, one Joop had gotten from the Gibbs woman. I searched the faces of the patients for one that resembled the one in the photograph, but I couldn't spot her. I had to check the chart attached to the foot of each bed.

One was labeled Amanda Owen. In the bed was a waxy, hollow-cheeked imitation of a woman who bore a superficial resemblance to the woman in the photograph. Her head was wrapped in white gauze, and a pale fluid dripped stingily from a clear plastic bag into a tube sticking in her arm. A thick, yellow fluid oozed through another tube running from under the sheet.

She smelled bad. Her arms were outside the sheet, exposing her sculptor's muscles. I wondered how long it would be before those muscles wasted away. I touched her shoulder, just above the sheet. Her skin was cool and rubbery, like an inner tube, and I understood why the staff avoided touching the patients.

"Excuse me." A nurse smiled antiseptically at me. "Can I help you with something?"

I looked at Amanda, then at the photograph I was carrying. In the picture she was laughing, holding a glass of wine in one hand and pushing her hair out of her face with the other. It must have been taken at a party.

"Sir? Can I help you?" the nurse asked again.

All I could do was shake my head. "No."

Joop Wheeler

Friday Night

Kozinsky's is a working-class bar. A guys' bar. With a beat-up old pool table and a TV over the stick that's always tuned to sports. Most of the guys who drink there work for a living. I'm not talking about men who are *employed,* I'm talking about guys who work. Guys who have jobs instead of careers.

The Friday-night crowd isn't all that different from the Thursday-night crowd. Or the Wednesday-night crowd, as far as that goes. Kozinsky's isn't the sort of place you'd bring a date. Or expect to pick one up. It's a bar where guys stop off after work and have a few pops—a reward for having done a good day's work—before they go home to their wives and supper. Or else they drink to pass the evening because they don't have wives and suppers at home waiting for them. A guys' bar.

If it's a payday, maybe they'll stop for a quick pop on the way home and come back later with the wife or girlfriend in tow. Maybe have a little supper and a few laughs. But as a rule, they won't stay out too late. They have to get up in the morning and go back to work.

I sort of like Kozinsky's. The folks that drink there are nothing more than what they seem to be. Which is sort of refreshing.

Kozinsky's is not the sort of place you'd expect to meet a transsexual lesbian.

Deirdre was already there when I arrived. She was sitting in a booth near the kitchen, talking to a waitress who looked like she was probably married to, or divorced from, a Kozinsky's regular.

I slid into the seat across from Deirdre. She ordered us

both a beer and a shot of Jameson's, with an eye in my
direction in case I had any objections. Which I didn't.

I leaned back and smiled out of sheer pleasure. There's
no other job in the world where you can get paid to sit in a
cracked leather booth in a working-class Polish bar, drinking
shots and beers with a transsexual lesbian.

Deirdre fussed with her purse while we made small talk.
I let her take her time getting around to the point. When the
drinks arrived, I sipped the whiskey and looked at the basketball scores and highlights on the television over the bar.

After a few moments of silence, Deirdre asked, "Aren't
you going to ask me why I wanted to talk to you?" She
sounded hurt.

"Sure," I said. "Why'd you want to talk to me?"

"You don't seem very interested."

"Sure I am. I'm very interested. But the way I figure, you
got something you think is important. And I figure whatever
it is, you want to tell it to me. Or you wouldn't have asked me
to meet you here. So I also figure you'll tell me when you get
ready to tell me." I spread my hands apart. "I'm ready when
you are."

She smiled and nodded. "I don't know if it's important or
not. But it might be. I wanted to tell you, just in case."

"Okay." I waved her on.

She knocked back her shot of whiskey. The easy way she
did it made me wonder if she'd been a regular at Kozinsky's
when she was a man, and what her name had been then.

"Okay," she said. "I guess I'd better tell you. But before
I do, you ought to know that I really like Anka and I don't
want anything bad to happen to her. She was a friend to me
when not many were."

I nodded.

"She never judged me, or asked me rude questions, or
made snide remarks about me," she said. "She just accepted
me for what I am."

I kept nodding.

"So I don't like to say anything that might get her in trouble, you know?"

"It's okay," I said. "The truth never hurts." Which may have been the biggest lie I'd told all evening.

Deirdre rolled the shot glass between her palms. "I hate to say this, but I think Anka might have—you know—done it. Tried to kill Amanda, I mean. She was acting really weird that night. I know she's supposed to be crazy and all, but I never saw her like she was that night. She was—well, she was different." She shook her head.

"In what way?"

Deirdre made a face. "Well, one thing, she came on to me, which is something she'd never done before. Not that I wanted her to, you know. But she did."

"When and where did this happen?" I asked.

"In the hall near the bathroom at the Zone. It was just me and Anka. It happened just before she and Stevie left."

"Go on."

Deirdre frowned. I tried to decide if it was a man's frown or if I was just seeing it that way. "She was a little drunk . . ."

"A little?" I asked.

Deirdre smiled. "Well, okay, she was hammered. It happens to everybody now and then."

I nodded again. "Don't I know it."

"Well, in the hallway she came up to me and told me . . . she told me she felt like . . . like getting really physical. She said she wanted to get in a fight, or— I don't know how to say this."

"Just blurt it out," I said.

"She said she felt like she was going to explode. She said she wanted to get in a fight or go someplace and really fuck her brains out. Man or woman, she said. She didn't care, she just wanted rough sex. Or violence. Or something."

"Ah." This did not sound good.

"She wanted me to go with her, but I said no, I wouldn't. Maybe I should have. Maybe if I had, none of this would have happened. Maybe if I'd helped her get it out of her system, Amanda would be okay."

"Maybe," I said. "I doubt it, but it's hard to say."

"But I'm not into that stuff. You know?"

I nodded. But I didn't really know. How the hell could I know what sort of stuff a transsexual lesbian would be into? My mind boggled at the possibilities.

She looked at me, then back at her shot glass. She must have known what I was thinking. "You know, don't you?"

"Know what?" I asked.

"That I'm a transsexual."

I nodded. "Yeah, I guess I do."

"You must think it's really weird, me being a transsexual and a lesbian."

I shrugged. "I don't think I know what's weird anymore," I said. "It's a new one to me, I'll admit. But weird?" I shrugged again.

She tapped a fingernail against her glass. I was pretty sure it was a fake nail. It was too perfect.

"After, you know, the surgery, I tried going out with men," she said. "Sometimes it was nice. But not very often. I guess I've always liked women better than men."

"I can understand that," I said. "I feel the same way."

Deirdre smiled. "I don't know. It must sound really weird to you. It even sounds weird to me."

"What happened with Anka?" I asked. "After you told her you wouldn't go with her?"

"Oh, yeah. First she got sort of mad. Then she tried to, I don't know, get seductive. But she'd had too much to drink, you know? She told me she wanted—she said she'd always wanted to sleep with me."

"Sleep with you?"

"Well, actually what she said was she wanted to fuck

somebody who knew fucking from both sides. She said she wanted to know what it was like to suck the memory of a cock."

I nodded. Nice line.

"When I still wouldn't go, she started to say really mean things to me. Things about me being a transsexual."

"She normally wasn't like that?" I asked.

"No, she wasn't." Deirdre shook her head. She smoothed her hair back in place and I saw that her nails were real. No seam on the underside.

"Anka was really nice and really understanding," she said. "I mean, it was really tough, you know, at first. When I started hanging out at the Zone, some of the women gave me a hard time. Except for the ones who were into gimp fucking. They were all over me."

"Gimp fucking?"

She nodded. "You know the type. Get hot for anything out of the ordinary. Amputees, scars, mutilation, stuff like that."

I thought about Michelle of the red satin eye patch. Whether the patch was to attract gimp fuckers or for real, it helped explain her resentment over my question.

"But Anka wasn't like that," Deirdre said. "Anka was always really nice to me. That's why I think maybe she really did try to kill Amanda. Because she wasn't really herself that night. She was like this crazy woman. I really thought for a minute she was going to attack me when I said I wouldn't go with her. Her eyes got really scary."

"Then what happened?"

"Well, nothing happened. She seemed to get over it really quick, and then she left."

"She left?"

Deirdre nodded. "Yeah, she and Stevie both. I think Stevie was worried about her. I don't think she wanted to leave Anka alone, like she thought Anka might, I don't know, do something crazy. And I guess maybe she was right."

"Did Anka mention Amanda at all that night?"

"Not to me, she didn't."

"To anybody else?"

"Not that I know of."

The waitress came over to check on us. I told her I was fine. Deirdre raised her shot glass and nodded for another.

So I drank about half my shot. It wasn't that I was worried about being outdrunk by a lesbian transsexual. But I wanted to put up a respectable defense.

"Anka say where she was going?" I asked.

"Nope. But I've heard they both went to Schotzie's."

That was what Stevie said. But it was nice to have it confirmed.

"I knew Anka wasn't about to go home," Deirdre said. "She was too hyper for that. I figured she'd just keep going from bar to bar until she got what she wanted, you know? Until she got in a fight or found somebody to, you know, to fuck her brains out. I was even afraid she might try to pick a fight with Stevie, get it out of her system. That's how bizarre she was."

"If she was looking for rough trade," I said, "where would she go?"

Deirdre shrugged. "Schotzie's. Maybe the Pink Wazoo."

"The Pink Wazoo?" I grinned. "I never heard of it." Me, the bar expert. I was getting an education about some strange and interesting bars.

She grinned back. "You wouldn't. It's a private club down closer to Boston proper. And it's about what you'd expect from a place with a name like that."

"God help us all," I said. "Listen, Deirdre, one more question. If Anka *was* after something rough, is there anybody in particular she might have gone looking for?"

She shrugged. "I don't know. I keep away from that stuff. I wouldn't even know who to ask about it."

"Who would know who to ask?"

"Stevie, I guess."

"Stevie Gibbs?"

She nodded. "Stevie has a great network. She knows almost everybody who's into almost anything."

"Ah."

"Besides, everybody's sort of in love with Stevie. Anka used to call her the Bachelorette of the Month. I think even Amanda had a crush on Stevie."

"Oh, really?"

"I don't think they ever slept together, though," Deirdre said. "In fact, I don't think Stevie's been sleeping with anybody since Kate. At least not on a regular basis."

"Kate?" I asked.

"Yeah. Kate Wiggin. After they split, Kate went to study in Barcelona."

The waitress brought Deirdre another shot. Which she downed like a construction worker.

"Kate was Stevie's . . ." I wasn't sure I wanted to hear this.

"Her lover. Big time."

I tossed back the rest of my whiskey. Just my luck. Red hair, freckles, good Southern manners, red lightning. And a lesbian. I thought about ordering another round, to drown the red lightning, make it sputter out.

"I guess it's getting sort of late," Deirdre said. "I should probably be going."

I waved for the tab. "Deirdre, I appreciate your help."

"You think it's important?"

I shrugged. "Don't know. But every little bit helps."

I paid the tab over Deirdre's mild objections, but let her leave the tip. Outside, a street washer drove slowly by, leaving the streets looking incredibly black. When I was a kid, I wanted to drive a street washer. It always sounded like a great job, cruising the streets at night, driving about five miles an hour, listening to music. It still sounded pretty nice.

"I'll walk you to your car," I said. My old momma would die if I didn't walk a lady to her car. Even if I wasn't allowed to use the word "lady" anymore. And even if the lady had once been a man. Manners are manners.

"I don't have my car," Deirdre said. "I don't drive when I go to bars."

"Probably a good policy."

"I'll just catch a cab."

I wanted to keep my mouth shut. I wanted *not* to be polite. But I'm damned if I didn't open my mouth and say, "Why don't I give you a lift?" right out loud.

She shook her head. "Oh, no, I don't want to bother you."

That almost always means "Yes, but I want you to insist so I don't feel like a mooch." "It's no bother," I said.

"Well, if you're really sure."

I wasn't sure of anything. Except that it was late. And I was tired. And that Stevie Gibbs had turned out to be a lesbian, after all. And that the last thing I wanted to do right then was drive a transsexual lesbian home.

"No trouble at all." I smiled. "My pleasure."

She also lived in Moose Creek, about six blocks from Stevie Gibbs. I double-parked in front of her apartment, thinking I'd done my gentlemanly duty and could go home. But the light was burned out over the entryway. And it wasn't the safest neighborhood. So I had to walk her up the steps and see that she got safely inside.

She unlocked the door and held it open. "Thanks," she said.

"No problem," I said. "Nice night for a drive."

"Well, it's really very kind and thoughtful of you."
I waved that away.
"Well, thanks again." And then she leaned forward and she gave me a quick kiss. Right on the lips.

Kevin Sweeney

Saturday, Late Morning

When an unbalanced lesbian poet shacks up with an affluent lesbian sculptor, you don't expect them to live in the suburbs. Certainly not an upper-middle-class, electric-garage-door-opener, Volvo-station-wagon, backyard-patio-with-Weber-grill suburb. The neighborhood was a proper White Anglo-Saxon Protestant outpost.

The location made a bit more sense when I remembered the house was a relic of Amanda Owen's former life as a heterosexual housewife. A pair of plastic pink flamingos wearing Ray Bans in the front lawn were the only hint that the residents of the house were not perfect suburbanites. Still, the neighborhood was so far removed from what I'd expected that I checked the mailbox to make sure I had the right address.

Anka Stiffel's name wasn't on the mailbox, but I could see where it had been painted it out. She'd been given the boot only a week or so earlier, and already her name had been painted out. Amanda Owen must have been serious about breaking up with Anka.

The neighborhood was quiet, more like a Sunday than Saturday morning. It reminded me of a science-fiction movie—all the people had mysteriously vanished. Saturday morning in my neighborhood was never so quiet, especially a few weeks before school started. Maybe proper upper-middle-class Anglo-Saxon Protestant kids were different. Maybe they were all down at the country club, playing tennis.

Marty Coyle had said that Callie Dobson, the neighbor who found Amanda Owen unconcious in her own back yard, lived directly next to Amanda's house. It was easy to pick out Dobson's house: It was the one with the woman standing half in and half out of the door, watching me. A nosy neighbor, Marty had said. Nosy neighbors are a detective's delight.

She saw me looking at her and said, "Can I help you with something?"

"Yes, I think you can." I pulled a business card out of my pocket and approached her house with a smile. "My name is Kevin Sweeney, and I work for one of the women who live next door." I nodded at Amanda's house.

"I'm Mrs. Dobson," she said. "Which one do you work for?"

"Anka Stiffel."

She nodded. "The crazy one," she said.

I nodded and smiled. "That's the one." I walked slowly up her sidewalk and handed her my card without going onto the porch. Nosy neighbors, as a group, are easily spooked.

"I need to ask you a few questions about her," I said. "And about Amanda too."

"What sort of questions?" she asked. She was in her late thirties, with that settled look people get when they've lived in one place long enough. She was wearing an unimaginative ankle-length skirt and a long-sleeved blouse. There is something odd about a woman wearing a skirt around the house in the daytime. It's something you don't see outside of television commercials.

I had the strong impression that Mrs. Dobson had leaned around that door in the same way many times, talking with neighbors or the mail carrier or delivery people, unwilling to actually leave her home but reluctant to go back inside and miss the conversation and human contact.

"The usual sort of questions," I said. "Were they good neighbors? Did they get along with the other people in the neighborhood? Did they get along with each other? Like that."

She looked at my card again. "Are you really a private

detective?" she asked. "I mean, you're not a reporter or something, are you?"

"No, I'm not. I'm really an investigator. Would you like to see my license?"

"May I?"

I dug it out of my wallet and showed it to her. She carefully examined both sides of the license.

"Well, now," she said, smiling. "I never really believed private eyes existed. Outside of movies and books, I mean."

I smiled. "I hope I haven't disappointed you."

"Oh no, no. I didn't mean that at all."

"It's okay," I said. "I've heard it said before. It's not the worst thing people have said about me."

She smiled again and gave her head a funny half-bob, the way a horse does.

"Maybe if I ask you some questions, it'll convince you I'm real," I said.

"Going to give me the third degree?" She cocked an eyebrow.

"Oh, I think we can stick with the first degree." I smiled. "It's still too early in the day for the third degree." It's odd how people tend to trust you if you tease them.

She thought about it for a moment. "Would you mind if we sit here on the steps?" she asked.

"Not at all. It's a lovely day for sitting on the steps."

I sat on the lowest step and leaned back against the rail. Mrs. Dobson sat on the top step, tucking her skirt tightly around her legs, so I wouldn't be tempted to peek.

"This is about Amanda, I assume. And what happened next door."

"Yes, it is."

She nodded and said, "I was the one who found her, you know."

I made a noncommittal gesture with my head. "It must have been horrible for you."

"Oh, it was. I've never seen anything like it. It's not like that in the movies."

"No, it's not."

"In the movies people might be all bloody, but they don't look the way Amanda looked. She looked so fragile, lying there like that." She frowned and examined the backs of her hands, and I knew she was seeing it again.

"How did you happen to see her?" I asked.

"Well, I'd gone out back to put out some sunflower seed for the birds. The cardinals love sunflower seed, and I like to feed them before I do my breakfast dishes. That way I can watch them out the kitchen window while I wash the dishes." She smiled shyly. "That sounds silly, doesn't it."

"Not at all," I said. "My wife does the same thing." And who knows, maybe it was true. Mary Margaret likes birds and we have a window over the kitchen sink. It was possible.

"I think it's so important to take care of birds, don't you? All year round, I mean, not just in the winter months."

I nodded. "I agree. People take birds for granted, and I think it's very nice of you to be so concerned. So you were putting sunflower seed out for the cardinals. In the back yard?"

She nodded.

"What did you see?"

"Well, I looked over the fence—I don't know why I did, I guess I must have had a funny feeling—and I saw her there, lying on the ground. On the stone path."

"Stone path?"

"Yes, the Lowells laid a fieldstone walk from the back door to the garage."

"The Lowells?"

She nodded. "Charles and Amanda. Oh, I know she went back to using her maiden name after Charles moved out, but I still think of her as Amanda Lowell. Is that legal? To use your maiden name even if you're not divorced?"

"I don't know," I said. "Do you think you could you show me this stone path?"

She hesitated.

"If it makes you uncomfortable . . ."

"Well, sort of."

I smiled. "Mrs. Dobson, I certainly don't want to make you uncomfortable. But this is an important case."

She frowned and looked at my business card again. "I know I'm probably being silly, but . . ."

"Not at all," I said. "You're being very sensible. I'd like to think my wife is this careful when I'm away."

She tapped the card against her palm. "Well, I suppose it'll be okay." She stood and smoothed her skirt. She led me around the house and into the back yard. A tall wooden privacy fence separated her yard from Amanda's. I could barely see over the fence and I wondered how Mrs. Dobson had been able to see Amanda.

An aluminum ladder was propped against a tree with a bird feeder. She opened the ladder, climbed to the third rung, and pointed over the fence. "She was lying right there," she said.

I climbed up the other side of the ladder.

"Look." She pointed. "You can still see bloodstains on the stones."

And so you could, a rust-colored smudge on the flat stones that led from the screened back porch to the garage. It didn't seem like much blood for a head wound.

"How was she lying?" I asked. "On her stomach? On her back?"

Mrs. Dobson frowned. "She was sort of on her side and sort of on her back."

"Which way were her feet pointing?"

"Her feet? Toward the porch."

"What was she wearing?"

"A robe. An Oriental robe. Like a kimono."

"Did you notice if she was wearing anything under it?"

Mrs. Dobson blushed, but shook her head. "Nothing."

It wasn't hard to conjure up the image of a woman, the woman I'd seen in the hospital bed, lying on the pathway, dressed only in a kimono, her head in a pool of blood.

"Where was the sculpture that was used to hit her?" I asked. "Did you see it?"

"I don't think so," she said. She climbed down from the ladder and gave a Gallic shrug. "I don't remember."

"Try to see exactly what you saw that morning," I said. "She was sort of on her back and sort of on her side. Close your eyes and picture it in your mind."

She closed her eyes and frowned.

"Can you see it?" I asked.

She nodded.

"Where is the sculpture?"

She shook her head. "I don't see it." She opened her eyes. "That's important, isn't it, that I didn't see it."

I smiled at her. "You'd make a fine detective."

She blushed again and made a confidential gesture. "Well, you know, I read mystery novels," she said, smiling. "And I can almost always tell who did it. As long as the author is fair. So many aren't, are they? Holding back clues until the very end."

"Not at all fair," I said. "What did you do when you saw her lying there like that?"

She cocked her head to one side and considered the matter. "First I shouted to her. She didn't answer, of course. And I could tell she was hurt. The blood and all. So I went around the house and tried her gate, but it was closed and locked."

"How was it locked? A padlock? A lock set in the gate?"

"The gate has a lock set in it, with a keyhole."

"Very good. You were by yourself? Your husband, he'd already gone to work then, had he?"

She shook her head. "He was out of town," she said. "On business."

"Okay. The gate was locked. Then what?"

"Well, I hurried to the front door and knocked and rang the bell." She laughed shyly. "Actually, I pounded on it. I was never so scared."

"I'll bet. Then what?"

"Nobody answered, which I should have expected. So I—"

"Why should you have expected nobody to answer?" I asked.

"Well, if somebody had been home, they'd have found her, wouldn't they? And besides, I knew her friend wasn't living there anymore."

"When you say 'her friend,' do you mean Anka?"

She nodded.

"I'll want to ask you about that in a minute," I said. "You pounded on the door and nobody answered. Then what did you do?"

"You'll never believe," she said, fanning herself with her hand. "I climbed over the gate."

I grinned. "Good for you."

"And then I hurried around back and, oh, she was such a mess, all the blood. I didn't know what to do. I've never even had a first-aid class. So I went inside and used her telephone to call 911 and asked them to send an ambulance."

"You went in Amanda's house?"

She nodded. "The back porch door was open."

"Open open, or unlocked open?"

"Open open." Suddenly her face lit up. "Wait a minute. Just inside the door there was a piece of sculpture. On the floor. About this big." She held her hands apart indicating a piece about the size of a honeydew melon. "I think it was South American."

Back door was open, sculpture on the porch. "So you called 911. Do you remember what you said?"

She cocked her head again. "I don't know. It was something like 'There's been an accident and there's a woman hurt. We need an ambulance immediately.' I know I told them 'immediately,' because I remember when my husband's mother had her heart attack. It seemed like hours before the ambulance arrived. Oh, and I told them my name and gave them the address. Amanda's address, not mine."

"So you thought it was an accident at first?"

She looked surprised. "Why, I guess I must have." Then she smiled. "You really are a detective, aren't you? That was so clever. Did you do that on purpose?"

"I don't know," I said. "I've been doing this so long, I don't know what I do on purpose anymore. But let me ask you this: If you thought it was an accident at first, what made you change your mind?"

She shook her head. "I don't really know. I guess it must have been the police. They came and asked questions and they must have told me that Anka did it."

That was possible; cops usually decide on a perpetrator early on in the investigation, then spend their time building a case against that person.

I wondered how long Amanda had been lying there. "Was Amanda bleeding?" I asked.

"A little, I think. There was blood oozing out, but not very fast." She shuddered a little. "I thought she was dead, the way she was lying there."

"I'm sorry if this is disturbing," I said. "But it's very important."

"It's okay. The more I talk about it the better. At least that's what my therapist says. Maybe if I talk about it enough, I won't have any more nightmares."

The poor woman. I normally don't have much sympathy for the rich or the suburban upper-middle class. But here was this woman, home all alone while her husband is out of town making enough money—probably by cheating some working-class stiff—to keep her locked up with her microwave and vacuum sweeper in this hopelessly sterile neighborhood. She was totally unprepared for bloody reality, poor woman. No wonder she had nightmares. The great wonder was that she didn't run screaming through the streets in horror of her own life.

"Tell me, do you think Anka is capable of doing that?" I asked. "To Amanda?"

"I guess she must be capable. The police think so."

"But what do you think?"

"Oh, I don't like to say."

I smiled. "It's okay. All I want is your opinion."

She took a deep breath. "Okay. I think she might have. She is a very disturbed person, you know."

I nodded.

"And you know they're lesbians," she said.

"Yes, I know."

She nodded, as if she'd just explained something. Maybe she thought it was common for lesbians to bash in each other's heads with artwork.

"Can you give me a specific reason you think Anka might have been willing to do such a thing to Amanda?" I asked.

"Well, they fought a lot."

"Oh? When you say they fought, do you mean they hit each other, or that they yelled at each other?"

"Well, I never actually saw any hitting."

"Did you hear blows struck?"

She shook her head. "No, not really. When they fought, they would go inside the house."

"Did they fight often?" I asked.

"What do you mean by 'often'?"

I told myself to be patient. "Let's try it this way—how often did they fight?"

"Well, there were periods where they got along very well. And then there were periods when they fought a lot. And they could be very bitter fights, the names they called each other."

"What sorts of names?"

"Well, mostly it was the other one who shouted names," she said. She was unwilling to repeat any of the names, but said they were obscene references to what she called "naughty parts." Amanda, she said, sometimes yelled back, but never used vulgar language.

"How did you get along with them personally?" I asked.

To my surprise, she blushed again. "Oh, well, I don't know. We were just neighbors." She shrugged. "I knew some lesbians in college back in—well, back in college. Or at least everybody said they were lesbians. It might have just been vicious rumors. I didn't know for myself."

"No, of course not."

"Anyway, I wasn't as shocked as some of the neighbors. My parents were liberal Democrats. Or at least my mother was—my father was more sensible, I'm happy to say." She fanned herself with her hand. "What I'm trying to say is that I got along with both of them tolerably well, though they weren't really part of the neighborhood."

I nodded. "I see. Did you . . ."

"Of course I got along better with Amanda. We had more in common. Education, background. That sort of thing. And her friend is Jewish, you know."

"Yes, I know."

"Amanda was always a lady," she said. "And, of course, I knew her from when she was still with her husband."

"What was he like?"

"Oh, you know. Like all husbands. Maybe he was a little too engrossed in his career, but he was a good provider. He was certainly better for her than, well, you know."

"Anka?"

She nodded.

Not a glowing recommendation. Slowly, bit by dreary bit Callie Dobson told me what she knew about Amanda and Anka. The neighborhood didn't know what to make of them. Not only were they artists in a community of managers and executives, they were an openly lesbian couple in a heterosexual enclave. Some neighbors didn't mind, some did. Some were outraged.

Amanda, she said, was polite but reserved; Anka was friendly and outgoing, but very weird. Mrs. Dobson couldn't understand how Amanda could put up with someone so peculiar.

They often had parties, though the neighbors weren't always invited. Mrs. Dobson would attend if her husband was out of town. He didn't approve of Amanda and Anka, as much for the pink flamingos in their lawn as their sexual orientation, and wouldn't enter their house.

At those parties Mrs. Dobson met several of Amanda and Anka's friends, but she couldn't recall any of their names. The name Amanda Standish was not familiar to her.

"You said earlier you knew Amanda and Anka had split up," I said. "How did you find out about that?"

"Amanda told me. I saw her painting over her friend's name on the mailbox and I asked. I'm such a snoop." She smiled.

"Did Amanda tell you why she and Anka broke up?"

She shook her head.

"Why do you think they broke up?" I asked.

"Well, they weren't very compatible. Socially, I mean. And in other ways. I never really understood what Amanda saw in her. She was so—I don't know. Extreme. She was either very common or very bizarre. I mean, you have to make certain allowances for artists, but that woman's behavior was simply unacceptable. What poor Amanda went through."

"When was the last time you saw Anka?" I asked.

She considered the question for a few minutes. "Probably four or five weeks ago," she said.

She didn't have much more to add. After a few more minutes she walked me back to the front yard. I asked her to call me if she thought of anything else.

I decided to nose around Amanda's house as long as I was in the neighborhood. The front door had a police crime-scene seal on it. The gate to the back yard was still locked, so I followed Mrs. Dobson's example and climbed over it.

A skinny tabby cat was sitting on the back porch steps. Its head swiveled to follow me. Cats always look like they're thinking murderous thoughts. Joop had said Amanda and Anka had four cats—this must have been one of them. God only knows where the others had gone.

I stooped to look at the bloodstains on the stone path. Not much there. Must have been a lot of internal hemorrhaging.

As I approached the porch, the cat slid off the side of the steps and disappeared behind a hedge. The door was closed and sealed by the police. Through the windows I could see some small wooden sculptures. It was hard to tell what they were, but they were all modern and had a soft, pleasing shape. Amanda's work, I assumed.

When I felt like I'd trespassed long enough, I turned to leave. Mrs. Dobson was standing on her ladder, watching me over the fence. She waved to me as I left.

J o o p   W h e e l e r

Saturday Night

I should have listened to Stevie. I don't ever seem to be listening when people tell me things I ought to be listening to.

My momma told me I was pigheaded even when I was a baby, said I wouldn't ever once listen to reason. Like when we were kids and my brother and sister used to catch honeybees in jars. They'd hold the jars up to their ears and listen to the bees buzzing. I wanted to try catching the bees with my hands—I wanted to *feel* them buzzing. My momma told me she couldn't for the life of her understand where I got such a fool notion and if I wanted to catch bees, which she also couldn't understand, then I should catch them in a jar like my brother and sister and not worry her so.

I did it anyway, of course. Caught a bee and held it in my hands. Got the snot stung out of me. But when I felt that tiny little thing bumping around and buzzing in my hands, I knew it was *alive*. That's something you can't ever know by looking and listening through a jar.

All the same, I should have listened to Stevie. She warned me I wouldn't get a friendly reception at Schotzie's. That it wasn't like any other gay bar I'd been in. But I figured what the hell, a bar is a bar and I can get along with anybody, no matter what their sexual alignment is. I'm a tolerant guy. I don't much care who or what a person sleeps with. People can have sex with goats for all I care. Long as the goats don't object.

So I followed Stevie into Schotzie's about ten-thirty Saturday night, feeling confident. And I got to tell you, I fell dead in love with the place directly from the start. The first thing I saw was a huge old beauty of a pool table. Leather strap pockets, and a green felt top about the size of Fenway Park. I wished I wasn't working so I could grab a cold beer and a cue and shoot a few racks.

Unfortunately, my infatuation with the bar only lasted until I tore my eyes off the table and noticed the customers. They were what you'd call hostile.

Schotzie's had the feel of a killer biker bar. The sort of place where fat guys with beards and tattoos get together a few nights a week and shed some friendly blood. The kind of place the cops get called to a lot. Where folks get themselves beat up and stabbed but nobody ever sees anything.

Only these folks were all women. I don't mean to imply that they *looked* like bikers. They didn't. Hardly any of them were fat and none of them were bearded, though I suspect a few of them did have tattoos. Mainly what they had was the rowdy who-gives-a-shit attitude of serious bikers. Coupled with a healthy dose of don't-fuck-with-me.

Which I had absolutely no intention of doing. Not in any sense of the term. There were some tough-looking women in that bar. There were also some very attractive women. But I ignored them studiously. I might not have had enough sense to stay out of Schotzie's, but I knew better than to make eye-flirts with the women there. It might have irritated some of them. And there were women in that bar who'd gladly snip off my testicles and toss them in with the chef's salad.

Stevie smiled and spoke to several of the scowling women as she led me toward the bar. I nodded hello and gave them my most gender-neutral smile.

When we got to the bar, Stevie announced: "This is Joop Wheeler." It was almost like she'd called a meeting, the way the women stood quietly, looking at me and listening to her. I've never seen anything like it in any other bar I've ever been in. "He's working for Anka Stiffel. You know Anka's been arrested and accused of assaulting Amanda. I realize not everybody here is on Anka's side, but this man is only trying to protect Anka's rights. He'd like to ask you some questions."

Stevie nodded at me. I tried to look as inoffensively male as I could, and said, "I'm sorry for interrupting your Saturday night. But this is pretty important. We know Anka was in here the night Ms. Owen was assaulted. What I need is to talk to anybody who saw her that night. If you did see her, I'd appreciate it if you'd come talk with me." I nodded to a table in the back. "I'm just going to go sit over—"

"You're not going to sit anywhere." I turned and saw a woman glaring at me. "You're going to get your ass out of our bar," she said.

She was a strongly built woman who'd obviously spent a chunk of time in a gym lifting weights. I had maybe twenty pounds and five inches on her, but she looked like she could bench-press more weight than I could. She had that balanced appearance that bodybuilders work for, every body part symmetrical and defined. She wasn't actually flexing her muscles at the moment, but I had the feeling she was prepared to.

I nodded. "I can appreciate how you might feel that way," I said. "And I'm sorry that—"

"You're going to be a hell of a lot sorrier if you don't haul ass out of here," the woman said. "I mean right now."

Stevie spoke to her. "Hannah, why don't you give—"

"You keep out of this, Stevie," said the woman next to Hannah. At least this one was smiling. She seemed amused by the situation. "Hannah knows what she's doing."

"Listen, Cotton . . ." Stevie began. She was interrupted by Hannah, who stepped forward and said, "You never should have brought him here."

I thought for a moment Stevie might back down, but she was tougher than that. She put her hands on her hips and said, "Hannah, he didn't come here looking for trouble. He's here to help Anka." Then Stevie took a small step forward and gestured toward me. "This man is here as my guest, and I don't want him harassed."

Stevie's little step forward fired off the red lightning again, and set me to grinning. Which was a bad mistake. There is a time for grinning and a time for not grinning. And this was a time for not grinning.

"Hannah's not going to harass him," Cotton said. "She's just going to show him out." She turned to me. "You'd better wipe that grin off your ugly face and start thinking about going."

I wiped the grin off my ugly face. "Look, I just want to ask a few questions. I'm not—"

Hannah went into a sort of kung fu crouch. "Get the fuck out," she said. "Right now."

I took a deep breath and tried to decide what to do. But Hannah decided for me. When I didn't move, she started waving her arms and walking toward me in a goofy series of karate steps. I tried not to grin again, but something must have slipped out. When an already pissed-off woman sees you grinning, she thinks it means you're not taking her seriously— which I'm afraid was true, I wasn't—and it pisses her off even more. Which it did.

Hannah started throwing punches and little kicks at me. I sort of pushed them aside with my open hands, the way my older brother did when he taught me how to box. She'd obviously taken some martial-arts lessons somewhere and maybe had some odd colored belts to show for it. But learning to throw punches and kicks in a classroom doesn't really prepare you for a fight.

Now I've been in a few fights, and a lot of it is attitude. And in that I was as handicapped as Hannah. I hadn't been taught to fight in a classroom, but I *had* been raised a proper Southern boy. And despite my recent training in the politically precise ways of the East Coast, I was having a tough time giving serious consideration to hitting a woman. So I just backed up and tried to protect myself.

And as long as I kept backing up, I was able to deflect her

kicks and punches without too much fuss. Then I backed into the pool table. Which startled me and gave Hannah an opening. She caught me a good clip—a short, nasty right. I was able to close up and take most of it on the shoulder, but it had some power behind it and it hurt like a son of a bitch.

It came to me that the whole situation was just too weird and it was time to change plans. There was no way I was going to pull this off. Regardless of what I did—or didn't do—to Hannah, the crowd wasn't going to be cooperative. I was wasting my time. So I decided to make for the door and get the hell out of Dodge.

I feinted left and ducked right, under another nasty shot. It was a real pretty move and it should have worked. But Hannah must have had a good teacher. When she missed with her left, she kept spinning around and kicked me. It was a vicious kick, which would have caught me right in the balls if I hadn't twisted enough to catch it on the thigh. It threw my timing off and I took another backhanded right off the top of my head. I was able to partially block her follow-up left, but it had enough power to get through and catch me over the right eye. I knew the eye would be swelling shut pretty quick.

I don't think I made a conscious decision to dump my hesitation at hitting women. It was just that the situation no longer involved gender. What it involved was keeping my ignorant Southern ass from getting kicked all over Schotzie's barroom floor. Hannah was going to do me some serious damage if I didn't catch up with the times real quick.

So I dropped my left guard just a tad, just enough to suck Hannah into throwing a right. I let the right slide by and gave Hannah a little push on the shoulder. Not too hard. Just hard enough to put her off balance. She did a good job of regaining herself and was canny enough to fall into a defensive position against the attack her training taught her ought to be coming. All in all she did exactly the right thing. At least it would have been the right thing in a classroom.

But we weren't in the classroom. In the classroom nobody picks up a little wooden bar chair and chucks it at your head. Which is what I did.

Some folks might object to the casual use of bar chairs in a fight, regardless of whether the opponent is a man or a woman. All I can say is this: You don't want to get hit with a bar chair, then don't pick a fight with me.

I didn't throw it hard, mind you. It was more like a lob. And it wasn't meant to hit her. I threw it just high enough that she'd have to look up and just hard enough that she'd have to catch it. Which she did. Snagged it real pretty, in fact, like she'd been catching bar chairs since she was just a little girl.

While she was busy catching the chair, I hit her in the stomach. It was as pretty an uppercut as I've ever thrown. I got my feet set and brought the punch right out of the floor. Caught her just below the ribs, low enough to avoid busting any but high enough to knock the air clean out of her.

Hannah dropped the chair and sat down hard, her eyes wide with the desperate look people get when they can't breathe. It took the crowd a moment to figure out what had happened and move to help her.

While they were busy, I grabbed a pool cue from off the rack and started for the fire exit, yelling for Stevie to follow.

And my luck ran true. The fire exit was blocked on the outside. Trash cans or something—I didn't look too closely. It didn't much matter *what* was blocking it, all that mattered was that it was blocked and I couldn't get out. I wasn't worried about fire regulations, after all. I was worried about my country ass.

I spun around, pool cue at port arms, and about half puked with fear when I saw all those angry faces. I really think they might have killed me if the woman named Cotton hadn't stepped in.

"Back off," she shouted. "Hannah's okay. She's just had

the breath knocked out of her. Everybody, back off. Back off. Leave him alone."

Stevie hadn't followed me to the fire exit. She stood by the pool table, next to Cotton. She didn't seem to be in any danger herself, but she didn't look like she was having much fun. She looked exasperated, is how she looked. Like I'd started it. Like it was my fault. Which I suppose I did and it was

The crowd held itself back while Cotton walked up to me with a swagger, grinning like a pirate. "You did that on purpose, didn't you," she said. "Got her to catch the chair and then hit her in the gut to knock the breath out of her."

I nodded.

"Why? How come you didn't kick her in the knees when you had the chance? Or in the cunt?"

"I didn't want to hurt her," I said. "I just wanted her to leave me alone."

Cotton grinned and nodded. "Yeah, that's what I thought," she said. "Listen, maybe we can talk. Put that pool cue down and I'll buy us a beer."

I shook my head. "I don't think so."

"Why not? We're not going to hurt you."

I shook my head again. "I figure there's maybe twenty or thirty women in here who could stomp me into juice one on one. I drop this pool cue, I could be in a world of hurt." The truth was that even *with* the pool cue, they could whip me to a bloody pulp. If they didn't mind taking a few lumps first. And there were women there who could take the lumps.

"It's okay." She grinned. "I promise we won't hurt you."

I hesitated for a moment, then shook my head once more. "I don't think so," I said to Cotton. "I don't know you that well. No offense."

Stevie spoke up. "Joop, Cotton's promise is good." She sounded irritated.

Cotton's grin widened. I couldn't believe it. I'd just told

the woman I didn't trust her and she was grinning like it was a compliment.

"You think we'd bust you up?" she asked.

"I don't know if you would or not," I said. "But why take the risk?"

"Okay. Have it your way." She made a theatrical wave toward the door. "Take off."

I slid around the wall and waited while Stevie opened the door. I backed into it, then stopped. I'd regained a bit of my composure once it looked like I might not actually get butchered. The situation seemed to call for some sort of closing line. But I couldn't think of anything. So I just nodded at Cotton. She was standing beside Hannah, who was sitting on the same bar chair I'd thrown at her.

Cotton nodded back and grinned.

"I'll leave the pool cue with Stevie," I said. And backed out the door.

Stevie was quiet until we got in the car. I let her drive. I was a little shook up and my right eye was beginning to swell shut.

"Are you insane?" she finally asked. "Was that necessary? Was *any* of that necessary?"

I shrugged. "You never know, do you."

"I did," she said. "I knew. And as much as I hate to say 'I told you so . . .' "

Why does everybody say they hate to say that? People *love* to say it. "You told me so," I said.

"Next time," she said, "maybe you'll listen to me."

"Yeah." Maybe so.

Kevin Sweeney

Saturday Midnight

The Roadhouse Motel was a different place at night. During the day it looked shabby enough, but you could see it had once been a decent little motel. Not so at midnight Saturday night. The front of the long cinderblock building was lit by neon, and the place had a desperate, nasty 1950s look. The units farthest from the street—where most of the cars were parked—were illuminated only by a few moth-embattled sixty-watt bulbs.

I had a mental image of Ed Harriman, the night clerk at the Roadhouse. I saw him as a wizened old man with bad teeth and three-day stubble, a man who chain-smoked unfiltered cigarettes and fought the bottle with limited success.

He wasn't like that at all. Ed Harriman was in his mid-twenties, just out of college, he said, with an MFA, whatever that is. He was industriously tapping away at a laptop computer when I walked into the office of the Roadhouse.

He was, he told me, working on a novel. "You can't just *write* about life," he said. "You've got to go out there and live it. Am I right?"

"Sure." I started to show him my license.

"I mean, what is life without experience? That's what I'm getting here. Experience. The things I've seen here have been invaluable. Absolutely invaluable."

"Well, that's why I'm here," I said. "I want to hear about the things you've seen. Especially the things you saw last Tuesday night. Or early the next morning."

"I mean, the ambience of this place alone is worth more than any college diploma, am I right? I mean, who could work here and not soak up scads of ambience?"

"Ed—can I call you Ed?"

"Sure." He grinned.

"Ed, I want you to pay attention for a moment." I showed him my detective's license and told him why I was there. "What I need from you—"

"Oh, yeah, right." He bobbed his head. "Gigi said you'd be around asking about that. I've been sort of expecting you."

"Good. Shall we get right to it, then?"

"Sure. This is about the woman who Gigi had to report for disturbing the peace, right? The woman who was howling?"

"That's correct."

"Don't know anything about it." He shook his head cheerfully. "I wasn't here when it happened. I get off at seven. Usually go out for breakfast—I've found this diner, the place is just chock full of the most fascinating people—then I go home and sleep for a few hours. So I wasn't here when it happened."

"But you were here when she checked in."

"Oh, yeah." He nodded. "That's right."

"Can you describe her for me?"

"Describe her?" He shook his head. "Nope. Wish I could. The police asked me the same thing."

"When did you talk to the police?" I asked.

"Couple of days later. They came to my apartment and woke me up. I told them I don't do interviews before noon," he grinned. "They didn't think it was funny."

"What did you tell them?"

"What *could* I tell them? Woman checked into a room. That's all I know. Don't know who she was, don't know what she looked like, don't know a thing about anything."

"Let's look at her registration card," I said. "Maybe that will help refresh your memory."

"Sure, why not." Ed found the card and studied it. "Amanda Standish," he said. "Unit twenty-seven. Checked in at one fifty-five A.M."

"Does that help you recall her?" I asked.

He thought for a moment, then shook his head. "Nope." He tapped his forehead. "Total blank."

Truer words were never spoke, I thought.

"What's this about, anyway?" he asked. "The police wouldn't tell me anything. 'Just answer the questions,' they said."

I decided to tell him, in the hope it would inspire him to think harder. "The woman the police found howling in that room Wednesday morning has been charged with attempted murder."

"Murder? Oh wow. How'd she do it?"

"Attempted murder," I said. "And it's only an accusation. We're trying to find out whether or not she did it. But it was done with a small stone sculpture."

He grinned. "Get out."

I nodded.

"A stone sculpture. Now, that's something." He let his attention drift. He was probably trying to work it into a story.

"So you can see how important this is," I said.

"Yeah, you bet."

"Good. Now, do a lot of people check in during your shift?"

"Nope. Not during that shift. Most people who check in here do it late afternoon and late evening. That's the reason I took the job. Time to write. And the ambience, of course."

"Of course." I leaned forward over the counter. "Ed, let's try to picture the last few people you've checked in, shall we?"

"Sure."

"Did anybody check in last night? That's Friday."

"A few." He said, nodding. "Friday's a big night."

I had him describe, in very general terms, the people who checked in. Then, with the aid of the registration cards, we did the same for the night before, and then the night before that. And finally the night before that, the night the woman calling herself Amanda Standish checked in.

"There were only two people who checked in during my shift that night." He examined both registrations and nodded. "Yep. Her and a guy who said he was from New York." Ed broke into a grin. "I remember the guy, all right. He said he was from New York, but still wrote down his Massachusetts license plates. Can you believe it?"

I told him I was capable of believing almost anything. "But Amanda Standish, do you recall if she checked in before or after this guy?"

"After."

"Okay. Was she alone?"

He shook his head and pointed at the registration card. "Says right here, double occupancy." He grinned at me. "And I thought you were a detective."

"Did you *see* anybody with her?"

"Oh. Stupid me." He shook his head. "Nope, I didn't see anybody else."

"The woman who checked in, did she do or say anything that made you think she was with somebody else?"

"You mean other than marking the double-occupancy box?"

"Other than that."

"Uh, well, now that you mention it, yeah, she did, while I was getting her change—she paid with two twenties and the room charge was only thirty-five bucks. I remember she walked over to the door and smiled, like there was somebody outside waiting in the car."

"Good. You're doing fine, Ed."

"I am, aren't I?" He grinned proudly. "It's being a writer, you know. Learning to pay attention to details. You ever read anything by—"

"Ed, now I want you to describe her for me."

"Describe her?"

"That's correct. I want you to visualize it," I said. "She walked over to the door and smiled out. Use your writer's eye, Ed. Close your eyes and see her standing at the door, smiling. You can see that, can't you?"

He closed his eyes, lowered his head, and frowned. "Yeah, I can see it."

"What's she wearing?"

"Uh, uh, white blouse sort of thing. And tan pants. I think. Yeah, tan pants."

"Good. How tall is she?"

"About my height. Maybe a little shorter. I'm five nine."

"How much does she weigh?"

He shrugged. "Maybe one-thirty."

"What color is her hair?"

"Brownish."

"Light brown or dark brown?"

"Sort of medium brown. Shoulder length."

We worked through the rest of it—no accent, no unusual mannerisms, no obvious display of temper or emotion, no nail polish, no limps or stutters or other defects. Just a brown-haired woman in her early thirties, a little taller than average, a little heavy in the hips, wearing good-quality casual clothes.

I showed Ed the photograph from the jacket of one Anka's books, the photograph of small, dark, intense Anka Stiffel.

"Is that the woman who checked in that night?" I asked.

"She's a writer?" he asked.

"Is that her?"

"Nope," he said, and shook his head. "Not even close."

J o o p   W h e e l e r

Sunday Morning

"This? This is nothing," I said. I was on the couch, flat on my back, and Stevie was putting a cold compress on my eye. Which had swollen to about the size and shape of a boxing glove.

"My cousin Dumar," I said, "he got himself thumped in the head once by a deer."

"A deer?" Stevie said.

"Yeah. Dumar shot the poor thing—did I mention he was poaching? Well, Dumar's not much smarter than a box of rocks. He shot the poor thing and when it flopped over and fell down, he just assumed it was dead. He walked over to it and damn if that deer didn't hop right up and start to running. Ran smack-bang into Dumar, whacked him upside the head with an antler. He wasn't much to look at to begin with, Dumar, and he wound up looking like somebody had surgically implanted an eggplant on the side of his head. Served him right for shooting the poor thing out of season."

Stevie sat on the floor beside the couch and shook her head. "Men never really stop being boys," she said. "Do they?"

"I suppose I must sound silly," I said.

She nodded. "Yes, you do."

Ask a stupid question . . . "I suppose I must look pretty silly, too." I felt the lump under the compress. Which hurt. So I poked at it with my finger. Which hurt even more.

"Stop fussing with that," Stevie said. "Why are you worrying about how you look? You ought to be worrying about whether or not you've got a concussion. You ought to go see a doctor."

I'd made that same suggestion to Cousin Dumar, back when he was lying on his momma's couch after getting thumped by that deer. Dumar told me to stop being such a pussy. Which was a line I didn't think I ought to try on Stevie. Instead I just made a face. Which also hurt.

She shook her head disgustedly. "Does it hurt a lot?"

I started to nod, but figured that would hurt too. "Just about everything hurts," I said. "Which pretty much sums up what you call the human condition."

Not that I had many complaints at the moment. Stevie had surprised me half an hour earlier, calling me on the phone, saying she had a message for me and asking if she could stop by in five minutes. Of course I said yes, even though I was supposed to be meeting Sweeney for breakfast. I spent the next five minutes rushing around the apartment, furiously trying to tidy up. Which hurt, of course.

When I let her in the apartment, Stevie took one look at my eye and turned into Florence Nightingale. Or the feminist equivalent, whatever that would be. Dr. Nightingale, Chief of Neurosurgery. Unless mainstream medicine is too male-focused. Which it probably is.

She made me lie on the couch while she bustled around the apartment doing God knows what. In the end all she did was soak a dish towel in cold water and put it on my head. Not a lot of health care for the amount of bustle involved. She'd been so busy I thought she was going to start boiling water and ripping up petticoats for bandages.

Not that I'd have minded. I was just glad she was there. I'd have liked it more if I hadn't been flat on my back with a cold towel pressed to my misshapen head, rattling on about my ridiculous family, while Stevie sat on the floor next to the couch and shook her head at the stupidity of all men. The stupidity of men wasn't a topic I cared to discuss at the moment.

"You said you had a message," I said. And immediately

wished I hadn't. The sooner she gave me the message, the sooner she'd probably leave. I still had about a force five crush on her, lesbian or not. And when she went all medical on me, the red lightning went skidding out of control again. That's the problem with red lightning. No real grasp on reality.

Stevie nodded. "From Cotton," she said. "The woman who . . ."

"Who hauled my ass out of the fire," I said. "I remember Cotton. How is her friend, Hannah? She okay?"

"Cotton says she's a little sore."

"Only a little? Damn. I got to learn to hit harder."

"Hannah probably wouldn't admit it if she were hurt," Stevie said. "She's as macho as you are."

"Machoer," I said.

"Cotton said she's willing to talk to you about Anka."

"Why the change of heart?" She'd said the same thing the night before at the bar, but I hadn't believed her. I wasn't sure I did now.

"I don't claim to understand it," Stevie said, "but she seems somehow pleased that you fought with Hannah."

"Ah." I thought understood it. It didn't have anything to do with fighting with Hannah—it had to do with something else. Respect, I guess you'd call it. I'd respected Hannah enough to fight dirty. I understood it, but I wasn't sure I could explain it to Stevie. It's sort of a guy thing.

"Okay. When does she want to get together?" I asked.

"She said tomorrow evening, if you're up to it."

I grinned. I was beginning to like Cotton. "Where?"

"My place? She didn't think you'd feel comfortable at Schotzie's, so she suggested my place."

I forgot what I was doing and nodded. Which hurt. "What are the odds that I'm getting set up?" I asked. Just because I was beginning to like Cotton didn't mean I trusted her.

"Set up?"

"Yeah, set up. You know—I'm walking to your place and I get jumped by twenty heavyset women with tire irons. Set up."

Stevie was shocked. "I cannot believe you're saying that." She acted like I'd just accused her of something horrible—penis envy, maybe, or being a Republican. "You think because Cotton is a woman that she's vindictive?"

I shook my head. Which hurt and made the cold towel slide off. "It's got nothing to do with her being a woman. It's got to do with— Well, I don't know what it's got to do with. Something else. Saving face. Cotton might feel I embarrassed her somehow. She might think I need to be taught a lesson."

Stevie shook her head. "I don't think you'll be set up," she said coldly.

"Okay," I said. "Just asking. Nothing personal."

"You insult my friends and say it's nothing personal?"

"Look, I'm just being careful," I said. "It's not an insult."

"Of course it is," she said.

I adjusted the towel on my eye. "Tell you what. You tell Cotton what I said. Let her decide if it's an insult."

"What makes you think you can trust *me*?" she asked. "Maybe I'm in on this plot to set you up."

All this was putting a damper on the red lightning.

"Look, if you trust her, I'll trust her," I said.

"I trust her."

"Fine. Then we're all set."

Stevie shook her head. "You don't really believe Cotton would set you up, do you?"

I didn't want to argue. I was sore and tired, and unhappy that we were arguing over something this stupid, and I felt more like crying than I had in years.

"Stevie," I said, "I can't tell you the last time I ever really believed anything. I don't know the woman. If she set me up, I wouldn't be surprised. If she *didn't*, I wouldn't be surprised.

And in the end, it doesn't much matter whether I trust her or not. I still have to go."

I closed my eyes and covered them with the wet towel. I could feel her looking at me. Or at least I thought I could. She could have been looking at a magazine for all I know; I kept my eyes closed. Which was about the only thing I could do that didn't hurt.

She readjusted the towel over my eyes. "You're in a lot of pain, aren't you? I'm sorry. I shouldn't be badgering you."

"It's not so bad," I lied.

She shook her head again. "I declare, you're such a boy."

That's a line I've heard all my life. Usually when I'd done something stupid and was trying to get myself out of trouble. But in the past, it was always said with affection. It was a sort of compliment, and I'd just grin and accept it. Because bad boys get by with a lot. But when Stevie called me a boy, there wasn't a smidgen of compliment in it. All I could hear in her voice was the sad recognition of a true thing.

She stayed another ten minutes or so and we had something approaching a pleasant conversation. Before she left, she put a glass of ice water and a bottle of aspirin on the table beside the couch. She told me she'd call later to see how I was doing.

One of the problems with having a force five crush on a lesbian-feminist is it makes you think about things. Which I normally enjoy doing. But that doesn't mean I want to *change* my way of thinking. I'm used to my way of thinking. I've been thinking this way for as long as I can remember.

But I couldn't help it. I thought about Cousin Dumar's remark. Which I'd always thought was stupid, but funny. Now it was less funny. Hell, it wasn't hardly funny at all.

And I thought about a sign I'd seen once in a VFW hall. "No weapons. No fighting. And no girls shooting pool." I'd always thought that was funny. Stupid and offensive, but funny. Now I found myself wondering if I'd have thought it was funny if the sign said, "No niggers shooting pool."

It's not easy, being the victim of feminist red lightning. It ruins some things for you. Which is a different sort of hurt.

I told myself to stop whining. I told myself to get up and hurry to the diner. Sweeney was there waiting for me. I told myself there was too much work to do for me to be lying around and cutting the fool

I know what Cousin Dumar would have told me, if he'd known I was lying on a couch, nursing a swollen eye I'd got in a fight with a woman, thinking about the things I was thinking about.

Cousin Dumar would have told me to stop being such a pussy.

Kevin Sweeney

Sunday Morning

I'd eaten half my breakfast by the time Joop finally showed up. Mary Margaret was visiting her mother at the nursing home over at St. Anne's, like she does every Sunday after mass. She's not that old or decrepit, Mary Margaret's mother, but she's drifted a little farther out to sea than is good for her, and she needs watching. I'd visit her with Mary Margaret, and gladly, because I like the old woman, but sometimes she gets upset when I'm around. She gets confused and thinks I'm her oldest son, Tim, who was killed in a truck accident years back serving a tour in Korea.

Joop looked bad. His right eye was swollen and he walked like an old man, stiff and bent over, from taking a few shots in the ribs. You could tell he hurt, but he was still grinning, partly out of embarrasment over the predicament he'd gotten himself into and partly because Stevie Gibbs had just visited his apartment.

"I think she likes me," he said.

"She's a lesbian," I reminded him. "She's not going to like you the way you want her to like you."

He waved it away. "I just like her," he said.

So I let it go. There's no point in trying to convince Joop to be rational about women. No point in trying to convince Joop to be rational about anything, as far as that goes.

I turned the conversation away from women and the damage done and onto the investigation. Joop filled me in on the interviews he'd done, including his meeting with the transsexual Deirdre.

"She kissed you?" I asked. "You let her kiss you?"

Joop nodded. "Nothing I could do."

"Tongues?"

"You're a disgusting man, Sweeney," he said. "It was just a little thank-you peck."

"Aren't you worried about AIDS?"

"You can't get AIDS from a kiss," Joop snapped. "Don't you ever read the newspaper?"

Joop was beginning to get testy, either about the topic or because his eye hurt. So I reported my progress. "While you were out scrapping with lesbians," I said, "I was out working."

"Getting your ass kicked *is* work," Joop said. "That's one of the reasons I don't like it.'

"This you'll like," I said. I told him what I'd learned from Ed Harriman at the Roadhouse Motel & Café.

He gave me a thumbs-up, then asked, "What are the odds that our boy Ed is talking out his ass?"

I had to admit the odds were fairly good. "He wants to be a writer," I said, "so we have to assume he has an active and unhealthy imagination. He could be pulling it out of the air."

"On the other hand, what reason would he have to lie?" Joop asked.

"I'm not saying he'd be lying," I said. "All I'm saying is that he might be remembering things that didn't happen. Maybe he saw the real Amanda Standish . . ."

"Or a woman who *called* herself Amanda Standish," Joop said. "Or none of the above."

"That's about it," I said. "He's either right or he's wrong."

"Well, that narrows it down." Joop sipped some tea and winced. Probably cut in the mouth, I figured, which can hurt like the devil. But the boy shouldn't be getting in fights.

"Still, it's the best indication we have that Anka might be telling the truth," I said.

"What's Kath say?" Joop asked.

"I haven't told her yet."

"Why not?"

I shrugged and smiled. "I was thinking if you didn't have anything else to do, you might enjoy calling and letting her know. Unless you're too smitten with lesbians and transsexuals."

Joop grinned. "You're a dog, Sweeney."

I sipped my tea. Joop looked up and waved. Mary Margaret was walking down the aisle, done with the weekly maternal visit.

Mary Margaret fussed over Joop's injuries, scolded him for getting in a fight—especially a fight with a woman—and gave him half a dozen remedies to reduce the swelling and discoloration.

Even though he was in pain, Joop stayed at the diner until Mary Margaret ordered and ate her breakfast. His Southern manners wouldn't allow him to leave earlier.

On the way home, Mary Margaret and I had a small argument, which is the only kind we seem to have, thanks be to God. She wanted me to take the day off and go on a picnic while the weather was still nice. I told her I had to work.

"But it's Sunday," she said.

"Sorry. Maybe when the case is over we can go on a picnic."

"Even the Lord took the one day off," she said.

"He could afford to," I said. "He didn't have a client looking at a potential murder charge."

"Is taking off one day—just one day—really going to matter?" she asked.

"It will if Amanda Owen dies."

"Why?"

"Because murder is different. Right now all the police have is an assault. Maybe attempted murder, though that's harder to prove in court. But if Amanda Owen dies, then the whole process escalates. More detectives get involved, and more forensics guys and more of everything. The prosecutor will work harder to get a murder conviction than he would for an assault conviction. And while they pour more resources into the case, it's still just us looking out for Anka."

And that was the end of it. She was quiet for the rest of the ride home, but it wasn't a hostile quiet. It was a sad quiet. She's a smart woman, Mary Margaret. She knew I'd take the day off if I could, and she knew I hated the thought that I couldn't. I suspect she felt let down that I chose work over her, but the dear woman decided not to make both of us more miserable by worrying at it. She also decided to call a friend and go on a picnic without me.

Is it any wonder I'm in love with her?

After dropping Mary Margaret off, I drove out to the home of Willis and Barbara Owen, Amanda's parents. Although they weren't listed in the telephone book, I'd been able to get their address through the electric company: 4 Culverton Circle.

I'd heard of Culverton Circle, although I'd never had any reason to go there, either as a cop or as a P.I. Rich people lived on Culverton Circle. The Owen house wasn't difficult to find, since there were only four houses on the street. Four huge houses. Four mansions.

I sat in my car, stared at the house, and cursed myself for a coward. It was only a house, I told myself. A damn big house, no mistake, but I'd seen bigger. I was on vacation when I saw them and had to pay an admission fee to get in, but they were bigger houses all the same.

I told myself there was nothing to be nervous about. It didn't mean anything that Amanda's parents lived in a house so large that the entire Sweeney clan—brothers, sisters, parents, grandparents, aunts, uncles, and the thousands of cousins—could have fit in it without jostling each other. I told myself I was too mature to let myself be intimidated by the trappings of the upper class.

At least that's what I told myself.

Even so, I had to fight the feeling that I should go round to the back door, hat in hand, the way my Irish ancestors did when reporting to the resident British magistrate to repair the ironwork. I knew how they must have felt—the nervous smile and the knuckle to the forehead, hiding the fear and resentment. Get the work done and get out without humiliating yourself and leaving a mess.

Well, that was all I wanted as well.

I got out of the car, grinning but ashamed of myself. The collective Irish working-class inferiority complex ran strong in me. I was glad Joop wasn't there to see me so unnerved. It wouldn't have bothered him, the house. Joop has that easy, old-family, I-fit-in-anywhere confidence. He'd have gone straight up to the front door and knocked, or rung the chimes, or banged the gong—however a person announces themselves at a house of that grandeur.

So I pretended I was Joop. I walked up the steps and banged a little too hard on the door, trying to drive the cheap willies away. A frail, white-haired woman answered. She was dressed entirely in what appeared to be well-worn L. L. Bean clothes. She looked like the vicar's wife, setting out on a nature walk.

"Yes?" she asked. She had a voice like Katharine Hepburn, a little harsh and wobbly, but somehow strong all the same.

"Mrs. Owen?"

"Yes?"

I introduced myself and gave her my card. "I'm sorry to be bothering you on a Sunday, Mrs. Owen, but I need to talk to you about your daughter Amanda."

She looked at me, then back at the card. "Oh. Ah, won't

you please step in?" She held the door for me. "My husband is in the family room."

She led me down a long carpeted hall and into a large room jammed with big, comfortable furniture. Her husband was in a reclining chair with one Sunday paper on his lap and another on the table beside him. He was the perfect picture of the retired ultra-capitalist—tall, ruddy-complected, aging but still fit enough to wield the throttle of commerce.

"Dear, this is Mr., uh . . ." She looked at my card.

"Sweeney," I said, and it never sounded more working-class Irish Catholic in my life. "Kevin Sweeney."

Owen put his paper aside and stood. He had a nice firm handshake. "Sweeney," he said, smiling. "Don't believe I've ever met anybody of that name before."

"No, sir." And not likely to, I thought.

"Mr. Sweeney is here to see us about Amanda, dear."

"Oh? I see. A policeman." He nodded, as if that explained why this lout Sweeney was interfering with his hard-earned day of rest. He sat back down and put the chair back.

"No sir," I said. "I used to be. Now I'm just a private investigator."

"I see." He nodded. "And how can I help you, Sweeney?"

I decided to blurt it out. "I'm working for the attorney Kathleen O'Mara, who has been assigned to represent the woman charged with the assault on your daughter."

His eyes went hard, and I knew I'd have to play this gently. Willis Owen was the sort of man who could—and would happily—call his friend the mayor and try to have my license lifted.

"We're trying to gather as much background information as possible on both Ms. Stiffel and your daughter," I said. "We need to know—"

"You want information to use against my Amanda in

court," he said. He sat forward in the chair. "You want to dirty her name."

I shook my head. "No, sir. My job is just to gather facts. I'm not interested in—"

"That woman you're working for—and I'm using the term 'woman' loosely—is a dangerous pervert and I'll be damned if I'll say a single word that will help her. She—she seduced my daughter. She took a fine, healthy, normal young woman—a happily married woman—and turned her into a sexual degenerate." He sat back in the big chair and picked up his newspaper.

"Mr. Owen, I don't—"

"No, sir," he said. "No, I have nothing to say to you and I'll ask you to leave my house."

"I'm sorry if I've . . ."

"It's best if you leave," Mrs. Owen said. "I'm so sorry."

"Don't apologize to him," her husband growled, without raising his head from the newspaper. "Out of the house, now, before I notify the police."

Mrs. Owen held up her arm to guide me out of the room. At the door she apologized again. "It's very difficult for him, you know. He so very much wanted a perfect family."

"I'm sorry if I've upset him," I said.

"No, no. It's just—well, that he feels it so deeply, you know. He feels responsible."

"Responsible? How?"

She looked back over her shoulder for a moment. "Oh, the usual obsession of the busy man," she said. "If only he'd been home more often, he could have done something. It's all nonsense, of course. I think Amanda was just born—that way. But my husband thinks he can and should control everything. So he feels responsible when things go wrong." She shook her head. "Of course, he also still blames Amanda."

"Why?"

She shook her head. "I don't know," she said. "But I

know he does." She glanced back toward the family room again. "And now, Mr. Sweeney, you really had better go."

"Thank you, Mrs. Owen."

"You're very welcome, Mr. Sweeney."

Halfway down the steps I stopped and turned around. There was one question I had to ask. "Mrs. Owen?"

"Yes?" She looked fearfully behind her.

"If your husband feels this so deeply, why is he at home reading the newspaper instead of at the hospital?"

I could see the wounded look creep over her face, and I cursed myself for a mean-hearted, vindictive bastard.

Mrs. Owen lowered her head and softly closed the door.

Sunday Night

I was back on the uncomfortable futon sofa thing in Stevie's apartment, sipping on a glass of iced tea. With mint. Stevie was having white wine. No mint. I'd have gone for the wine myself, or something stronger, except I wanted to be perfectly sober when Cotton and Hannah arrived. In case Hannah was feeling rowdy and felt like trying to rupture my spleen.

I'd arrived early. Despite Stevie's assurances, I wasn't totally convinced that Cotton wouldn't set me up. I didn't say that to Stevie, of course. I just apologized for being early.

Stevie was talking about a movie she'd recently seen, something about women political prisoners in the U.S. I gave her about half of my attention. Just enough to carry on my part of the conversation. Which was mostly the appropriate "Oh?"'s and "They did what?"'s.

Mostly, though, what I was doing was waiting for the Midol to kick in. I was still stiff and sore and I had a king hell headache. A few hours earlier, Kath O'Mara had given me a fistful of Midol to help me through the evening. Midol was all she had. Kath said she hadn't used even an aspirin in years, but she still had some Midol from when she was in law school. Which was fine. I once heard a woman compare menstrual cramps to physical assault, so I figured it would do the job.

I'd called Kath from a pay phone as soon as I left Sweeney. And I got her out of the shower. I blamed it on Sweeney.

"I've got some interesting news," I said.

"Joop, I'm dripping all over the floor. Let me call you back in a few minutes."

I grinned at the thought of her hopping from foot to foot,

dripping on the floor, towel artfully disarranged. "I'm not at home," I said. "I'm at a pay phone."

"Where?"

I told her. She hesitated for about the time it takes for your heart to beat three or four times. "That's only about half a mile from here," she said. "Why don't you just come over. Say fifteen minutes."

Fifteen minutes later there was a happy Southern boy ringing her doorbell. A happy Southern boy with a head shaped like a diseased gourd. I'd forgotten to tell Kath that I'd been in a scrap and looked like Quasimodo's brother. The ugly one.

Kath took one look at my great lump of a head and went medical on me. First Stevie, then Mary Margaret, now Kath. I don't know if it's something women learn, or if it's something innate, like what makes baby kangaroos climb up into their momma's pouch. Whatever it is, women seem to get an inordinate amount of gratification out of taking care of a person who is beat all to hell.

Kath sat me down on a little love seat and fussed over me for a few minutes before asking me to run through the story about how I got whacked in the head. I didn't mind telling it again, even though I was getting sick of it. The reason I didn't mind was because Kath sat right next to me, nodding and frowning, while I ran through the story. And she smelled like soap. Soap and Johnson's Baby Shampoo.

It sparked a modified red-lightning effect. A softer version. Red lightning didn't exactly *lighten* through my blood; it sort of *wriggled* through it. Like a salamander in soft mud.

After the melodrama, I told her the real news. Which was Sweeney's having found a witness who said the woman who checked into the Roadhouse Motel wasn't Anka Stiffel.

"It doesn't clear Anka," I said. "Not by a long shot. But what it might do is cast a little doubt in the minds of a jury. And reasonable doubt is all we need."

Kath frowned. "It's pretty iffy," she said.

"Yeah, but it's the only thing we've got that shows Anka *might* be telling the truth. Or something approaching the truth."

"At least about going to the Roadhouse with another woman," Kath said. "And if a jury'll buy that, maybe they'll buy the whole package."

We looked at each other for a moment. Then shook our heads in unison. "Pretty iffy," we agreed.

"Can we find this other woman?" Kath asked. "It would be great if we could prove Anka didn't leave the motel that night."

"I thought it was their job to prove that she did."

"It is," Kath said. "But you know juries." She got a faraway look in her eyes. "If we could verify the time she left Schotzie's. And that she left with this Amanda Standish. And that she spent the whole night at the Roadhouse . . ."

I told her I'd already arranged a meeting with Cotton and Hannah. "Tonight at Stevie Gibbs's apartment," I said.

She frowned and bit her lip. "Maybe it's not such a good idea," she said.

"I don't see any option."

"Well, be careful," she said. "It could be a setup."

And zing—there it was, back again, that old familiar red lightning, flashing at the most unlikely things. Like shared paranoia.

"I'll try," I said. "What the hell, I've still got one eye that works. If things go like last time, you and Sweeney can enroll me in a school for the blind."

We talked about the case a while longer, then I reluctantly said I had to go. I was tuckered, as my uncle Amos would say. I wanted to go home and take a nap before going to Stevie's.

So Kath offered to let me take a nap there. Right in her own bed. The one she slept in her ownself.

And I hesitated. Which right off convinced me I must have suffered some serious brain damage in the fight. When she saw me hesitate, Kath said she had plenty of chores to do and she'd keep very quiet.

I managed to suppress a whole bunch of inappropriate remarks and agreed to nap there. How could I refuse? I figured it this way—a quick nap, then ask Kath out for a little dinner, maybe a little semi-innocent flirting over the table. See how things went.

The quick nap turned into three hours. When I finally woke up and dragged myself out of Kath's bed, I was about half stupid with sleep. Half stupid and about two-thirds crippled. Getting beat up makes you feel old.

Kath had cooked up some sort of chicken casserole thing. Which she invited me to eat with her. And which I did, after begging some sort of painkiller off her. Midol, like I said, was all she had.

I ate the Midol, gimped around trying to work out the stiffness, and then set to the chicken casserole. We talked and laughed a little while we ate. And it was —well, it was nice. No real flirting. At least not the way I think of flirting. Which has a seductive edge to it. Instead Kath just acted like I was welcome there in her house and like she was comfortable with my company.

I stayed until it was time to go to Stevie's. I gobbled a few more Midol when I got there, and then did my minimal conversational duty. By the time Stevie's doorbell rang, I was feeling something like okay.

I stood up when Stevie let Cotton and Hannah in. Partly out of courtesy and partly because I didn't want Hannah to catch me sitting down.

Hannah looked a lot smaller than she had the night before. I smiled and shook hands with them both. Cautiously.

Stevie, the perfect Southern hostess, fetched drinks and we all sat down. I watched Hannah to see if she was stiff. If she was, she hid it well. Nobody mentioned the ruckus of the night before.

Cotton got right to down to business. "You wanted to know about Anka, right?" she asked me. "That night at Schotzie's? About Anka and Amanda getting into it?"

"That's right."

"Now, Stevie says you're working for her. Is that right?"

"For her lawyer, right."

"Who's her lawyer?"

"Kathleen O'Mara." I think it gave me a few extra points that I was working for a woman. I was hoping it would. So I underplayed it, like it was no big deal. Which it wasn't. But if they thought it was, I'd use it.

Cotton nodded. "Okay," she said. "What do you want to know?"

"Let's start with Amanda. She was there when Anka and Stevie arrived, is that right?"

They both nodded.

"Did she come alone?"

They said she did.

"Was she there to meet anybody?"

They didn't think so.

"But she was dancing with somebody when Anka and Stevie arrived," I said.

They agreed that she was.

"Who?" I asked.

Cotton looked at Hannah. "What's her name?" She screwed up her face. "She works for that public-relations firm."

"Vicky?" Hannah said. "Something like that. Victoria."

"Victoria. That's it." Cotton turned to Stevie. "You know who we're talking about?"

Stevie nodded. "Victoria Gilbois." She told me the name of the company the Gilbois woman worked for. I wrote it all down like a good little detective.

"Were Amanda and Victoria, uh, involved?" I asked.

All three women shook their heads.

"Are you embarrassed to say 'fucking'?" Cotton asked. "Or does it bother you to think of women fucking women?"

"Cotton," Stevie said, frowning.

Cotton raised her hands, as if to say "Okay, I'm sorry, it just slipped out." Hannah didn't even blink.

"Why don't we just move on to what happened when Anka walked in," I said. "Tell me what happened then."

Cotton told it. She told it pretty much the way Stevie had told it. Which was pretty much the way Detective Marty Coyle had told it. Which was probably pretty much the way it had happened. Which is about all you can ever ask for.

When Stevie and Anka walked into the bar, there were Amanda and Victoria Gilbois. Dancing. Anka went straight up to Amanda and started pushing her and calling her names. Amanda pushed and slapped back. Then Anka pushed or knocked Amanda down.

"That's when it got confusing," Cotton said. "Stevie got in between the two of them. Anka was trying to get to Amanda, who was sitting on the floor, trying to kick Anka. Everybody was shouting and pushing. It was sorta fun." Cotton grinned evilly.

"Then what happened?" I asked. Cotton was on a roll and my job had been reduced to taking notes and giving prompts. Which is all a good detective ought to do.

"Then Anka left," she said.

"Alone?" I asked.

"Far as I know." Cotton looked at Hannah.

"I saw two or three women going out after her," Hannah said.

"When you say they were going out after her, do you mean they were simply leaving at about the same time? Or that they were looking for her?"

"I think they were looking for her."

"Why do you think that?" I asked. It's a trick I learned from watching Sweeney. If folks can tell you *why* they think something happened, they can usually dredge up a more accurate account of the event.

"Because of the way they were moving," Hannah said. "One of them had her hand out like she was trying to get Anka to wait." She demonstrated the gesture.

"Do you know the names of these women?" I asked.

She shook her head. "I really wasn't paying that much attention."

"Was Victoria Gilbois one of them?"

"Maybe. I don't really remember."

"What about Amanda Standish?" I asked.

Cotton and Hannah looked at each other. I couldn't tell if the look was a question or a warning.

"Who the hell is Amanda Standish?" Hannah asked.

"Never heard of her," Cotton said. "She's not somebody who hangs out at Schotzie's."

They didn't have much more information. I quizzed them about a few other details, but it was mostly a waste of time. Which is what a lot of detective work is.

Cotton helped Stevie take the glasses to the kitchen area of her loft apartment. Hannah nodded at me.

"Sorry about your eye," she said. "Does it hurt much?"

I started to lie about it. Habit, I guess. But then I decided to 'fess up. "Yeah, it does. So does my shoulder. And my ribs. And just about everything else. How about you?"

She shook her head. "I was a little sore this morning, and it was hard to work out . . ."

Work out? I thought. Damn.

". . . but now I feel fine." She came close to smiling.

Lying bitch, I thought. And immediately mentally withdrew the "bitch." I was getting more politically correct by the minute. As politically correct as you can get and not feel any remorse for throwing bar chairs at women.

"Can I ask you a question?" Hannah asked.

"Sure," I said. "I've been asking questions all evening. I guess it's about your turn."

"It's about last night," she said. She looked at her hands for a moment. "You know, you learn things in class, but you're never really sure if they'll work in real life. Or if you'll be able to do them. You know?"

"Yeah. Was that your first real fight?" I asked.

She nodded.

"And you want to know how you did?"

The smile escaped. "I guess so."

"You were doing fine," I said. "That's why I chucked the chair at you."

"That was a pretty dirty trick."

I smiled and nodded. "That's why I did it. That's why it worked."

"If you hadn't thrown the chair at me, I'd have taken you," she said.

I shrugged. "Maybe. Maybe not." I leaned forward. "Can I give you some advice? As a person who's been in a few real fights?"

She half shrugged, half nodded. Like she wasn't going to ask me for advice, but was willing to listen to it if it made sense.

"Don't ever get in a fight unless you're willing to throw a chair at somebody," I said. "Or a brick. Or whatever is handy."

She smiled again. But I could see she didn't really get it. Somehow, somewhere she'd been handed the notion that a fight has rules and etiquette. Which is stupid and will get you hit with a bar chair if you're not careful. Fighting is what you do when you have no other choice, and then the only rule is you do whatever you can to keep the other person from hurting you. You put the other person on the ground and you run away. You don't have winners in a real fight. You only have survivors.

It's not a thing they teach you in classes. It's a thing you learn by dodging bar chairs.

Kevin Sweeney

Monday Morning

Charles Lowell, Amanda Owen's husband-in-name-only,
must have had hemorrhoids the size of cantaloupes. Nothing
else could have accounted for the pained expression he kept
welded to his face during our interview. It might have been
an attempt to look sincere, or displeased, or even angry, but
whatever it was, it wasn't pleasant to see.

He hadn't seemed surprised to see me, even though I'd
arrived at his office unannounced. I suspected that Amanda's
parents had warned him I might be around.

Charles Lowell ran a small, very successful architecture
firm. Dr. Rifkin had said that Amanda's parents had financed
the firm as a wedding gift. It appeared they'd made a good
investment. If the photographs on the wall were examples of
his work, he was talented.

When we were seated—him behind a broad wooden
desk, me in a deep, cloth-covered chair—his secretary stuck
her head into his office and asked if we'd like coffee. Lowell
shook his head and dismissed her, without even a glance in my
direction. I would have liked coffee.

"You're here about Amanda," he said.

"Yes sir, I am."

He nodded. "I can give you ten minutes," he said. Without any prompting, he recited their vital statistics—the date
they were married; the length of time they had been married,
in years and months; the date he moved out of the house.

"I don't know what else I can tell you," he said. "I
haven't seen Amanda for nearly a year. Maybe longer."

"You haven't visited her at the hospital?" I asked.

He got a little flustered. "Well, yes, I have been to the

hospital. I meant, well, before she was . . . you know, injured. I meant I hadn't, you know, seen her for a year or so before the, uh, assault."

I nodded. "I understand the two of you are still married."

He nodded, tight-lipped. "Yes, we are."

"Is there a reason neither of you has asked for a divorce?"

"I suspect you've already formed your opinion regarding why we are still married," he said primly.

I gave him a friendly smile. "Mr. Lowell, I try not to have too many opinions. I just collect the facts. Why don't you give me your facts, then maybe I'll form an opinion."

His face took on a constipated ultra-Protestant look. "Most people seem to think my reasons are mercenary," he said. "They think I married Amanda for her money and that I stay married to her for the same reason. I freely admit that her parents were very generous to me. Still are."

I remembered that Dr. Rifkin had said Amanda's parents gave him some sort of stipend to keep him from divorcing their daughter. I nodded for him to continue.

"But I married Amanda for one reason and only one reason. Because I loved her. And I stay married to her for that same reason."

"You still love her?"

He nodded. "Yes sir, I do." He said it almost defiantly. I liked that.

"Do you think there's a chance she'll change her mind?" I asked. "Do you think she'll come back to you?"

He didn't hesitate. "Yes, someday I think she will. I hope and pray she will."

"Has she given you any indication that she might change her mind?" I asked. He seemed to feel comfortable discussing her as if she were still healthy, as if she still had a mind to change, so I did the same, though it made me feel uneasy.

He shook his head. "No," he admitted.

"When you were together, how did you get along?"

"I thought we got along pretty well. Better than most of the married couples we knew. I was wrong, obviously. But I still don't understand why she left. To this day, I simply do not understand."

It seemed fairly obvious to me: She'd left him because she fell in love with somebody else. That isn't the sort of thing you point out in an interview, though.

"Amanda is a very kind woman," he said. "Kindhearted. Even when she told me about— about her, well, her involvement . . ."

"With Anka Stiffel?"

"Yes. Even then she was kind. She didn't tell me she was seeing this, this other woman at first. She simply told me she needed some space, some time for herself."

"Were you surprised when you learned about her relationship with Ms. Stiffel?"

"Surprise doesn't express it," he said. "I was in shock. But eventually I began to understand it. In some warped way, it even made some sense."

"Oh?"

He nodded. "Yes, Amanda is very nurturing. A quality you don't often find in modern women. When I learned that this woman suffered from emotional problems—well, I knew Amanda was probably taken in by that. She felt strongly for the suffering of others. She always made me give money to the United Way."

He smiled, as if to himself. Then his smile faded. "I can understand that intellectually, but at the gut level, I simply cannot understand it," he said. "I gave her everything. When she started the sculpture thing, I went along. I didn't grumble, even though the supplies cost me a small fortune and she was always a mess. Meals were late. Sometimes she didn't cook at all and we had to order in Chinese. And when she started

consorting with all those artist types, I went along with her.
I even went to their parties, though God knows I didn't enjoy
them. But I went. For her I went."

And probably let her know what a big favor that was, I
thought.

"And when she told me she wanted to separate, I went
along with that too. Of course, I tried to get her to see a
marriage counselor, somebody who could help her see what
she was risking, what she was throwing away. But she
wouldn't do it. So eventually I moved out of our house."

"It must have been very hard for you," I said.

"Mister . . ." He looked at my card. ". . . Sweeney, I can't
begin to tell you what it was like. At first I thought perhaps
it might have been me, that I was somehow at fault. I mean,
I worked some long hours. And I probably wasn't as attentive
as I should have been. But it takes a lot of work to get a
business going and make it a success."

I said I supposed it did.

"But when I learned she was, well, involved in an affair
with, well, with a woman—and an emotionally disturbed
woman at that—well, then I knew it wasn't me. I knew it
wasn't my fault. I knew something was wrong with Amanda,
that she was suffering some sort of emotional crisis as well. I
advised her to see a psychiatrist, but of course she wasn't
willing to listen to me."

I nodded and made some sort of sympathetic male noise.
"Mr. Lowell, I hope you'll excuse this next question. But I
need to ask it." I gave him a grave, man-to-man look. "What
exactly is your financial arrangement with Amanda's parents?"

He cocked his head to one side. "I don't think that is at
all relevant, is it?"

"Well, sir, I just don't know. It might be." It never hurts
to "sir" and "mister" guys like Charles Lowell.

"I fail to see how," he said.

I gave it some thought. "Well, it's hard to say," I said. "You may be right. It may not be relevant. But there's no way I can tell if it's relevant until I know your answer."

His eyes got wider. "You're not suggesting I had anything to do with this incident, are you?"

"No, of course not," I said. "But in this job we have to look at everything. Just the way you have to construct a solid foundation before you can build the building."

He considered it for a moment, then shook his head. "No, I don't think I care to answer that question. It doesn't have any bearing on the matter. I trust you'll understand."

I nodded. "Yes, of course," I said.

We talked for another twenty minutes. Nothing else he said was of any interest. Nothing, that is, until I was getting ready to leave. He stood and shook my hand.

"Mr. Sweeney," he said. "Like I told you, I love my wife. Despite everything she's done to me and her poor family, I love her. And I would have done, and still would do, anything for her. Amanda was my most prized possession."

As I walked down the stairs, I found myself silently glad that Amanda Owen had left her husband and previous owner. I doubted he had much to do with Amanda being a lesbian, but he was certainly capable of putting a person off men. I'd spent less than an hour with him and I was beginning to hate the bastards myself.

Once outside, I took a short walk. There were three banks within two blocks of Charles Lowell's office. He probably kept his money in one of them.

I had a contact at a suburban branch office of one of the banks. A quick telephone call revealed that Charles Lowell's finances weren't handled by that bank.

But you don't need contacts in every bank, so long as you have contacts who have contacts. That's how all business works, even the detective business. I phoned an associate, one who specialized in financial matters. After a little haggling he agreed to check out Lowell for me in exchange for a small fee and a case of Guinness.

Less than two hours later, he called me at the office. Every other week $3,500 was automatically transferred from Willis Owen's account to Charles Lowell's NOW account. That came to just over $90,000 a year, a serious chunk of money—money that would be lost if Charles Lowell and Amanda Owen ever decided to get a divorce.

Large sums of money can make people irrational. Maybe irrational enough to whack somebody in the head.

Joop Wheeler

Monday Morning

"It's a dybbuk," Marty Coyle said. He used both hands to hold up a large plastic evidence bag. Sealed inside was a light-colored stone sculpture. After looking at it from both sides and grinning, Coyle set the bag on the bench. "I think it's the first time in the history of Hobsbawm, Massachusetts, that a dybbuk has been used to commit a felony."

We were in the evidence room of the police station. The sculpture, even though it was in the same type of evidence bag as the guns, the beer bottles, the paint cans, and the other bits of evidence, looked out of place. It looked like it belonged in a museum warehouse.

"It's a what?" I asked.

"A dybbuk," he said. "Here, read it for yourself." He handed me a forensic report, which said: "The statue depicts a dybbuk (from the Hebrew *dibbūq*), in Jewish folklore an evil spirit that enters the body of a living person and controls his actions." If I'd been hanging out with Stevie Gibbs, I'd have made a comment about the report's sexist language. But it didn't seem worth mentioning to Coyle. The report also noted that this particular dybbuk was carved out of aplite, which the report said was a type of granite. I didn't know there was more than one type of granite. Not that it mattered. Aplite did the job.

"Oh," I said. "A dybbuk."

"Right. Your basic dybbuk."

"Your basic aplite dybbuk," I said. I held up the report and cocked an eyebrow. "You're not going to tell me you've got a guy here who can recognize different types of Jewish demons?" I said. "And who can also distinguish types of granite?"

Coyle shook his head. "Naw. That was the FBI. We sent this down to them hoping they'd be able to use some of their high-tech laser things to produce some fingerprints. Waste of fuckin' time. They didn't find any more prints than we did, but you know the FBI. Got to show off. Since they couldn't give us anything we could really use, they got one of their whiz kids to put a name on the thing and find out what it was made out of. Fuckin' FBI jerk-offs."

"Are you saying there were no prints at all?" I asked. "It had been wiped?"

"No identifiable prints," he corrected me. "Surface is too rough to take a good print. There's smudges all over it."

"May I?" I indicated the evidence bag.

"Knock yourself out," he said. "You can't open it up, but go ahead and look. You look on the back, down around the dybbuk's butt, you can see some of the victim's blood and hair."

The thing must have weighed ten pounds. It was a squat nude female figure, crouching, her knees drawn up directly beneath her breasts, her hands by her feet. Her face was drawn into a tight grimace, showing a mouthful of straight teeth. And sure enough, on the butt, there it was—blood and and a few strands of hair.

"That's a dybbuk," I said. "No getting around it."

"Odd coincidence, that," Coyle said.

"What?"

"Here we got us a Jewish woman who acts like she's possessed accused of whacking her lover with a statue of a Jewish demon what possesses people. Odd coincidence, don't you think?"

I agreed it was an odd coincidence.

"Jury will love it." Coyle grinned.

"Nobody ever said a jury was smart," I said. "A jury is

just twelve folks who aren't smart enough to avoid jury duty."

I looked at the dybbuk a bit longer. It was ugly as incest. But it had a certain sort of power. "Is it old?" I asked.

"Don't know," Coyle said. "Looks it. Those jerk-offs at the FBI didn't say shit about how old it is. For all I know, the victim might have made it."

I put the sculpture back on the evidence bench.

"Hell of a thing, isn't it," I said.

"What's that?" Coyle asked.

"To have your head beat in by a dybbuk's butt?"

"A hell of a thing," he said.

"A dybbuk is generally thought to be an especially cling-ing demon," Stevie said. "Very reluctant to leave its host and harder than most demons to exorcise."

I'd called Stevie from a pay phone right after leaving the station. Since she'd taught courses on women's mythology, I thought she might have some info on dybbuks. Besides, I thought it would be a pleasant way to spend lunch. Talking dybbuks over drinks.

And it should have been a pleasant way to spend lunch. We were on the deck of a nice restaurant overlooking the harbor. The weather was spectacular. The food was excellent. Everything was perfect. But . . .

"Well, that's fascinating," I said. I'd already learned a lot more about dybbuks and the demonology of the ancient He-brews than I thought really necessary. What I'd hoped would be an entertaining, semiflirtatious lunch had turned into a lecture. I hate lectures.

"Tell me," I said, when I could interrupt her without being overly rude, "have you ever seen this dybbuk?"

"Pardon?" Her eyes widened.

"This particular dybbuk. The one that was used to . . . in the assault on Amanda? Have you ever seen it? Like when you visited their house. You *have* visited their house, haven't you?"

She nodded and said, "Many times. But I don't know if I've seen the dybbuk. What does it look like?"

I described it to her, leaving out the blood and hair on the dybbuk's butt. "It was found on the back porch, if that's any help. Of course, just because it was found there doesn't mean that's where it was normally."

"Sorry," she said. "It doesn't sound familiar. I'm sure if I'd seen it I would remember. It sounds . . . distinctive."

"Distinctive is what it is," I said. "Does it sound like the sort of thing Amanda would carve? Or sculpt. Or whatever it is she does. Or did."

"No, not really. I know Amanda always wanted to work in stone, but most of her work was done in wood or metal. And demons weren't really her subject matter."

"Oh." I fussed with my food. Stevie fussed with hers and frowned. A couple of herring gulls sat on a nearby piling and screeched at us for scraps.

"It's an odd coincidence," Stevie said. "A century or two ago Anka might have been said to be possessed by a dybbuk."

"That's what the police said," I told her. "Almost word for word. An odd coincidence."

"Oh."

I threw a few french fries to the gulls. Just to get them to shut up.

"It's a problem, isn't it?" Stevie asked.

"Could be. Juries eat that stuff up like cream gravy."

She flung a few fries to the birds. Who hadn't shut up at all. In fact, the food seemed to encourage them to make even more noise.

"But it's not really relevant, is it?" Stevie asked. "I mean anybody could have picked up the dybbuk and hit

Amanda with it. Just because it's a dybbuk doesn't mean
Anka did it."

"Nope. Doesn't mean that at all," I said.

But it *was* an odd coincidence. And a jury *would* eat it up.

Monday Afternoon

"You want to fuck me, don't you," Anka said.

Kathleen O'Mara looked at her, then turned her surprised eyes to Dr. Rifkin, then over to me, then back to Anka. "No," she said. "I'm a lawyer."

"It's okay," Anka said. "Most women want to. She does." Anka nodded at Dr. Rifkin.

Dr. Rifkin waved her hand as if to say "See, I told you."

"He probably does, too," Anka said, indicating me. "But I don't fuck men. Unless I feel like it."

Dr. Rifkin nodded to Kathleen. "I'm afraid we're not going to get much today," she said.

"You're not going to get much from me, I can tell you that," Anka said. "The nurses wouldn't like it. They want to fuck me too. I don't mind if they want to. Do you like it when somebody watches?"

We were standing in a small interview room of the close-custody psychiatric ward at St. Albans. It was oppressive, no mistake, but probably better than being in jail. There were windows, at least, and a person could look out. The windows were covered with a wire mesh screen and were a little dingy, but you could look out of them.

St. Albans is a modern psychiatric facility, which means it looks a lot like a junior high school. I prefer the State Mental Health Institution, with its red brick and slate roofs. The State MHI looks more like a hospital. Joop has pointed out to me that architecture is probably not the best criterion for choosing a psychiatric hospital, and he's right. Inside, they were both dreary.

Kathleen and I had been escorted through four sets of

locked doors before we met Dr. Rifkin, who led us through two more sets of locked doors before we got to Anka's ward.

Dr. Rifkin had warned us that Anka probably wouldn't be able to answer our questions. It had been only a few days since her arrest, and while she'd apparently stopped hallucinating, she still showed signs of what Dr. Rifkin referred to as marked delusional thinking.

We'd wanted to try to learn more about Amanda Standish—who she was, where they'd met, and, most important, where we could find her, but Dr. Rifkin suggested we avoid mentioning the name "Amanda" altogether. In the first five minutes, all we'd been able to establish was that Anka thought almost everybody in the state of Massachusetts wanted to have sex with her.

Kathleen tried again. "Anka, this is very important. Try to think back to the night before you got arrested. You went to a bar called Schotzie's, remember? With Stevie Gibbs?"

"Of course I remember," she nodded. "I wonder if I could have a cigarette." She walked over to the door of the small room and peered out the little window. "Schotzie's. I went there with Stevie Gibbs."

"That's right. And do you remember who you left with?"

Anka banged on the door and a nurse's face appeared moonlike at the small window. Anka mimed like she was puffing on a cigarette. The nurse nodded, held up a finger, and disappeared.

"Anka," Kathleen continued, "do you remember who you left Schotzie's with?"

"Didn't leave with anyone," she said.

"Then did you meet somebody later? At another bar, maybe?"

Anka frowned and nodded. "Yeah, I guess I did."

"Who was she? What was her name?"

Anka shrugged. "She was just some woman who wanted to fuck me." She cocked her head and looked at Kathleen.

"Are you sure you don't want to fuck me? I like to be certain I understand what's going on."

"Where did you meet this woman?" I asked.

Anka shrugged. "I don't know. Someplace."

"Can you tell us what she looked like?" I asked.

Anka closed her eyes and let her head drift lazily from side to side, like Stevie Wonder at the piano. "Oh, she had the most wonderful little pores. Like she was made out of ceramic."

"Pores?" I asked.

She nodded. "Yes. And she looked surprised when she came. And she smelled of cognac when she sweated." Anka opened her eyes and smiled a little. "Thank you. I'd forgotten."

"What about her hair?" I asked. "What color was it?"

Anka dismissed the question with a wave of her hand.

Kathleen tried again. "Anka, do you think you could tell us how tall she was? Or how much she weighed? Maybe how she was dressed?"

"Of course, she only wanted to fuck me," Anka said. "That's what they all want." She smiled. I hadn't seen her smile before. She had a nice, sad smile. "But, oh my, it was fine."

The nurse knocked on the door and opened it without waiting for permission. "Here are your cigarettes and matches," she said. She let Anka shake one cigarette out of the pack and lit it for her. Then she took the cigarettes and matches and left.

Dr. Rifkin cleared her throat. "Excuse me. It might be that Anka feels uncomfortable with so many strangers," she said. "Over the years she and I have developed a rapport. Perhaps I might try it alone?"

Kathleen turned the idea over for a brief moment, then said, "We'll wait right outside. You know what we're interested in."

In the hallway, a short, fat woman was talking urgently into her cupped hands. She looked at us over the tops of her fingers, then turned her back to us and continued talking.

"So what do you think?" Kathleen asked.

"I think it's a job for Joop," I said. "We send him round to the lesbian bars looking for a woman with small pores and skin like ceramic, who smells like cognac when she sweats. He'll love it."

"We're wasting our time, aren't we," Kathleen said.

"Pretty much. But there was no way to tell until we came."

Kathleen nodded. We sat on a pair of old Naugahyde chairs. After a few minutes, Dr. Rifkin came out of Anka's room. She shook her head. "Sorry," she said. "No luck."

"Maybe I should try it again," Kathleen suggested.

"I wouldn't advise it."

Kathleen tried to explain. "But we need to know what happened if we're going to put on a decent defense," she said. "Otherwise she's probably going to go to prison."

Dr. Rifkin frowned. "If you feel you must try, then let Mr. Sweeney try."

"Please, call me Kevin," I said.

"Why him?" Kathleen asked. "I thought she didn't like men."

"She doesn't *dislike* men," Dr. Rifkin said. "She just likes women more. Mr. Sweeney . . ."

I started to remind her to call me Kevin, but she caught herself.

". . . Kevin"—she smiled a wonderfully homely smile—"might actually seem less sexually threatening to her right now. Maybe that will help."

Kathleen looked at me. I shrugged and said, "I'll give it a shot if you'd like."

Kathleen considered it for a moment. "What the hell," she said. "Go ahead. You can't do any worse than we did."

I asked Dr. Rifkin to give me five minutes, then have the nurse bring Anka another cigarette. Sometimes an outside distraction like that can provide a sort of bond between the people who are interrupted. It was a long shot, but we were down to long shots.

When I walked into the room, Anka was making odd gestures with her hands. She stopped and looked over my shoulder.

I started with something nonthreatening. "I saw your old neighbor a few days ago," I said. "Callie Dobson. She said to tell you hello." That was a lie, but I thought it might help.

Anka made a face. "Callie. Prissy Callie. I used to think she wanted to fuck me," she said. "But she really wanted to fuck Amanda."

There was something in her voice and her expression, something so far removed from us and what we were there for, that I felt—no, I *knew*, with absolute certainty, with a certainty that would stagger priests—that there was no point in asking Anka any real questions. She simply wasn't connected.

So I decided to ask her the thing I really wanted to know. "What's it like?" I asked.

Anka cocked her head. "What's what like?" she asked. But you could tell from her voice that she didn't care what I was asking.

"What's it like to hear voices? Is it wonderful? Or does it frighten you?"

She turned and at looked at me, directly at me, for a moment. Then turned away again.

"I probably shouldn't be asking, I know. But this may be the only chance I'll ever have to find out. I mean, I could read books about it, but what's a book? That's just somebody writing down the things somebody else told them. I doubt it's the same."

Anka stood up and walked toward the door.

I decided to try again. "Would you stop it if you could?"

She put her hand flat against the door and lowered her head. "Do you think I like being like this?" she asked.

I shook my head. "I don't know. But I don't think it has anything to do with liking it, or not liking it. The question is would you stop it if you could."

She turned toward me and looked at my shoulder. "Life would be a lot easier if I didn't hear this voice."

"But would you stop it?" I repeated. "If you could."

She dropped her head again. "No." She didn't move for several moments. Then she began to open and close her right hand, slowly. She watched her hand, as if it were the most amazing thing. As if she'd never seen such a thing before.

"I don't know if I envy you or feel sorry for you," I said.

She stopped opening and closing her hand, but continued to stare at it. "Why would you envy me?" she asked.

"Because you experience something I never will, something I can't even begin to understand."

"It's true," she said. "You really can't. It's impossible for anybody to understand. I hate it and I love it. And I wish it would be torn away from me. But I wouldn't give it up, not on your life." She looked at my shoulder again. "I wish you *could* understand it. I wish just one person could understand, could hear it the way I hear it. I wish just one person could."

There was a knock on the door, and the nurse entered with Anka's cigarettes and matches. I silently cursed myself for being too clever. The distraction was going to hurt instead of help.

The nurse made nurse chatter while she let Anka shake out another cigarette. I stared at the nurse, hoping she would pick up on my signal and hurry out. But she took her time, chatting professionally and waving the matchbook.

The matchbook made me sit up straight. I started to reach out for it, but the nurse was finally on her way out, all smiles and efficiency. I almost called her back.

Anka drew hard on the cigarette and let the smoke curl slowly out of her lips. I put thoughts of the matchbook aside and returned to work. "What were you about to say?" I asked. "If one person could . . ."

Anka shook her head. "I don't know."

We sat quietly while Anka smoked her cigarette and watched her hand. She moved one finger, then the next, then another. It seemed pretty clear nothing was going to happen.

So I decided to take a trick from Joop. I've seen him charm his way into the good graces of a hostile witness with a personal story. If it worked for him, it might work for me.

"When I was just a boy," I said, "my mother used to read to me and tell me stories, mostly about Ireland, where her parents were born. One of the stories she told me was 'Suibne Geilt.' In Irish that means 'Mad Sweeney.' Sweeney was a minor Irish king back about thirteen hundred years ago.

"He was a bad-tempered man, this Sweeney, and one morning he was awakened by the sound of a bell ringing. He went to see who was causing the racket and he found a priest ringing a bell and singing while he laid out the measurements of a church he was going to build. This was back in the days when Christianity was just beginning to carry some weight in Ireland.

"Maybe he was hung over, maybe he was just a late sleeper—I don't remember. But Sweeney's temper wasn't improved to learn this priest was planning on setting up shop in his village, never mind ringing bells at such an early hour. Being a bad-tempered man, Sweeney grabbed the priest and chucked his psalter into a pond."

"What's a psalter?" Anka asked. She'd stopped staring at her hand and was looking in my general direction.

"A psalter is a book of psalms," I said. "Sweeney threw the psalter into the pond and was getting ready to throw the priest in after it when his servant came and told him there was a big battle taking place nearby, at a place called Mag Rath.

Sweeney was a warrior and had to join the battle. So he dropped the priest, grabbed his sword, and took off. The priest, instead of thanking God for saving his butt, asked God to curse Sweeney. Back in those days it seemed God was always willing to stick it to some poor guy who'd upset one of his priests. And do you know what I'm going to tell you? In the middle of the battle, Sweeney took leave of his senses."

"He went insane?" Anka asked.

I shrugged. "I don't know. 'Took leave of his senses' is how my mother always said it. Maybe it was the priest's curse, or maybe it was some sort of early Celtic post-traumatic stress disorder. I don't know. Whatever the reason, Sweeney left the battlefield thinking he was a bird."

"A bird?" Anka shifted her attention to my forehead.

"A bird," I said. "And for the rest of his life, poor, mad Sweeney wandered naked through Ireland, sleeping in trees and bushes, writing poetry, and being hounded by people who wanted to kill him."

"A poet." Anka smiled. "What did he write about?"

I tried to remember. "I recall the story better than the poems. He wrote about trees, I think. Trees and animals and birds. And I seem to recall that somehow through his madness he could remember a time when he preferred the company of men and women to that of birds and animals. But I don't think he could remember why."

"What happened to him?" she asked.

"Oh, he died," I said. "He died horribly, like all good Irish heroes."

"Mad Sweeney," she said. She looked at the wall for a moment, then went back to watching her hand open and close.

I sat there for another moment, feeling a perfect fool for telling Irish folk tales to a Jewish schizophrenic, and blaming it on Joop. I stood up.

"Anka, I have to go," I said. "But I want to thank you for telling me about the voice."

She was still looking at her hand when I left. Dr. Rifkin and Kathleen were waiting for me at the nurse's station.

"Well?" Kathleen asked. "She tell you anything?"

I shook my head. "She didn't. But I think I might have learned something from the nurse."

"From the nurse?" Kathleen looked confused.

I asked the nurse if I could see Anka's cigarettes and matches. She looked at Dr. Rifkin, who shrugged and nodded. The nurse brought them to me.

"Did Anka have these cigarettes and matches with her when she was admitted?" I asked.

"Yes, she did."

"What's going on, Kevin?" Kathleen asked.

I flipped her the shiny green matchbook.

She looked it over, opened it up, closed it, and read the outside cover. "Jenever, Truro, Cape Cod." She looked up at me. "So what?"

"So I have another matchbook just like it," I said. "Back at the office."

"Yeah, so?"

"So I found it at the Roadhouse Motel. In Anka's room."

J o o p   W h e e l e r

Monday, Late Afternoon

"Well, what do you say?" I asked Stevie. "Want to hang out on the Cape for a few days? All expenses paid?"

I got to admit I felt funny asking her to go away with me like that, what with Kath sitting right there, dead solid lawyerly behind her desk, listening. I don't know why I felt funny. It wasn't like I was planning on anything carnal with Stevie. Fantasizing, maybe. In a hopeless sort of way. But not *planning*. Mainly because I knew Stevie wouldn't go for it.

But I felt funny all the same.

Just before Stevie and I left the restaurant I called the answering service, and they told me I should call Sweeney at Kath's office. Sweeney told me to haul ass over to her office pronto. Stuff was happening, he'd said. So I not only hauled my ass over to Kath's office, I hauled Stevie's as well.

I didn't need to. Sweeney had told me not to dawdle, but I probably had time to drive Stevie back to her Moose Creek loft. The problem was that I had this irresistible urge to see Stevie and Kath together. In the same room. So I brought her along.

I get these self-destructive impulses now and then. All Southern folk do. Normally, if I'm interested in more than one woman—and that's happened more often than I care to admit—I try to keep them separate. Only makes sense.

To my surprise, Kath invited Stevie to sit in with us while we discussed the situation. So there I was, sitting stupidly on Kath's office couch, between two women who set red lightning torching through my veins. I was about half afraid of some sort of cataclysmic red-lightning polarity reaction—two opposite and contrary charges sparking at the same time.

Which would probably make my head explode. Or just melt down like an out-of-control nuclear reactor.

I must have been insane.

But—no red lightning. After I'd given them the dybbuk news, all we'd done was discuss Sweeney's matchbook discovery. Sweeney had been the golden boy on the case so far. He'd found the Motel Witness; he'd discovered the Nosy Neighbor; and now he'd made the Matchbook Connection.

All I'd managed to do so far was see some blood and hair on a dybbuk's butt and get beat up by a small lesbian. Not a balanced division of labor.

So when they suggested I head down to the Cape and hang out in lesbian bars, I figured the trip would give me a chance to redeem myself. So I asked Stevie if maybe she'd like to come along.

Actually, Kath suggested it first. She thought Stevie might give me some legitimacy. That she might help convince folks to talk to me. Or at least not beat me up. Kath thought it was a great idea.

I wasn't so sure, my ownself. Some small, disturbed part of me was a little hurt that Kath was so willing to pack me off to Cape Cod with another woman. Even if the woman was a lesbian. What it meant, I figured, was that the worst-case scenario was correct; I hadn't sparked a hint of the red lightning in Kath.

But, since Kath suggested it, I tried to sound especially cheerful when I asked Stevie if she wanted to go to the Cape.

She took about half a second to think it over. "I have a friend who has a house in Wellfleet," she said. "That's just down the road from Truro. She's in Barcelona right now, but I have the key and we could stay at her place."

"Great," Kath said. "How soon can you go?" It was like driving a stake through my heart.

"Tomorrow morning?" Stevie said, looking at me.

"Fits in with my schedule," I said. Like I had a schedule.

"Then tomorrow it is," Kath said. She got the address and telephone number of Stevie's friend in Wellfleet. Just in case.

I made them go over the whole thing one more time— their initial talk with Anka, Sweeney's private talk with her, and then their subsequent discussion with Anka about the matchbook.

After Sweeney got the matchbook, he and Kath and the shrink had gone back in to talk with Anka. She told them she'd never heard of the bar and didn't know where the matchbook came from. She said she might be able to remember more if she could get a full night's sleep. Which she couldn't because folks kept harassing her, they kept waking her up all night, wanting to hop in the sack with her.

"I'm not sure I understand the significance of these matchbooks," Stevie said.

"It's simple," Sweeney said. "This is the first physical evidence we have that Anka might have spent the night with another woman. If *she* didn't pick up these matches in Truro, then who did? The other woman. Amanda Standish, we hope."

Stevie cocked her head. "Does this mean Anka is innocent?"

Kath and Sweeney and I, after exchanging looks, hemmed and hawed and dodged the question like politicians in an election year. But Stevie wasn't easily put off. I finally had to tell her what it meant.

"What it means is that Anka is maybe telling the truth when she says she shacked up with another woman," I said. "And that's about all it means."

"But if she was with this Amanda Standish, doesn't that mean she's innocent?" Stevie asked.

I shook my head.

"But . . ."

Kath looked peevish. "Look," she said. "Maybe Amanda

Standish exists. Despite what the clerk at the Roadhouse says, I wouldn't bet my paycheck on it. Those matchbooks could have been left there by an earlier customer. But even if Amanda Standish does exist, and even if Anka did go to the motel with her, it still doesn't mean Anka is innocent. They might have had some fun, then after an hour or so Anka could have booted her out, gone to Amanda's house, caved in her head with the statue, gone back to the motel, and started howling."

"Oh," Stevie said. "So then you think she's guilty."

"What I *think* doesn't matter," Kath snapped. "All that matters is that we do our job, and that means protecting her rights and giving her the best possible defense. Period."

I understood Kath's irritation. There are things you don't much talk about in criminal-defense work. Like guilt and innocence. Like Kath had said, it didn't really matter if Anka *had* bashed in Amanda's head. Not to us, anyway. A jury would decide that. All we had to do was make the prosecutor *prove* she'd done it. If he could, Anka would go to prison. If he couldn't, Anka would walk. That's all there was to it.

Stevie, having been properly raised by a good Southern mother, sensed she'd violated a rule of etiquette even though she didn't quite know what it was. So she nodded and said she understood, even though it was clear she didn't. Which sent a small shiver of red lightning through me.

Kath eventually shooed us out of her office, saying she had other work to do. Stevie took a cab home. Sweeney and I went to Mick Croker's for a couple of jars, as he'd say. Beer.

We had arrived at the darts stage of the investigation. That's the point where Sweeney and I drink beers, toss darts, and try to figure out just what the hell we're doing. And what we ought to be doing. For some reason, this process always seems to require beer and darts.

"What we need," Sweeney said, darts in hand, "is somebody to pin this on."

"Now there's an idea," I said. "Got anybody in mind?"

He shook his head. "Anybody. Somebody who will distract a jury away from Anka."

"How about I go down to the Cape and find the real killer," I suggested. "Would that help?"

"Nobody's been killed yet," Sweeney pointed out.

I looked at my watch. "You called the hospital recently?"

He thought about it. "Okay. But what if you don't find the real killer?" he asked. "Or what if Anka *is* the real killer?"

"I vote for her father, then. We'll pin it on him. He sounds like a cast-iron bastard. Couldn't stand having a deviant daughter, so he whacks her with an obscene sculpture. What do you think?"

"I don't think so." Sweeney shook his head. "He's too rich and too Protestant. Protestants don't have that sort of passion. He'd never get that upset over anything but taxes."

I reminded him I was a Protestant. "We're as bloodthirsty as the next gang," I said. "We've done our share of senseless slaughtering. Maybe more than our share."

"I still don't buy it," he said.

"Okay. Then you pick somebody better."

We threw darts for a few minutes.

"Your transsexual," Sweeney said. "Deirdre."

"She's not *my* transsexual," I said.

"Sure. I don't hear about her tongue-kissing anybody else."

"There weren't any tongues," I said.

"She's perfect all the same. Listen to this—she slips off from the Loading Zone and meets Anka at the Roadhouse Motel. Remember they had that private conversation? Maybe they were arranging to meet at the motel later."

"It's not bad. But where does whacking Amanda in the head come in?"

"Oh, yeah." He frowned. We threw darts for another minute. "Okay, how about this? She meets Anka at the motel, they slide around for a while, Anka tells her about the fight with Amanda. Deirdre goes to Amanda's to, to . . . Well, I don't know why she goes to Amanda's."

"To patch things up between Anka and Amanda?" I offered. "Or maybe to get some clothes for Anka? Or how about money? Deirdre knows Anka is broke and Amanda has cash to spare."

Sweeney nodded. "Any of those. They argue about whatever it is, and she hits Amanda with a Jewish demon."

I threw my darts. "Deirdre's probably strong enough."

"Oh, that's even better." Sweeney smiled. "That's perfect. I forgot her name's Deirdre. It gets even better."

I watched Sweeney for a moment. He was lost in thought, grinning to himself. "I hope you're planning on explaining that," I said. "And it's your darts." I waved him up to the throwing line.

"It's an old Irish story," he said, carefully setting his toe to the line.

"Is there an Irish story that's not old?" I asked. "And do I have to hear another one?"

"Deirdre of the Sorrows," Sweeney said.

I shook my head. "Not the sorrows," I said. "Didn't anything *happy* ever happen in Ireland?"

"She was the loveliest woman ever born in all Ireland—"

"Which is saying a lot," I said. "Having seen Mary Margaret Sweeney."

"I'll tell her you said that." Sweeney smiled.

"I knew you would. That's why I said it."

"The king falls madly in love with her, of course. Deirdre."

"Kings," I said. "They always do that. Fall madly in love with the prettiest woman in the kingdom."

"But she doesn't love him."

"Of course she doesn't. How could she? She loves some other guy, right?"

Sweeney nodded. "Naisi."

"Gesundheit."

"It's a guy's name," Sweeney said. "They run away together, Deirdre and Naisi. The king chases them all over
Ireland."

"I got a feeling he catches them," I said. "And something
horrible happens."

Sweeney shook his head. "He doesn't actually catch
them. They let themselves get talked into just giving up. They
turn themselves in and throw themselves on the king's
mercy."

"That's a damn stupid move. You never confess and you
never turn yourself in."

Sweeney grinned. A little drunkenly, I thought.

"That's the last thing I'd do," I said. "Assuming I ever
ran away with the prettiest woman in all Ireland and some
king in heat was after my butt. I declare, I've never heard a
single story where a king has had a penny's worth of mercy."

"This one was no better than the rest," Sweeney said.
"Naisi gets killed. And what do you suppose Deirdre does?"

"Joins a convent? Takes up a hobby?"

He shook his head and smiled sadly. "She kills herself."

"Ah."

"She smashes her head in," Sweeney said. "On a rock."

We ordered more beer and threw more darts and
thought about it for a while.

"It would be tough for Kath to introduce an old Irish
story as evidence," I said.

Sweeney nodded. "Probably so."

"Nice story, though."

"Thanks."

"How about the husband?" I asked. "Amanda's husband, I mean. Not the guy in the story. What was his name?"

"Charles." Sweeney nodded. "I like him."

"You *like* him?"

"As the real killer, I mean." Sweeney was most definitely getting a tad lit. "He's got a great motive."

"The money," I said.

"There it is."

"Except didn't you say he said he loves her? Or something like that?" Perhaps I was getting a tad intoxo my ownself. But Sweeney was too drunk to notice.

"I did, in fact, say something like that," Sweeney said. "Another thing, he says Amanda was his most prized possession."

"Ooh," I nodded. "Let's pin it on the bastard."

We threw more darts. Ordered more beer. Got more stupid.

"There's a thing I've been wanting to ask," Sweeney said.

"Ask away, O friend of my youth."

"What's the matter with you?"

"It's the eye," I said. "Getting whacked in the eye throws off my darts game. That and maybe the amount of beer we've had."

Sweeney shook his head. "I don't mean your darts. Your darts are always this bad. I mean what's going on between you and Kathleen? And between you and the lesbian, for that matter."

"Her name is Stevie," I said.

"Stevie, then."

I examined my darts. To make sure the points were sharp. I hate a dull dart.

"Joop, old buddy, listen to your old uncle Kevin. Don't you be doing anything stupid."

I threw my darts. Not very well. But with spirit. And, I think, a certain elegance.

"I can see it coming, Joop," he said. "You're working up a serious crush on both of them, aren't you? Why do you always do this?"

I didn't say anything.

"Joop, we're going to have to get you neutered before something terrible happens."

I fetched my darts and drank some beer. I like the way a beer glass balances the weight of the darts.

Sweeney was giving me one of those looks, like I'm a bull goose idiot and shouldn't be let out in public.

"I got it under control," I said. "All under control."

He shook his head. "No you don't," he said. "You're going to do something stupid." He shook his head and sort of laughed. "I can feel it. Something wildly stupid."

"Not a chance," I said. "Everything is under control. Perfectly under control."

Sweeney shook his head and smiled sadly. "Well, whenever it happens, whatever it is, remember one thing," he said. "Okay? Just one thing."

"What's that?" I hate being lectured by a drunk Irishman. About as much as I hate a dull dart.

"If you need to," Sweeney said, "you can hide in our cellar until it's safe to come out."

Sweeney's not a bad guy. For a drunk Irishman.

Kevin Sweeney

Tuesday Afternoon

"May I help you?"

"Victoria Gilbois, please."

"Do you have an appointment?" The receptionist reached for her appointment book. She was afflicted with the perkiness common among young receptionists.

I admitted I didn't have an appointment. You might as well tell the truth when a lie can be easily detected. The young receptionist, however, didn't seem particularly impressed with my honesty.

"May I tell her who is calling?" she asked.

I gave her my business card. She looked at it and raised an eyebrow. "May I tell Ms. Gilbois what this is in reference to?"

I smiled and shook my head. "It's nothing very mysterious, I assure you. But I'd rather discuss it with Ms. Gilbois."

She gave me a sidelong glance, then asked me to have a seat. She wandered away.

The office decor of HeadLong Enterprises, the public-relations firm Victoria Gilbois worked for, was painfully trendy. But the office itself had a good feel to it. The people all seemed busy, but enjoying themselves. There was a buoyant energy that took the edge off the trendiness. I liked it.

I found myself wondering what public-relations people actually did. And if it was as much fun as it seemed to be. And how well it paid. I don't find trendy furniture attractive, but it's not cheap.

I picked up a recent copy of *Advertising Week* and thumbed through it. While I was waiting I might as well see what the industry was up to.

This should have been Joop's job, but he was on his way down to Cape Cod with his lesbian friend, trying to follow up the lead on Amanda Standish. I was stuck following Joop's lead on Victoria Gilbois, the woman Amanda Owen was said to be dancing with at Schotzie's when Anka interrupted. Joop, I felt, had got hold of the better end of the stick.

"Mr. Sweeney?" A woman stood near the receptionist's desk, her glasses in one hand, the other resting on her hip. She was obviously bewildered.

I put down the magazine and stood up. "Ms. Gilbois?"

She nodded. I was prepared to like her, in part because of the bemused smile on her face and in part because of the feel of the office. She was dressed in something that was neither a suit nor a dress. I'm not entirely sure what it was, except that it looked comfortable and attractive, and somehow tribal, if that means anything.

She held my card up and waved it, doubling her puzzled look.

"Is there someplace we can talk?" I asked.

"I'm not sure," she said. "What's this about?"

"Do you think you should call legal?" the receptionist asked.

She shrugged and turned to me. "Am I in some sort of trouble?"

"Not at all." I smiled.

She grinned and made a relieved sound. "It's a little scary to be told a private detective wants to talk to you."

"It's nothing at all scary," I said.

"I'm so glad to hear it. But what is it you want?"

"I just want to ask you a few questions about a couple people you know. Anka Stiffel and Amanda Owen. It'll only take a few—"

"I'm sorry," she said, "but I'm extremely busy right now. Perhaps some other time." It was hard to tell, but I thought she'd turned a little pale.

"That's all right, I can wait," I said. "I'm free all afternoon."

She shook her head. "Today isn't good for me. I have your card." She held it up. "I'll call you when I have time." With that, she turned and walked away.

The receptionist watched her walk away, then looked at me and shrugged. She was clearly surprised by Gilbois's abrupt change in attitude.

So was I. But there wasn't anything I could do but leave. I didn't go far, though—only across the street. I bought an ice cream cone and sat on a wooden bench, where I could see the door to HeadLong Enterprises.

Victoria Gilbois's reluctance to talk to me might be a good sign. It probably meant she was hiding something. What she was hiding might not be related to the case, but it couldn't hurt to find out what it was. I checked my watch: just after three o'clock. Victoria Gilbois had to come out of her office sometime, and when she did, I'd be there waiting for her.

It was a pleasant summer day, sunny and warm, perfect for sitting on a bench, eating a double dip of mint chocolate chip, and waiting for a twitchy witness to leave her office.

Shortly after four, traffic began to pick up and I decided to cross back to Gilbois's side of the street. It wouldn't do if she came out of her office and I was caught on the other side of the street because of traffic.

As I was waiting to cross the street, an older model Ford stalled in the intersection, blocking traffic. Other motorists began honking and shouting at the driver, a white-haired woman who looked a lot like Mary Margaret's poor old mother. She sat very still in the driver's seat, staring straight out the windshield, with her hands shaking and covering her mouth.

I glanced at my watch, cursed quietly, then went to her window and tapped on it. She spooked a little, but rolled down the window a couple of inches.

"Are you okay?" I asked. I couldn't tell if she was about to start crying or if her eyes were just rheumy.

"I can't get her started again," the woman said. "She just stopped and I can't get . . . She just stopped on me."

"Try turning it over," I said, "and let me take a look." She looked blank.

"Turn the key," I said, making the universal sign for turning the key. "Try to start it again."

"Oh, yes," she said. "Henry used to take care of the car, don't you see. I'm afraid I'm not very mechanical."

"It's okay," I said. "Try it again and we'll see what happens."

She turned the key and absolutely nothing happened. I had her turn on the emergency flashers and pop the hood, though I'm not mechanical myself. The old woman seemed reassured, though. She took her hands away from her face and tried to smile.

While I puttered under the hood, trying not to get too dirty, the woman stuck her head out the window.

"She stalled once before," she shouted over the traffic. "Henry did something with the carburetor."

I told her it wasn't the carburetor this time. I didn't know what it was, but I knew it wasn't the carburetor. Something electrical, maybe. I jiggled some wires near the battery, exhausting my mechanical skills, and asked her to try it again.

Still nothing.

I went back to her window. "I think we're going to have to call a tow truck," I said.

"A tow truck?" she asked. "Is it serious?" She kept touching her hands to her face, as if she was trying to convince herself that she was real and this was really happening to her. "Who should I call? I don't know anything about tow trucks."

"I'll deal with it," I said. "There's a pay phone right over there. Would you like to come with me? Or would you rather wait here in the car?"

"I'd better wait here," she said. "Henry always said if there was a problem I should stay with the car."

"Good advice." I gave her a cheerful smile and threaded my way through the angry traffic, wondering where the hell Henry was when she needed him.

By some fluke, the telephone directory in the booth hadn't been trashed. I looked up the nearest towing company and scribbled the number on the side of the booth, beside all the other numbers people had written there. Then I dropped a quarter in the slot, and dialed the number for HeadLong Enterprises. Business first.

"Hi, I'm returning Ms. Gilbois's call. Is she in?" I asked.

"Yes, sir, she is. Can I tell her who is calling?"

"Yes, this is . . . Oh, damn. Can you hold for a second?" I covered the receiver slightly with my hand and said, "What is it, Jenkins?" I paused. "Well, can't Randalls handle it?" Another pause, then I spoke back into the receiver. "Listen, I have a problem here. Will Ms. Gilbois be in for another half hour?"

"She normally leaves work about this time," the receptionist said. "But I could ask her to wait."

"Would you? It's rather important and I'd really appreciate it. Tell her I'll call back in thirty minutes."

"Could I have your—"

"Forty-five minutes tops," I said. "You're an angel." I hung up, jacked another quarter in the slot, and called the towing agency. After I told them I didn't know if the old woman was a member of Triple A, that I didn't know what credit cards she held, and that I didn't know what the problem was, they agreed to send a truck.

I went back to the old woman and told her help was on its way.

"Oh, thank you so much," she said. "I've been dreading something like this since I lost Henry. He always took care of, well, of everything."

Henry, she insisted on telling me, was her late husband. Dead nearly nine months. While we waited for the tow truck, I listened to her talk about Henry, who had died of testicular cancer, and her children, who were all grown and too busy with their own lives to give her much time. She was having a hard time getting used to being alone, she said, and felt like everything was racing out of control. She couldn't remember where the flashlight batteries were, or when the auto insur ance was due, or how to cook for only one person instead of a household of five. She felt lost and betrayed, and now even the car—Henry's car—had turned on her.

As I stood beside the car and listened to the old woman talk, I saw Victoria Gilbois walk out of her office building and stroll down the street. It had been less than ten minutes since I called; either she hadn't gotten my message or she was totally disregarding it. Even though the message had been a lie, I was irritated by her lack of regard for a customer. That's no way to run a business. I ought to write a letter of complaint to HeadLong Enterprises.

The old woman must have seen me glance at my watch and the look of irritation on my face. "I'm sorry to be such a bother," she said. "I'm just a silly old woman."

"Not at all," I said.

"Would it be too much trouble for you to stay with me until the tow truck arrives?" she asked.

I watched Victoria Gilbois turn the corner and disappear.

"Of course I will," I said.

Joop Wheeler

Tuesday Night

"You know what I like about you?" Stevie asked.

I didn't. But I surely wanted to.

We'd only just arrived at her friend's house near Well-fleet. Stevie had neglected to mention that the house was right smack dab on the beach. And that it had a deck with a view of the ocean that made you just want to go limp.

We'd stowed our stuff—in separate bedrooms, of course—and made straight for the deck. We ought to have been working on some sort of strategy, a plan of action for our evening at Jenever. Instead we leaned on the deck rails, looking at the ocean change colors in the early evening light. I'd been talking some nonsense about having grown up by the ocean when she asked the question. If it was a question.

"Is it my distinguished profile?"

She shook her head and smiled. "What I like about you is that you talk like a woman."

I was pretty sure she'd just given me a compliment. Or at least she thought she had. I wasn't so sure.

"That's about the nicest thing anybody has ever said to me," I smiled. "What does it mean?"

She put her hand on my arm for a moment. And I swear tiny sparks leaped off her fingertips and made my arm tickle. "It means you don't get caught up in the information exchange that most men think of as conversation. You know. Men talk *to* people, women talk *with*. Men push bits of information and opinions at each other. Women talk about people and feelings and who did what and what's going on."

I thought about that for a moment. "I guess I talk like a

woman," I said. I hoped my cousin Dumar never found out. I just knew what he'd say I talked like.

But just then I didn't care. Being in a house beside the ocean was like going home. A peacefulness, is what it was. A feeling of belonging.

The sun was doing spectacular things to the ocean. And some terns were doing impossible things over the waves. And the air smelled like it had just been made. And Stevie was smiling at me. And I was on the verge of saying, and maybe doing, something wildly stupid, just like Sweeney had predicted, when Stevie sort of cleared her throat.

"We should probably be going," she said. "I've arranged for us to have drinks with some people before we go to Jenever."

I took a deep breath and held it. "Some people?" I hoped she wasn't going to try to play detective.

She smiled again. Very prettily. "Some friends of mine who are active in the gay and lesbian community here. I hope you don't mind. I thought they might know something about Amanda Standish. At the very least they'll be able to tell us something about Jenever."

"Do they know why we're here?" I asked.

She shook her head. "No, I just told them I was down for a few days. And that I'd brought a friend."

A friend. "All right. Sounds like a fine idea." Not half as fine as the idea I'd had thirty seconds earlier. But probably much better in the long run.

We met Stevie's friends up the road in Provincetown. Which has to have more gay folks per square inch than any other paved or semipaved area in New England. Cousin Dumar would have had conniptions.

Stevie's friends turned out to be a pair of artsy-looking women and a pair of equally artsy-looking men. We met them in the bar of a restaurant with an unlikely Egyptian-sounding

name. I was somehow relieved to see them all drinking beer.
Corona, and with a lime, but beer just the same.

They were all gay and seemed to assume I was as well.
An assumption Stevie didn't correct. Which about half bothered me. For some reason it seemed sort of important to set
them straight. So to speak. But I couldn't think of a polite way
to do it. You can't just interrupt a conversation and blurt out,
"Oh, by the way, did I happen to mention I'm heterosexual?"

While Stevie caught up on gossip, I talked with one of the
men, who said his name was André. André did most of the
talking. What I did was I smiled and nodded a lot. And asked
myself was I losing my mind.

What he talked about was photographs. A guy named
Robert Mapplethorpe had apparently put some kink on
Kodak paper and upset a whole lot of folks. Which upset
André. He said that while "breeders"—which I took to mean
heterosexuals—might have their sensibilities offended by a
photograph of a man with a whip inserted up his rectum, it
was important art and documented a significant era in Green-
wich Village gay life. Didn't I agree?

"I'm afraid I haven't seen the photographs," I said. I was
a little uncomfortable. Partly with the topic. I have a difficult
time grasping the aesthetic qualities of a photo of a man with
a whip dangling out his ass. But mostly what made me uncomfortable was being in a moderately crowded bar and talking
in normal tones about a man with a whip dangling out his ass.
That's the sort of conversation that can draw attention from
the other customers. I know if I was sitting in a bar and I
heard somebody at the next table mention a man—or a
woman, for that matter—with a whip dangling out his or her
ass, my ears would perk right up. It's just the way I am.

But in Provincetown, in this particular bar, in the late
summer, nobody noticed. Nobody at all. Probably an actual
man could have walked through the kitchen with an actual
whip dangling out his actual ass, and wouldn't nobody notice.

"Even if you haven't seen the photographs," André's buddy chipped in, "don't you think the issue is important in principle?"

I wasn't all that sure what principle was at stake. "Is this a bullwhip we're talking about?" I asked. "Or a buggy whip sort of thing?" It was a minor distinction, but I had to ask.

They agreed it was almost certainly a bullwhip, though neither of them was too certain just what a bullwhip was. I think they just liked the sound of "bullwhip." A bullwhip sounds sexier than a buggy whip. At least that's the impression I got.

"This whip," I said. "Now, which end of it is actually, uh, inserted? If you know what I mean." From a purely technical point of view—which was about the only way I was prepared to look at the situation—I sort of thought the non-handle part would be more difficult to insert.

This unbalanced conversation continued until I heard Stevie bring up the name of Amanda Standish. She did it nicely. Like a pro. She'd been asking after friends and acquaintances and just included Amanda Standish in her list of folks to ask about. I felt sort of proud of her, it was so slick.

And she got an answer.

"Amanda should be back tomorrow," one of the women said. "Or the day after."

"Oh? Where has she been?" Stevie asked. Like she wasn't surprised to learn that Amanda Standish existed at all. My heart was thumping like an old air conditioner.

They weren't sure where Amanda Standish had been. But they knew she was doing the food for somebody's party on Friday, so they were certain she'd be back soon. Amanda, they said, had a way with fresh seafood and could do remarkable things with an avocado. Being a detective, I surmised she was a caterer. Or maybe a photographer of the Mapplethorpe school.

Between us, Stevie and I kept the conversation revolving

around Amanda Standish. We got her address and a description of her house and car, and we learned she'd recently been dumped by her lover of so many years and had talked about throwing herself into a period of promiscuity.

"Ah, promiscuity," André said. "Those were the days." He raised his glass. "Here's to a more innocent time."

We all raised our glasses and drank. I wasn't drinking to innocent promiscuity, though. I was drinking to Anka Stiffel. Amanda Standish was not only real, she was nearby. Or would be soon. All we had to do was wait for her.

By unspoken agreement, Stevie and I decided it was a night for celebration. The others picked up on our mood, and even though they didn't know what we were celebrating, they were all for it. I don't know if it's true of all gay folks, but I got to admit I'd never met a group of people so ready to celebrate as Stevie's friends. Anything at all, they'd celebrate. Argentina Flag Day. A pumpkin-judging contest. The tide coming in. Or going out. The reason didn't seem to matter so much as the idea of celebrating. I may not understand all their sexual needs and desires—that whip, for instance—but those folks had a dead solid lock on celebrating.

We went to a club with a reggae band and danced like demons. I danced with Stevie. I danced with her lesbian friends. Hell, I even danced a couple of times with André. Who, I got to admit, was a pretty good dancer. If Cousin Dumar could see me now, I thought, bouncing around a dance floor to a Jamaican band with a guy who spent more money on his haircut than I did on my clothes.

We danced, and we drank, and we laughed, and then we went to another club and started it all over again. At some point, poor André passed out. Nice guy. But a lightweight at the bottle. The others rolled him up and took him home. Stevie and I headed back to the beach house.

The wind off the water had a slight chill. So Stevie found a bottle of cognac in a cupboard over the refrigerator and cracked it open. We sat on the deck for a while, listening to the ocean, talking quietly, passing the cognac back and forth, sipping it straight from the bottle.

The moon was amazing. I swear it couldn't have been the same moon I'd been seeing all my life. It was bigger and stronger than the moon I was used to. It was dizzy-making. When I closed my eyes, I swear I could feel it making the tide run in my veins,

We decided to take a short walk. To sober up. But down at the water's edge we found ourselves dancing again—an intoxicated minuet that we began individually with the moon-lit waves. Then we somehow joined hands and began turning giddy hand-in-hand pirouettes, giggling like the Lord's own lunatics.

When we got too dizzy, we stopped dancing and sort of held on to each other. Partly for support, partly for warmth, and partly 'cause it felt nice. Stevie smiled at me and I felt such a rush of red lightning I thought my heart would stop dead.

I put my hand on her cheek. And it was the softest cheek I have ever in my whole entire life touched. Her eyes picked up the glint from the moon and they sparkled like marbles in water.

And I just couldn't help myself.

I kissed her.

Kevin Sweeney

Tuesday Night

After a quick dinner with Mary Margaret, I went back to work on Victoria Gilbois. I'd found her home address through that old reliable detective tool, the telephone book. She lived in a high-rise apartment complex about five blocks from the offices of HeadLong Enterprises. It was a "secure" building—no doorman, but an entrance that was always locked and a reception desk where visitors were supposed to be cleared.

I sat in my car until I saw a man approaching the building with a couple of grocery bags and his keys out. I timed it so I arrived at the door just as he was unlocking it. I conspicuously put my keys away and held the door open for him.

"Groceries cost a fortune now, don't they?" I smiled. He laughed as we walked together past the reception desk. Just like we were old friends. We both stopped in the mailroom—him to check his mailbox, me to learn which was the Gilbois apartment.

A minute later, I was knocking on her door.

"Who is it?" she asked through the door.

"Kevin Sweeney." I stood in front of the peephole and gave her my best choirboy smile.

I heard her put the chain on before she cracked the door open. "What do you want?" she asked. "I told you I'd call you when I had the time."

"I thought this might be a good time," I said.

"You thought wrong."

"I'd appreciate it if you'd make some time," I said, letting the smile fade. "I think it would be in your best interests to talk with me."

I let the implied threat hang there. It was important that

she take me seriously. I was counting—and counting heavily—on my impression that she was hiding something. People who have things to hide don't want to cause any commotion or attract attention. If I leaned on her a little, Victoria Gilbois might give in and talk to me.

But even if I was right, even if she was hiding something, it didn't mean she'd tell me what it was. She might be willing to stand to my bluff. If so, there was a chance I'd be facing the building superintendent real quick. Maybe even the police.

And, of course, there was always the possibility that I was wrong and she wasn't hiding anything.

Victoria Gilbois started to close her door.

Sometimes you have to gamble, to push your luck. So I put my foot in the doorway. "Don't do that," I said, shaking my head. "We have to talk."

She stared at me for a moment. "If I have to talk to you, I don't want to do it in the hallway. The neighbors."

I nodded. "Okay."

"Well, I can't let you in until I've taken the chain off the door," she said as if she was speaking to a child. "And I've got to close the door before I can take off the chain."

I studied her eyes. Sometimes you can tell if somebody is lying to you because their pupils will dilate. But I couldn't see anything in Victoria Gilbois's eyes.

I decided to run a small threat. "If we don't talk now," I said, "I'll be back at your office tomorrow morning. I don't think you want that."

She looked at me with something like contempt, a feeling I understood and even shared. Coercion is a nasty business. It's a terrible thing that it's so effective, and that I seem to be good at it.

But in the end, I had to trust her. There really was no other choice. I took my foot out of the doorway.

She closed the door, slid the chain off, and let me in. She'd changed from her tribal-looking outfit into a purple velour jogging suit that was totally unsuitable for jogging. Her apartment was proof that public relations paid well. Everything was ultramodern and it all matched. The couch with the chairs, the chairs with the bookcases, the bookcases with the lamps. She didn't have a television, she had a home entertainment center. It looked like something NASA would put together. Her apartment made my house look like it had been furnished from garage sales.

Without waiting for an invitation, I sat in the nearest chair. It looked like a modern version of a medieval torture instrument, but was surprisingly comfortable. Gilbois sat on the couch and folded her legs up under her, like a cat.

She seemed both nervous and depressed. "What's this all about?" she asked. "What is it you want? I don't know anything about Anka Stiffel."

"Maybe not. But you know something about Amanda Owen. You were dancing with her at Schotzie's the night she was assaulted."

She looked away from me and wrapped her arms tightly around herself. It's something women do, like folding their legs up underneath them. I've never seen a man hug himself like that.

She began to chew on the nail of her little finger.

I felt sorry for her. I'd intimidated her into letting me into her apartment; now it was time to offer some comfort, a role I felt more comfortable with.

"Look, you're not in any trouble," I told her. "Nobody's accusing you of having done anything wrong. I just need to know what you saw that night."

"I didn't see anything," Gilbois said. "Honestly. I don't know anything that can help you."

Anything that can help me, I thought. Sometimes that's a signal not to ask any more questions. But she was troubled about something and I felt it was important to discover what it was.

"Why don't you tell me what you know," I said, "and I'll decide if it's helpful. Take a few deep breaths, and tell me why you're so upset."

"Don't patronize me. I'm not upset," she said, making a visible effort to compose herself.

"Tell me about it," I said.

"About what?"

I shook my head. "This will be so much easier for both of us if you don't play stupid," I said. "This morning when I mentioned Anka Stiffel's name, the blood drained out of your face. Something is bothering you, something about Anka Stiffel or Amanda Owen, and I need to know what it is."

She stopped gnawing at her nail and studied the damage she'd done. I sat quietly and waited until the silence began to get uncomfortable. Then I stretched out a bit more in the chair. If the silence made me uncomfortable, it had to be terrible for her. Eventually she'd have to break it. It took about five minutes.

"Okay," she said. "The problem is that nobody knows."

I liked the sound of that. I sat up a bit in the chair. "Nobody knows what?" I asked.

"That I'm a lesbian."

"Ah." I was a little disappointed. It wasn't what I was looking for.

"It could cost me my job," she said.

"They can't fire you for being a lesbian."

"No, they can't *fire* me," she said, exasperated. "But if people found out, I'd lose all my best accounts. And that has the same result as being fired. Either way, if they learn I'm a lesbian, I'm out of business."

"I don't get it."

Gilbois looked at me like I was simple-minded. "Look, sex is part of the game if you're a woman. It's the fuel that makes public relations run. You flirt with the clients, you flirt with the opposition, you flirt with the partners. You do all that well enough, you get your way. You don't have to follow through, you don't have to actually *sleep* with anybody, but you have to flirt with the men. Men run the show."

I shook my head. "I don't get it."

"Look, men always want to *believe* there's a chance you will follow through."

And that made it clear. "If they know you're not really attracted to men, you'll lose business," I said.

She nodded. "And if I lose business, I'm out on my ass. HeadLong expects you to produce. You don't produce, you walk. It's capitalism."

"I see."

She shook her head. "I doubt it. There's a lot more to it than that."

"Tell me."

Gilbois looked at me for a moment, then seemed to decide it didn't really matter. "Men—heterosexual men—are afraid of lesbians," she said. "We threaten their manhood or something. If the men at the office find out I'm a lesbian, they'll feel threatened and angry. Some of the women, too. It won't matter how long we've known each other, or how close we've been. Most of them will cut me out. And in this business, that's the kiss of death."

I got the picture, but I couldn't see its relevance to our situation. "I sympathize with your position," I said. "But what has it got to do with Amanda Owen, Anka Stiffel, and the fight at Schotzie's?"

"If I talk about it, you'll probably want me to go to court. Can you guarantee me anonymity in court?" she asked.

I shook my head.

"No, I didn't think so. So if I go to court, people will find out. They're bound to. And then everybody will know. Everybody. Not just the people at HeadLong, but my family, my neighbors, everybody. It could—it *would* totally screw up my life."

"I'm sorry," I said.

She shook her head. "No you're not. My problems don't mean shit to you."

She had a point. I was more concerned about Anka Stiffel than about Victoria Gilbois's personal problems. Actually, I was more concerned with doing my job for my client, who just happened to be Anka Stiffel.

"I'll do what I can to keep you out of it," I said. "But if it comes to a choice between your secret or my client's freedom, I have to choose her freedom. So I still need you to tell me what happened that night."

"What if I decide not to talk to you?"

I raised my eyebrows. "Is that what you want?"

She looked at me for a moment. "I don't really have a choice, do I? If I don't tell you, you make a scene at the office. Right?"

I nodded. I don't know if I really would have made a scene at her office—I doubt that I would have—but it was important that Gilbois believe I would.

And she did believe it. I could see defeat register in her eyes. She was right; she really had no choice. She told me everything. Once she got started, she was perfectly open and, I think, honest.

She'd known both Amanda Owen and Anka Stiffel for a couple of years. Not intimately, but enough to know who they were. She was attracted to Amanda, but never did anything about it.

"Never had the opportunity to do anything about it," she admitted. "Amanda was all knotted up with her little poet. She didn't show much interest in anybody else. I'd heard that they'd split up, but I didn't put much stock in that."

"Why not?"

"Amanda Owen is the original Good Woman, the sort who always takes her lover back, regardless. She was that way when she was still pretending to be hetero, she's that way now. Amanda is the lesbian version of a Tammy Wynette song."

"A pushover?" I asked.

She shook her head. "No, just a good, tolerant woman. So we were all a little shocked when she showed up at Schotzie's all alone and looking for company."

"You're sure she was looking for company?"

She nodded. "Oh, yeah. No doubt about it. Amanda Owen, on the market. And we were all queuing up, hoping she'd pick us. She was looking for company, all right. Or at least she was until Anka showed up."

Her description of the argument and the fight was basically the same as the other versions we'd heard—the shouting, the pushing, ending with Amanda on the floor and Anka standing over her, threatening to bash her brains out. There were just enough minor differences to make it believable.

"Anka rushed out," she said, "followed by the artsy crowd and Stevie Gibbs. The rest of us hovered around Amanda, hoping."

"Hoping what?"

"That she'd go home with one of us."

"Did she?"

"No such luck. She left by herself."

"You're certain about that?"

"Absolutely. I was paying attention. I was hoping to go home with her, remember. But she left by herself."

"What was her mood like when she left the bar?"

"Amanda's? Her mood changed after the fight. Before, she was laughing and dancing and enjoying herself. After, she said she just wanted to go home and go to bed. She seemed so, I don't know, tired."

"Do you think there's a chance Amanda might have gone to another bar?" I asked.

"I doubt it." She shook her head. "So what do you think? Am I going to have to testify?"

"I don't know," I said. "I won't know until I discuss this with Ms. Stiffel's lawyer and find out whether she thinks what you've told me is important."

"You said you'd keep me out of it."

"I said I'd try."

She sat very still for a moment, toying with her hair.

There was no reason for me to stick around. I stood up and thanked her for her time. She refused to shake my hand.

"You don't have to thank people you bully into talking to you," she said. She let me out of the apartment and put the chain back on the door.

Night was falling as I walked to my car. The days were getting shorter. As I walked, I thought about Amanda Owen in her hospital bed, and about Anka Stiffel in her psychiatric ward, and about Victoria Gilbois sitting upstairs waiting for her world to come crashing down around her ears. And I thought about Joop, for some reason.

I wanted to hurry home, where Mary Margaret would be waiting for me. I looked at my watch and saw I'd get home in time to interrupt a ball game on television. But she'd be patient, we'd talk about the case for a while, then she'd watch the game while I sipped a small glass of Bushmill's and read. Later we'd go to bed—me on the right side, her on the left. We might make love; we might just cuddle.

I thought maybe I'd even go to mass with her next Sunday.

Joop Wheeler

Wednesday Morning

It would be unjust to call what I had a hangover. What I had was of a magnitude that made mortal hangovers pale. I had God's own hangover.

Spikes had been driven into my eyeballs from behind. My mouth tasted like something unnatural had died in it. My eyeballs felt like they'd been coated with sandpaper. I was sick to my stomach. And my left arm was about half numb— maybe because I'd slept on it, maybe because of brain damage. I didn't know and it didn't bear thinking about.

In short, I was about as miserable as I have ever been in my entire long and wicked life. If my bladder hadn't forced me out of bed, I might be lying there still. But during the night my bladder had swollen to about the size of a regulation soccer ball and it was demanding immediate attention.

I staggered out of bed, fought back pain and nausea while I pulled on a pair of hiking shorts, and followed the walls until I found the bathroom door. Which was closed. Behind it, I could hear Stevie humming in the shower.

Which is when I remembered what I'd done the night before. Remembered with vicious clarity. And I was rocked by a second assault of nausea and a brand-new sense of shame and horror. What I'd done was exactly what Sweeney had predicted I was going to do. Something wildly stupid. I'd put a move on Stevie Gibbs. Or at least I'd tried to. Drunk on wine and cognac and moonlight and the waves, I'd kissed Stevie Gibbs. And that probably would have been fine. But I hadn't just kissed her. I'd kissed her in a way friends don't normally kiss each other.

Wildly stupid, is what it was.

In the brutal light of day—and we're talking *brutal* light of day—I could see there probably wouldn't be many things more repugnant to a lesbian than a drunken Southern man trying to get affectionate. But it had seemed like a good idea at the time.

At first Stevie was just sort of shocked. Then she got angry. Angry like I haven't seen very often. Angry the way Norse gods used to get angry. And then she lit into me.

"I don't believe this," she'd said. "What in the hell do you think you're doing?" Without waiting for an answer, she began to shout. "You bastard. You think all you have to do is get me drunk and I'll let you fuck me? Is that it? You think 'Poor girl, the only reason she's a lesbian is because she never got it from a real man'? 'All she needs is a good fuck, turn her right around'? Is that it?"

I'd protested. I'd tried to tell her I didn't think any of those things. Which was true, I didn't. I'd tried to tell her that I was just very much attracted to her, and that the drink and the night and the ocean had shaken the common sense right out of my head. But the explanation hadn't done a lick of good. After she yelled at me for a while, Stevie stormed back up to the house and slammed inside.

I stood there on the beach for a while, feeling like I don't know what. After a while, the waves began tickling my ankles. So I went back up to the deck. I sat on a chair and looked up at the traitor moon and the Judas ocean. And started to work over the bottle of cognac. Which was a bad idea.

I was on a deep run of bad ideas.

It damaged me, that cognac. I leaned on the wall outside the bathroom door, feeling sicker than a trash-eating dog, hating myself. And nearer to pissing my pants than at any time since I was in about the fourth grade. The sound of the water running in the shower didn't help.

My bladder was becoming insistent. Something had to be done. I wobbled outside, thinking to urinate off the deck.

During the night, the sun seemed to have gone nova, it was so bright outside. I staggered for a moment, like Dracula in the old movies just before he died and putrefied.

But my poor abused bladder urged me on. I closed my eyes against the glare, steadied myself against the rail, and managed to get unzipped. But before I could let go, I opened my eyes just enough to look around.

The beach was crowded with people. Tourists. All of whom seemed to be staring directly at me. It might have been my drink-shattered imagination, but I *knew* they were all staring at me. Like I was a biblical leper. And I got a weird image of them pointing at me, shouting "Unclean!" and recoiling in horror.

I dragged myself back inside, trying to zip up as I went. I considered pounding on the bathroom door, demanding to be let in. But I figured Stevie had probably armed herself against further assault, and would willingly shoot me right through the door.

Then I saw an empty wine bottle on the kitchen counter. Even as I saw it, I told myself, "No, Joop, you will not stoop this low. This is just too disgusting to be considered."

But it wasn't. I not only considered the idea, I embraced it. Any port in a storm, as they say. I grabbed the wine bottle and managed to haul my repulsive self back up the stairs to my bedroom. I closed the door, leaned against it, unzipped again, and was suddenly overcome with despair at the technical difficulty of pissing into a wine bottle. It's not as easy as it sounds. It requires a delicacy of technique I wasn't certain I could muster, suffering as I was from a savage, brain-melting, hand-shaking hangover.

I managed it. With difficulty, I admit. But I managed it. The worst moment was when I went sort of weak-kneed in relief. I almost lost my concentration. Which is a critical element in the business of urinating into wine bottles.

Once I'd finished, I put the wine bottle on the dresser, sat on the side of the bed, and clutched my head in my hands. It wasn't just the hangover. I had to face the next dilemma. What does a gentleman do with a wine bottle about a third full of urine?

I almost cried. I was sick, both in body and spirit, and I was tired and ashamed. No grown man should ever have to sit on the side of a bed in a house where he's just humiliated himself, trying to figure out the best way to dispose of a urine-filled wine bottle.

After a moment, the despair passed and my brain began to work again. Though only on a limited, part-time basis. The obvious thing to do was to tote the bottle outside and empty it into the scrub grass next to the house. It took me about five minutes to work this out.

I struggled back to my feet and was heading down the hall, on my way to dump the bottle, when Stevie opened the bathroom door and stepped out.

If I'd been suffering from nothing more than a hangover, I'd have been able to face her. Even if I'd been suffering from just a hangover and the knowledge that I'd behaved horribly the night before, I'd have been able to face her. It would have been tough, but I could have done it. But to face her with a hangover, a guilty conscience, *and* a wine bottle filled with urine was too much. My nerves failed me.

I held up my empty hand, turned immediately, and without saying a word, walked right straight back to my bedroom, closing the door behind me.

Stevie followed and knocked on the door. "Joop?"

"Not now," I said.

"Are you okay?"

Was I okay? Was she insane? How could I possibly be okay? "Fine," I said.

"You sure?"

"Positive." The only thing I could do was smash the bottle and cut my throat with the shards.

"Joop?"

"Stevie, just give me half an hour, okay? Maybe forty-five minutes. Then I'll be fine." I just needed time to think. And maybe to pray. Though I wasn't quite hung over enough to actually believe in God, I figured a little prayer couldn't do any harm.

She hesitated, then said, "Okay. I'm going to walk down to the pharmacy. You want anything?"

Cyanide. "Aspirin," I said. "And Gatorade."

"Gatorade?"

"To replace the fluids."

"Oh. Okay."

I waited until I heard her leave, then rushed—as much as I was capable of rushing—into the bathroom to empty the bottle. Then down to the kitchen to toss the bottle in the trash.

I was on my way back upstairs with an eye toward a hot and cold shower, when the hangover caught up with me again. I sat on the bottom step and fought down the urge to vomit. To distract myself from thinking about my own concerns, I grabbed a magazine and began to flip through it.

It seemed to work. A few minutes later I felt capable of trying the stairs again. I started to toss the magazine back; then I noticed the name on the subscription. Kate Wiggin.

I knew that name. But I couldn't place it.

My head hurt too much to think. I went upstairs, turned on the shower, and slid in. The hot water seemed to rinse some of the poison out my system. I put my face as close to the shower nozzle as I could and let it beat on me.

The water beat some sense into me. Because I remembered where I'd heard the name Kate Wiggin. I'd heard it from Deirdre, the willowy transsexual. Kate Wiggin was Stevie Gibbs's ex-lover. I remembered Deirdre had told me she was in Barcelona.

The knowledge that we were staying in Stevie's ex-lover's house was a shocker. Stevie must still be in love with her. And I'd tried to put a move on her. In the one place that probably most reminded her of her ex-lover. "Wildly stupid" didn't begin to cover what I did.

I lay down on the tile shower floor, which felt cool and solid. And for the first time, I felt the nausea recede. Not so far that I forgot it, but far enough that I was able to ignore it. I listened to the water roll down the drain.

And I wondered if I could plug it up and drown myself.

Kevin Sweeney

Wednesday Afternoon

The sky went dark during the dessert. Mary Margaret and I sat at a window table at La Roma, the Italian restaurant she'd been wanting to try, and watched the sky turn bruise-purple. The temperature dropped twenty degrees, the wind started to blow, and it began to rain like the day Christ was nailed to the tree.

It wasn't what I'd planned. I'd planned on a slow, late lunch and a short walk on the beach—short because Mary Margaret would want to get to Fenway Park early. I'd arranged a pair of box seats to the Red Sox game that night, courtesy of an old client.

I wanted the day to be special for Mary Margaret. God knows she deserved it for being so patient. So if Mary Margaret wanted lunch, the beach, and the Sox, then she ought to get lunch, the beach, and the Sox.

But the weather had no respect for Mary Margaret or her wants. We lingered over the coffee, hoping the rain would ease enough for us to make it to the car without getting soaked. Mary Margaret was telling me about a parish-sponsored trip to Costa Rica and I, being a consistent idiot, was nodding vacantly and giving her a little less than half of my attention. I was thinking about Anka Stiffel and Amanda Owen, poor souls, both of them in the hospital.

Mary Margaret noticed my lack of attention and touched my hand. "It's a dreadful thing, isn't it," she said. "To be responsible for other people, and them hurting."

I put down my coffee. "How do you do that?" I asked.
"Do what?"
"Know what I'm thinking."

She grinned broadly. "Ni heolas go haontios," she said.

"You're showing off again," I said. "I know it's Irish, but I have no idea what you just said."

"I said, 'You must live with a person to know the person.' "

"Ah. Very clever people, the Irish."

She smiled and examined her coffee cup. "Can I make a suggestion?"

I told her to go ahead.

"It's not a day for the beach," she said.

"It's not," I admitted. "I'm sorry."

She smiled. "And I doubt the Sox will play in this rain."

I agreed that the game would be rained out.

She smiled. "So perhaps we can do something else, something to ease your mind."

"Ease my mind?"

She nodded and touched my hand with the back of hers. "To help you to relax."

I grinned. "A fine idea. Let's go home."

Mary Margaret dimpled and blushed a little. "You're a dirty-minded man, Kevin Sweeney," she said. "And I love you for it. But I was thinking of going to the hospital."

"The hospital?" I was suddenly disappointed. "Why would either of us want to go to the hospital?"

"To see your lesbian poet."

One of Mary Margaret's volunteer projects was to visit members of the parish who were in the hospital, and I assumed she saw this as an extension of her parish work. "I'm not sure Anka would appreciate the thought," I said.

Mary Margaret sipped her coffee. "Does the poor soul have anybody to visit her? Or bring her things? Other than lawyers and doctors?"

I shrugged. "She's on a locked ward. She's not allowed to have visitors except for her immediate family and her lawyer."

"What about her lawyer's investigators?"

"And her lawyer's investigators," I admitted. "But you're not an investigator."

She turned her head slightly to one side and smiled. "Are you saying you wouldn't tell a little white lie for your own dear wife?"

I hesitated. "Even if I could get you into the hospital, I'm not sure it would be appropriate.

Mary Margaret snorted. "Appropriate? Of course it's appropriate. It's always appropriate to visit them that's in trouble. 'Not appropriate,' indeed. What would Father Hannan say?"

I studied her face for a moment, and smiled. "Father Hannan would say you're a dear woman," I said. "And he'd be right."

She made a face and waved the compliment away, but I could tell she was pleased. She looked out the window and said, "I think the rain has slackened. Shall we make a run for it?"

I wanted to tell her how very much I loved her, and that she was the finest woman I'd ever known, and how grateful I was for her presence in my life. I wanted to tell her we'd been running for it since the day we fell in love. But all I did was nod and kiss her hand and tell her, "Whatever you want."

The guy in front of me in the express checkout line had a six-pack of beer, two large cans of chili with beans, and a bag of potato chips. The guy behind me had a six-pack and a fifty-pound bag of dog food. I had a large pink box of sanitary pads.

It was sanitary napkins that brought Mary Margaret and Anka Stiffel together. The first five or ten minutes of the visit were awkward to say the least. We'd brought Anka some cigarettes, which she accepted gracelessly. She was more lucid than she'd been last Monday, but no more courteous.

I introduced Mary Margaret and asked Anka if there was anything she needed. She just shook her head and lowered her eyes, so that she looked at us through a black scruff of bangs.

Mary Margaret was more accustomed than I to the artificiality of hospital visits. She started a steady stream of idle chatter and questions about trivialities and eventually discovered there was something unsuitable about the sanitary pads in the locked ward. For some reason, they didn't allow tampons, and their pads were either too thin or too thick, I never figured out which. Mary Margaret was outraged and sent me off to the nearest market with a note telling me which brand to buy.

The old man at the register raised an eyebrow when it was my turn. He traded a look with the man with the dog food, but rang up the pads without a word.

"They're for shining my shoes," I said.

"Ah." The cashier smiled. "They're for his shoes, Eddie," he said to the man with the dog food.

"Oh yeah, I've heard of that," Eddie said. "I got an uncle was in the Army, he did that, used those things."

The clerk raised his eyebrows. "You got an uncle used those things? Was that your uncle Shirley?" He handed me my change and put my sanitary pads in a bag.

"He used 'em on his shoes," the man said. "Asshole."

"Yeah, his shoes." The clerk grinned. "Hey, I got one for you. What do a ripe avocado and a woman on the rag have in common?"

"An avocado? How the hell should I know? I don't even know what the fuck an avocado is. You tell me."

The squeaking door drowned out the answer, but I heard them laughing as I left. On the drive back to the hospital, I tried to figure out what a ripe avocado and a menstruating woman had in common. I kept working on it as I parked the car and passed through the hospital and all the security that makes the locked ward the locked ward.

When I arrived, Mary Margaret and an attendant were chatting like old army buddies and playing cards with Anka. Only my wife could get a psychotic lesbian poet to play three-handed rummy.

I don't enjoy cards and I couldn't figure out the connection between the avocado and the woman on her period, so I fell back on what I understand. Work.

The charge nurse was a hard-nosed, by-the-book woman who refused to let me look at Anka's medical records without proper authorization. I told her a release-of-information form granting Kath O'Mara and associates the privilege of examining the medical records ought to be in Anka's file.

The nurse found the form, but still refused to allow me to touch the records until she'd received approval from the shift supervisor. While the supervisor was being paged, I watched Mary Margaret and Anka play cards. Anka wasn't smiling or laughing like the others, but she wasn't totally withdrawn; she was paying attention—to the conversation as well as the cards.

Eventually, the charge nurse received the approval she'd asked for, and grudgingly handed over a thick file. It covered the four most recent times Anka was hospitalized and hinted at earlier hospital stays.

Considering Anka and the nature of her problem, it should have been interesting reading, and the summary sheets were. But much of the file was very dull—laboratory results and nursing progress notes. If I'd cared to, I could have learned what Anka was given for each meal during each hospitalization, how much of it she ate, and how often she moved her bowels.

I decided to simply scan the nursing notes, thinking that a closer examination could be made later if necessary. But as

I flipped through the pages, I noticed a comment about physical restraints.

During Anka's second stay on the locked ward she'd assaulted a female attendant and had to be placed in leather psychiatric restraints. Anka had apparently hit the woman repeatedly in the head with a clipboard.

I heard the nurse clearing her throat. "Visiting hours are over in five minutes," she said.

"I'm not a visitor," I reminded her. "I work for Anka Stiffel's lawyer."

"You may work for her lawyer," she said. "But she doesn't." She pointed toward Mary Margaret, who was still at the card table. "She has to leave with the other visitors."

I nodded. "Five minutes," I said.

I turned back to the nursing notes, trying to learn more about the assault on the attendant. And it was right there in a report written by Licensed Practical Nurse Irmagard Mitchell.

Patient had repeatedly told me she had developed a
"crush" on me. After consulting with Dr. Rifkin, it was
decided that I should inform pt. that I was flattered but
that such a relationship was inappropriate and that, in
any case, I was not a homosexual. Pt. appeared to accept
this. However, this night pt. saw me conversing
(laughing) with another female pt. Pt. became verbally
abusive, calling me a "2-timing bitch" and attacked me,
striking me in the head several times with the clipboard
used for vital signs, which she had taken from me by
physical force and violence.

I closed the file. Two things bothered me about the report. First, Anka had committed an assault similar to the one against Amanda Owen, and she'd done it under similar circumstances—violence in a jealous rage. Second, and equally disturbing, this was an assault that Dr. Rifkin apparently knew about. And yet she hadn't mentioned it to us.

"Time's up," the nurse said. "Visiting hours are over."

Joop Wheeler

Wednesday Afternoon

Amanda Standish handed back my card and gave me a look that was both startled and disgusted. I'd seen a similar look once: on a woman's face in a restaurant when she discovered a potato bug in her salad.

I smiled in response. Not a very good smile, I'm afraid, on account of I was still badly hung over. But it's the thought that counts, is what my momma always told me.

"You're a private investigator?" she asked. She held up a half-shucked ear of corn like a question mark. She must have been fixing an early dinner or a late lunch.

"Yes, ma'am." I waved my hand at Stevie. "And this is my, uh, my associate, Ms. Stevie Gibbs. We work for Ms. Kathleen O'Mara, who is a lawyer." Once again, I was hoping to score points because I was working for a woman. It was a slim hope, but it never hurts to try.

But I could tell trying wasn't going to be enough. She kept giving me the potato-bug look. Which was supposed to make me feel bad. And it did. Though not in the way she meant it to.

What the potato-bug look did was give me a sick feeling in the pit of my stomach. A feeling as bad as the worst hangover. It's the feeling you get when you find the one person who could possibly break a case wide open and you *know* that person just plain doesn't like you and you realize there's not a damn thing you can do about it. There's some folks just aren't going to talk to you.

It was a cruel disappointment, is what it was. Especially after the discovery that Amanda Standish was real, that she wasn't just a figment of Anka's fevered imagination.

We'd found her where Stevie's friends said we'd find her—in a house a couple of miles inland. One of those old, ramshackle, tag-along houses they have in New England. The ones that look like each generation of owner has tacked another room or two on without regard for anything but immediate function. Sort of lackadaisical. Which is what makes them so odd. Lackadaisy is not a New England style.

Amanda Standish looked just about the way Ed Harriman, the night clerk at the Roadhouse Motel, had described. Which is unusual, a witness being so accurate in giving a description. But there she was, mid-thirties, maybe five foot six, 130, with brown hair that would have fallen below her shoulders if it hadn't been tied in a careless ponytail.

"What do you want?" she asked.

That was a difficult question. I couldn't just blurt out what I wanted. Which was to know if she'd been wrecking the sheets with Anka Stiffel at the time Amanda Owen was getting her head cracked open like a boiled lobster. That's a question you have to ease into.

"We just need to ask you a few questions," I said. "About a woman you might have met last week."

Anxiety and suspicion flooded her eyes. "Last week? I was out of town last week."

"Yes ma'am. This was up near Boston. In Hobsbawm. Would have been a week ago last Wednesday. Her name is Anka Stiffel."

She shook her head. "No, I don't think I know the name."

And then I made a mistake. I rushed it. "Well, does the Roadhouse Motel sound familiar?" I asked.

She gave me the potato-bug look again, this time with a twist of anger. Then she started to close the door. Some warped instinct made me stick my foot in the door. Which was a trick I'd seen Sweeney use with great results.

But I guess I hadn't watched Sweeney close enough. Because I made two critical mistakes. The first was I put my foot up against the door jamb rather than against the door. This is not good door-stopping technique. It allows the person closing the door enough space to put some muscle into the closing. Which compounded my second mistake. Which was wearing sneakers.

The doctor looked at my foot—which was turning twenty different shades of purple and had swollen to about the size and shape of a hippopotamus foot—and couldn't help herself. She had to make the joke. "Well, I guess you really put your foot in it, didn't you?" she said.

Hospital humor. "Is it broken?" I asked.

She held an X ray up to the light for me to look at and started to explain. Something about tarsals. Or metatarsals.

"Just tell me," I said. "Is the damn thing broken?"

She shook her head. "No. You've got a hell of a contusion," she said. "A very deep bruise. It's going to hurt like sin. You're not going to want to put much pressure on it for a while. But it's not broken."

"It's *going* to hurt?" I asked. "I thought it was hurting now. You're telling me it's going to hurt more?"

She smiled and pulled out a prescription pad. "I'm giving you a prescription for some painkillers," she said. "And I'll give you an injection in just a minute."

She stuck her head out the door of the treatment room and spoke to a nurse. A moment later a nurse brought in a syringe on a stainless steel tray. Classy joint. The doctor made me undo my trousers and roll over. A shot in the butt.

Afterward I asked, "Anything else I should do?"

"The best thing you can do now is stay off your foot for a few days," she said. "And wear something more solid than sneakers if you try that trick again."

I'd already figured that out. "Am I going to be able to walk?"

She nodded. "We'll get you a cane."

"A cane. Terrific." The perfect way to round off the day. I'd woke up with a hangover, suffered agonies of the soul at the recollection of my earlier foul behavior, been turned away from a key witness, had my foot deeply bruised, got a shot in the butt, and now I was going to have to walk with a cane.

"You ever have one of those days?" I asked.

"There's no need to keep you here any longer," the doctor said. "Let's get you into a wheelchair and out to your friends."

"Friends?" I asked. "Plural?"

She nodded. "Two women. Aren't they with you?"

The only person with me was Stevie. Amanda Standish had slammed the door shut while I was writhing in pain on her front porch. Stevie had helped me up from the porch, helped me hobble into the car, and then driven me to the emergency room.

A saint, is what she was. Earlier that morning, after she'd returned from the pharmacy, we'd sat on the deck and talked about what had happened the night before. We didn't agree on *why* it happened—Stevie felt the problem was that heterosexual men think if a woman dances and laughs with a man, she must want to have sex with him, and I thought the problem was simply the volatile combination of alcohol, moon, sea, and general lust—but we agreed it was an unfortunate incident and we shouldn't let it spoil our friendship. She apologized for getting so angry and I apologized for every sin I'd ever committed in her presence.

And the funny thing was, as the day wore on, it actually didn't seem to make much difference. We got along pretty much like we did before. Searching for Amanda Standish's house—she navigated, I drove—had been fun.

The only fun part of the whole day.

The nurse put me in a wheelchair and wheeled me into the waiting area. Where, it turned out, two women *were* waiting for me. Stevie Gibbs and Amanda Standish her own-self. They stood as I was wheeled in.

Stevie looked at my hippo-sized foot, which was loosely wrapped in a bandage since it was now too big to fit into my human-sized sneaker, and asked if I was okay. It was a silly question, but I gave her the deep bruise–not broken–stay off it report.

The nurse rolled me to the door, with Stevie and Amanda Standish hovering nearby. She handed me a cane—maybe the ugliest cane I've ever seen—and turned me loose with a stern admonition to take care of myself.

I hobbled to my feet, grunting freely with the pain, and sat on a bench while Stevie went to get the car. I only exaggerated the pain a little. For Amanda Standish's benefit.

"Oh, God, I'm so sorry," she said. "I don't know what got into me. I've never done anything like that before. I'm really so sorry." She was flustered and upset. Probably as much at seeing the extent of the injury as at her door-slamming behavior.

I nodded, trying to decide which was the best course to take in order to get her to talk—be forgiving or make her feel guiltier.

I decided on forgiveness. Which was hypocritical, since the whole thing was my own fault. Nobody told me to stick my damn foot in the door.

"It was my own damn fault," I said. "And I've never done anything like that, either. Sticking my foot in somebody's door, I mean."

"But still, I didn't have to slam the door on it," she said.

Which brought to mind a good question. So I asked it. "Why did you?"

"I don't know. It's stupid."

"What's stupid?"

She sat on the bench with me. "I thought you might have been with the Board of Health."

"The Board of Health?"

"Or the Centers for Disease Control. Or something. Whoever it is that notifies people when they've slept with somebody who has been diagnosed with an STD."

"Ah," I said. I knew what an STD was. A sexually transmitted disease. Herpes or syphilis. Or AIDS. "But didn't I tell you I was a private investigator?" I asked. "I even gave you my card. Hell, I even told you who we were working for."

"Yes, but as soon as you said 'Roadhouse Motel' my brain became paralyzed. All I could think about was AIDS. And I didn't want to hear what you had to say." She shrugged as if to say "I told you it was stupid."

And she was right.

I pointed to my foot. "You mean to say I got this because you thought I was with the disease police?"

She nodded and made a face. "That's why I followed you to the hospital. To apologize and face the music. And now I learn from your friend that you're only interested in that woman."

That woman. "Anka Stiffel," I said.

"If that's her name."

I wanted to ask about that comment, but just then Stevie pulled up in the car. "Is there somewhere we can talk?" I asked. "I really need to learn what you know about Anka Stiffel. She could be in a lot of trouble and you might be able to help."

"Okay. There's a little bar not too far from here," she said. "You could follow me in your car."

"Great." I started to stand, but felt sort of woozy. From the medicine, I guess. So I sat back down. But at least the pain wasn't so bad.

Stevie got out of the car to help me in. I told her the plan and, after waiting for Amanda Standish to fetch her car, we set off right behind her. We wound up at a relentlessly hip fern bar near the bay. But at least it was quiet; we were between the lunch crowd and the dinner crowd. And it had a deck overlooking the water.

Getting to the table, though, was a struggle. The drugs the doctor had given me at the hospital began to kick in. Between the cane and the drug-induced numbness, I was walking like a drunken sailor.

Before we got down to business, we ordered drinks. At least they ordered drinks. I was stuck with iced tea. Stevie told the waiter I was on pain medication and was not to be served alcohol. I didn't know whether to be touched or pissed off.

"Now," I said. "Anka Stiffel. How did you meet her? Where did you meet her? And what happened after you met her?" I realized I was asking too many questions at once, but I was too numb to figure out how to retract some of them. I was feeling distinctly odd. Sort of like I was hovering outside myself. I was aware enough to know what was going on, but unable to control my part of it.

Fortunately, Stevie was able to take over. She asked the questions and took the notes and generally did my job for me. I was proud of her and sort of distantly aware that red lightning was making its presence known.

The story Amanda Standish told was fairly simple. Like Stevie's friends had said, Amanda Standish had recently been dumped by her long-term lover. When her friends tried to comfort her, she told them she didn't mind. She was going to trash around a while, she'd said. Drink like a fiend and sleep with lots of strange women.

But she wasn't really interested in drinking and trashing around. So she went up to Boston for a few days. Just to be by herself. She visited the museums, saw the sights, and toured the coast from Boston up to Portsmouth, New Hampshire.

It was on her return from Portsmouth that she met Anka. Met her in a twenty-four-hour diner a couple of blocks from the Roadhouse Motel. Anka walked into the diner, looked around, spotted Amanda sitting alone, walked straight up to her, and sat down. After a few minutes of aggressive flirting, Anka propositioned her.

"She said there was a motel right down the road," Amanda said. "She wanted to take me there.

"I don't know why I said yes. I think it was because I was tired of being alone and I was feeling a little down. And because I'd said I was going to trash around, and here was the chance. And because it was sort of exciting, the blunt way she approached me. And because I'd eaten too much and I felt fat and wanted somebody to want me."

Stevie nodded. "I know that feeling," she said.

It was a new one to me. If I'd felt fat, the last thing I'd have wanted to do was let somebody see me naked. But women are different from men.

Regardless of her reason, Amanda Standish decided to go with Anka. She left her car in the diner parking lot; Anka drove them the block and a half to the Roadhouse. They stopped at a liquor store on the way, and Amanda bought a small bottle of cognac. She could tell Anka was a little drunk and she wanted to catch up. Besides, she was a little nervous.

Amanda had chosen to register and pay for the motel room because she said it made her feel like she had some control over the situation. But when she registered she couldn't remember her license tag number. Which the registration form required. So she made one up.

Stevie and I exchanged looks. We'd all of us assumed the license number on the register was intentionally false. Great detectives we are.

Amanda said they'd sat in the car outside the room for a few minutes, sharing the cognac and necking, while she worked up the courage to go in. Once inside, they hopped right in the sack.

"At first the sex was pretty normal," Amanda said.

I didn't know what "pretty normal" meant when it came to lesbians. But it couldn't be all *that* different from what men and women did together. At least I didn't think it could. Even in my drugged state, I knew better than to ask.

"But as the evening wore on," Amanda said, "she got more and more strange. I don't mind a little bondage. I even like it sometimes. So when she asked me to tie her to the bed, I did. She wanted me to force her to have oral sex with me. So I pretended to do that as well. But then she wanted me to call her names, and to pinch her and slap her and jerk her head by the hair. And to burn her with my cigarette. I said I wouldn't."

"What did she do then?" Stevie asked.

"She went totally insane," Amanda Standish said. "The thing that really got to me was she kept looking at the ceiling and hissing, 'I'm trying, I'm trying, leave me alone.'" Amanda's eyes were wide. "I couldn't believe it. The one time I try to be a little spontaneous and I get hooked up with a lunatic."

"What did you do?" Stevie asked.

"I left," she said. "I got dressed, I gathered my stuff, then I untied one of her arms so she'd be able to free herself. And then I just left. Drove up into Maine and stayed there."

"What time was this?" Stevie asked.

Amanda Standish shrugged. "Maybe two."

Plenty of time for Anka to untie herself, drive to Amanda Owen's house, whack her in the head with a dybbuk, and make it back to the Roadhouse in time to start howling at the rising sun.

There wasn't much else Amanda Standish could add. She didn't know Amanda Owen. Hadn't even heard her name—or Anka Stiffel's name, for that matter—except from us. And while she was spooked, if not terribly surprised, when Stevie told her that Anka was accused of attempting to murder somebody that night, Amanda Standish was doubly spooked when she learned that she and the victim shared the same first name.

"I can't tell you how weird that is," she said. "It's like something you'd read in the supermarket tabloids. Because you know why?"

We said we didn't.

"Because she didn't know my name. I never told her my name and she never told me hers. Or if she told me, I don't remember. I didn't know her name until you mentioned it at the hospital."

When it became clear she had nothing else to add, I excused myself and hobbled into the bathroom with my cane. I stuck my finger down my throat and made myself throw up. To get the pain medication out of my system. I was too muzzy-headed and I needed to be able to think clearly.

After I rinsed my mouth and washed my face, I gimped around until I found a pay phone and made a credit-card call to Kath.

"Joop," she said, "good to hear from you. How's the Cape?"

"Kath, there's too much to tell you over the telephone," I said. "But I will say this: there are places on the Cape that redefine the term weird. I'll tell you all about it when we get back."

"And when will that be?"

"Tonight."

"You learn anything important?" she asked.

"Lots."

"Like what?" she asked.

"Like don't ever stick your foot in a door if you're wearing sneakers."

"Joop, I don't think that's going to help much."

"There's more," I said.

"I hope so. Because I just talked to Detective Coyle. He said Amanda went into respiratory arrest this morning and almost died. They don't expect her to last the day."

Kevin Sweeney

Wednesday Night

"So basically what we've got is this," Joop said. He held up a finger. "One, we got no alibi."

"Right," I said. "There was plenty of time for Anka to untie herself, drive to Amanda's, commit the assault, and still get back to the Roadhouse in time to start howling."

"Two," Joop said, holding up another finger. "We got nothing that indicates Anka *didn't* smack Amanda in the head with a dybbuk's butt. Am I right?"

He was right. Although Anka was clearly telling the truth about Amanda Standish, there wasn't a shred of direct evidence to suggest she was innocent.

"And three," Joop said. "We got no hope for a plea bargain."

"None," Kathleen said. "The prosecutor is totally unwilling to even discuss a plea arrangement. He's certain Amanda's going to die soon and he's confident he can get a jury to convict Anka on second-degree murder. So he's got no incentive to offer a plea bargain."

We all sat around the dinner table, looking at the dirty dishes. It had not been a pleasant dinner, though it wasn't Mary Margaret's fault. She'd fixed a wonderful meal, including a salad from her own garden, and we'd gone through two bottles of wine and had started on a third.

But we were none of us in the mood to appreciate it.

Joop and his lesbian sidekick had succeeded beyond all our expectations. They'd found the woman we had all assumed was one of Anka Stiffel's hallucinations, the woman Anka had said she'd spent the night with—found her and spoken to her. Only to learn that Anka's alibi, like everything else in this case, was uncertain and insubstantial.

On top of that discouraging information was the knowledge that Amanda Owen might die at any moment. It's hard to have a cheery meal under those conditions.

Kathleen had called me as soon as Joop hung up. She'd said she wanted a strategy session as soon as he got back, but didn't think she could bear the thought of spending one more minute in her office. I'd suggested we all meet at the house and have dinner. We could talk afterward.

I was beginning to regret the suggestion. And poor Mary Margaret: This was one of the things she'd hated about me being a police officer—bringing work home with me.

But she seemed to be okay. In fact, she and Stevie Gibbs had hit it off immediately and had spent the evening in the kitchen laughing.

"We knew it was a long shot," Kathleen said. "We never really expected anything to come of it."

"That's right," Joop said. "Look on the bright side."

"What's that?" Kathleen asked.

"Well, I don't know exactly know what the bright side is," Joop said. "But there's got to be one. You figure it out. I can't do all the work for you."

"The bright side," I said, "is that the prosecution is almost as weak as we are. There's no physical evidence pointing to Anka, no eyewitnesses, and no solid facts."

"That's not exactly what I'd call bright," Joop said. "But it'll have to do." He was plainly tired and in some pain. He'd had his share of the wine during dinner. Maybe more than his share. Stevie Gibbs had confiscated his pain drugs, saying he could have them back an hour or so after he stopped drinking.

"Why don't we move out to the porch," I suggested. "We can drink wine and watch the fireflies while we sort this out."

Mary Margaret cleared her throat and stood up. "That's an excellent idea," she said. "And since Stevie and I cooked,

I think it's only fair that you people do the cleaning up." She gave us a sweet smile. "Take your time. We'll be on the porch when you finish, talking and drinking and watching the fireflies." She headed for the door. "Stevie, will you bring the wine, please?"

Stevie Gibbs grinned, grabbed the wine bottle by the neck, and stood up. "Yes, ma'am," she said. "I surely will."

Kathleen cracked her first real smile of the evening. Joop made a face and said something about consideration for cripples.

"It's your own fault you're injured, Joop Wheeler," Mary Margaret said sternly. "Sticking your foot in the door like that. What sort of person would do such a thing?"

A person like your husband, I thought.

But Mary Margaret's a sucker for Joop and she relented with a smile and a shake of her head. "Okay. Come along. You'd probably be breaking half the dishes anyway."

Joop stood with a groan. He turned his head so I could see his face and he grinned and winked at me, the bastard.

When Kathleen and I joined them a short time later, they'd almost finished the bottle of wine. Joop was on the porch swing, resting his leg and smiling drunkenly. Stevie Gibbs was in an old Adirondack chair, her legs pulled up in front of her in a sort of yoga position, also with a drunken smile. And even Mary Margaret looked a bit intoxicated.

Seeing their faces, Kathleen also broke into a smile. She leaned against the porch rail near Joop, took his cane, and twirled it like a baton.

"What's everybody grinning about?" I asked.

Mary Margaret waved her hand at the yard. "Have you ever seen so many fireflies?" she asked. "We're grinning because we live in a world with fireflies."

I scanned the area. There did seem to be an unusual number of fireflies.

"Kevin Sweeney," Mary Margaret said. "If you're any

sort of man at all, you'll have brought another bottle of wine with you."

I held up a bottle.

"Ah, he's a good man, my Kevin." Mary Margaret smiled, and she patted me on the shoulder and gave me a kiss on the cheek.

We drank wine and watched the fireflies, each of us quiet and lost in our own thoughts. Until Joop spoke.

"I vote for the husband," he said.

"Pardon?" Stevie Gibbs said.

"He's talking about work," I said, and everybody groaned.

"Look," Joop said. "We've nosed around full-time for a week. And the only strategy that holds an ounce of promise is the one we first thought of. Point the finger at somebody else. I vote for the husband . . . what's his name?"

"Charles Lowell," I said.

"Charles Lowell," Joop said. "I vote for Charles. What was it he said about Amanda?"

"He said she was his most prized possession," I said.

"He said that?" Kath asked. "That wasn't in your report."

"It didn't seem relevant," I said.

Kathleen nodded. "It probably isn't. But it's a hell of a thing to say."

The firefly mood was shattered, though it didn't seem to affect either Joop or Kathleen. It did affect Stevie Gibbs, though. She sighed and moved to the rail beside Mary Margaret.

I let myself get drawn back into the case. Kathleen and I argued the merits of trying to point a jury toward Charles Lowell. She was all for it, though I think that was partly because of his comment about Amanda.

Joop interrupted our train of thought again. "You know, it just doesn't make much sense," he said.

"But pointing the finger at the husband was your idea," Kathleen said.

"No, not that," Joop said, shaking his head. "I mean Anka." He screwed up his face. "I know she probably did it, but it doesn't make a lot of sense. I mean, how likely is it that she's going to untie herself from the bed—"

Mary Margaret smiled and said quietly, "People do find odd ways to amuse themselves."

"—drive herself all the way to the other side of town, smack her ex-lover in the head with an ancient Hebrew demon, then drive *back* to the motel? Doesn't make a lick of sense. Does it? It doesn't to me."

"As you keep pointing out," Kathleen said, "the woman is crazy. She doesn't have to make sense."

Joop nodded. "Yeah, but the *jury* will be trying to make some sense of it," he said. "Unless the jury is crazy, too."

As Kathleen examined this new angle, I found my mind turning back. "Do you know what I haven't done?" I asked. "I can't believe I'm such an idiot. Any rookie would have done it." I stood up and walked to the porch rail.

"What?" Kathleen asked.

I swatted at a moth. "I never asked anybody about the car. I didn't ask Ed Harriman if he heard a car leave the motel lot, and I didn't ask Callie Dobson if she'd heard one arrive."

"That's easy enough to fix," Joop said. "Don't get in a sweat about it. We'll take care of it tomorrow."

"She even told me she was a light sleeper," I said. "And I let it go right by me."

"What are you talking about, Kevin?" Kathleen asked.

"Callie Dobson," I said. "She told me she was a light sleeper. She said she used to wake up at night when Amanda and Anka came home late. She'd hear them arguing."

If Anka had driven to Amanda Owen's house, Mrs. Dobson would have heard her arrive.

"It was stupid of me not to find out about the car," I said.

"Don't worry about it," Joop said again. "We'll find out tomorrow. We'll go see her and ask." He frowned. "What are we going to do if she says she *did* hear a car?"

"God, let's not even think about that," Kathleen said.

"Well, she had to hear at least one car, didn't she?" Mary Margaret asked.

"Why?" Kathleen asked.

"She must have heard Amanda come home," Mary Margaret said.

"That's true," I said, and touched her hand. She's a clever woman, Mary Margaret.

"Well, if she did hear a car, she didn't mention it to Sweeney," Joop said. "I wonder if she mentioned it to the cops."

"We'll find out tomorrow, then, shall we?" I asked Joop.

He nodded and said his schedule was clear tomorrow.

"Then check it out," Kathleen said. "If we don't come up with something, I'm going to end up standing in front of a jury at a murder trial, trying to do tricks with smoke and mirrors."

"What will you do if there isn't any evidence that helps?" Stevie Gibbs asked.

"I don't know," Kathleen said. "I'll try to shovel some smoke at the jury. If that doesn't work, I guess I'll have to get angry."

"I don't understand," Stevie Gibbs said.

Kathleen leaned forward and spoke in a tired voice. "There is an old law-school maxim," she said. "If the facts are against you, bang on the law. If the law is against you, bang on the facts. And if both the facts and the law are against you, bang on the table."

J o o p   W h e e l e r

Thursday Morning

"I like the tie," I said, "The tie is a nice touch."

Sweeney ignored me and concentrated on driving. He'd picked me up on his way to interview Ed Harriman, the night clerk at the Roadhouse, and Callie Dobson, the nosy neighbor. We don't often work together like that. But since I was a gimp and couldn't drive, I insisted on going along.

He didn't need me. He'd have managed just fine without me. Maybe even better. But I knew if I spent the day confined to my apartment on account of my foot, I'd wind up as crazy as a roomful of Anka Stiffels.

"The tie is a very nice touch," I said. "Why are you wearing a tie?" Sweeney rarely wears a tie. Or a sport coat, for that matter. But here he was in both. It made him look like a cop. Which is no surprise, since that's what he used to be.

"I want to, uh, inspire confidence," he said.

"Oh. In whom?"

"Confidence in me, idiot."

"No, no." I shook my head. "In whom do you want to inspire this confidence in you? If you know what I mean."

He nodded. "In Mrs. Dobson. She was a little cautious before. I'm hoping the tie and jacket will make her feel more secure. Maybe we'll get more out of her."

We went to Ed Harriman's apartment first. Since he worked nights, Sweeney wanted to catch him before he went to sleep. Thoughtful guy, Sweeney.

Although Harriman had given Sweeney his address, it took us a few minutes to find his apartment. It was unmarked, and on the second floor in the back of an old cannery office building. It would have been a kindness to call the place a dump.

But he didn't seem to mind living in a dump. Probably thought it was "real." He answered the door and, when he recognized Sweeney, invited us in cheerfully. He'd done the best he could with the place. It was as clean as a dump could be.

Sweeney introduced us and we shook hands.

Harriman had a little laptop computer propped up on a shaky kitchen table. The computer probably cost more than all the furniture in the apartment. Twice as much.

I pointed at the computer. "Sweeney told me you were a writer," I said. "Are we interrupting your work?"

"Oh no, not at all," he said. "Please come in. I don't get a lot of company here."

And who could blame his company?

"Ed, we only need a minute of your time," Sweeney said. "Just a couple of quick questions."

"No problem," he said. He looked at my bandaged, shoeless foot. "What happened to your foot?"

"A witness closed a door on it," I said.

"Really?" Harriman grinned. "On your foot?"

"Yep." I pointed to my injured foot. "That one right there."

"Ed," Sweeney said, "we need to ask you about last week. The same night we talked about, the night Amanda Standish checked into the motel. Remember?"

"You mean the woman *calling* herself Amanda Standish," Harriman said. He shook a finger at Sweeney. Actually *shook* a finger. At Sweeney. I almost laughed. "We can't jump to conclusions, now, can we?" Harriman said.

"No we can't," Sweeney said. "You're absolutely right. But getting back to that night, do you recall if a car drove out of the motel lot during the night?"

"Nope." He shook his head, then inclined it toward my foot. "How'd it feel?"

"It hurt," I said. "Real bad."

I could see Sweeney restraining himself. "Ed, are you saying you don't recall if anybody left? Or that you do recall and nobody left?"

"I don't recall."

"Okay," Sweeney said. "*Would* you be able to tell if a car left your motel while you were on duty?"

"Well, sure." Harriman showed us a big grin. "The cars go right by the office window. I'd be bound to see any car that drove out of the lot, wouldn't I. Unless I was in the W.C."

"The what?" I asked.

"Water closet," Sweeney said. "The head. The bathroom."

"Oh." Why not just call it the bathroom? I thought.

"Or if I was engrossed in my writing," Harriman said. "Or if there was something really good on the television. Or if another customer came in. Or—"

"We get the picture," Sweeney said. "You'd notice any car that left the lot, unless you were distracted. Is that correct?"

"Exactly," Harriman said.

Sweeney spent a few more minutes trying to get the same info from different angles, but without any luck. I felt a little frustrated as we walked back to the car. But Sweeney didn't seem to mind. It's like he can flip a switch and it's all gone.

"So what do you think?" he asked, as we got back in the car.

I arranged my foot so it would be semicomfortable. "Ed Harriman has a peculiar way of looking at the world," I said.

"Ed Harriman is a waste of space," Sweeney said. He can be a tad critical at times, Sweeney can.

❊ ❊ ❊

Sweeney rang the bell. And June Cleaver opened the door. She was in a white blouse, a loose calf-length flower-print skirt, and an apron. An actual, honest-to-God apron. With little frilly things on the edges. Like my momma used to wear.

Mrs. Callie Dobson smiled. "Mr. Sweeney, isn't it?"

Sweeney nodded and smiled back, apparently pleased she'd remembered his name. He seemed fond of her. Which is a thing that happens sometimes. You meet a witness and, who knows why, you have an intuitive affection for her. Like me and Stevie. And the red-lightning effect. Only more limited.

But I never thought Sweeney was subject to even a limited RL effect. I don't know if I was pleased or disappointed to see that Sweeney was as human as I was.

"This is my partner, Wendell Wheeler," Sweeney said. I'd never heard him use my real first name before. Hell, till that moment I wasn't sure he even *knew* my first name. I would have stared at him, except I had to smile and shake the extended Dobson hand.

"Mr. Wheeler, so nice to meet you," she said. She turned back to Sweeney. "Well, I never thought to see you again."

"I'm afraid I need to ask you some more questions," he said.

"Oh?" She cocked her head to one side and looked puzzled.

He nodded. "Would you like to sit here on the steps?" he asked. "Or would you rather talk inside?"

"Well, my husband isn't home at the moment, I'm afraid."

"Business trip?" he asked.

She shook her head. "No, he's just at the office." She frowned for a moment. Then looked at my poor foot. "I suppose you might as well come in. I don't think . . . it's probably not necessary to sit out here on the steps." She gave an awkward toss of her head and a thin laugh.

She led us through an immaculate house to what would be called a family room, if a person had a family. Unlike the rest of the house, which was antiseptically clean, the family room was merely spotless. It looked like people might live in it. Very clean and neat people. There were a matched set of large stuffed chairs, a sofa big enough for Kareem Abdul-Jabbar to sleep on, a low table with magazines fanned out on top, and a television with a screen the approximate size of Utah.

I eased myself gently down into one of the stuffed chairs. Sweeney sat stiffly in the other. Mrs. Dobson sat on the edge of the giant sofa and smoothed her skirt. And waited.

"We're sorry to impose on you," Sweeney said, "but there are some questions I forgot to ask earlier."

She gave that jerky head gesture again. Like she'd been stuck with a pin and was trying not to show it. "Yes?" she said.

"The night Amanda was assaulted," he said, "do you recall hearing a car pull into her drive?"

"Oh yes," she said. "I always wake up when a car pulls into Amanda's driveway. Her driveway is right outside my bedroom window. Yes, of course I heard a car."

Pack your clothes, Anka, I thought. You're going to prison.

"I've already told all this to the police," she said.

Terrific. Sweeney's buddy Marty Coyle must have forgotten to mention that small detail.

"What time was it?" Sweeney asked.

Mrs. Dobson cocked her head to one side. "Amanda got home about two in the morning."

Both Sweeney and I perked up.

"You woke up when Amanda got home?" he asked.

She nodded.

"How do you know it was Amanda?"

"I looked out the window," she said. "I saw her."

"You *saw* her?" I asked.

She blinked and nodded.

Sweeney leaned forward. "Did you hear another car pull into the drive that night?"

She shook her head. "No, I didn't."

"And if another car *had* pulled into the drive, you're certain you would have heard it?"

"Oh, yes. Positive."

Sweeney nodded. "When you saw Amanda, was she alone?"

"Oh, yes." Mrs. Dobson bobbed her head. "All alone."

I tried not to grin. Mrs. Dobson had just stuck a pin in the prosecutor's case.

Sweeney made a few notes and asked a few more questions. But he did it mainly because he's a thorough investigator. We both knew Mrs. Dobson had given us some prime stuff.

We were out the door and in the car less than ten minutes later. Before starting the car, Sweeney turned to me and raised his eyebrows.

"What do you think?" Sweeney asked.

I gave him a grin. He deserved it. And I felt like giving it to him. "I think maybe we got ourselves ahold of some reasonable doubt."

"I think you could be right," Sweeney said. "I think if Mrs. Dobson didn't hear a car, then there was no car to be heard. And if there was no car, there was no Anka."

"She could have parked down the street," I said.

"Now why would she do that?" Sweeney asked.

"To keep from waking Mrs. Dobson up." Sweeney knew that. He was being boneheaded on purpose. And I knew the point he was looking to make. But I wasn't going to help out. I wanted him to *make* it, to convince me.

Sweeney loosened his tie. "If Anka parked down the

street, that would mean she was acting in cold blood," he said. "That would mean she planned the whole thing."

"Yep. And *that* would mean she didn't attack Amanda in a jealous lunatic passion like the prosecutor says."

Sweeney frowned and shook his head. "But that doesn't make any sense. If she planned the whole thing, why didn't she bring along a weapon?"

It was a good point. A would-be murderer couldn't count on finding a dybbuk's butt handy. "Maybe she wanted to make it look like a burglary," I suggested.

He shook his head again. "I don't buy it. I saw her. She's crazy. When you saw her at the police station, did she look like she was capable of planning something like this?"

"Nope." Anka hadn't seemed capable of planning to tie her shoes that night. Let alone plan an assault on an ex-lover. In fact, she'd acted crazier than a black dog in the summer sun.

"I don't buy cold blood either," I said.

Sweeney agreed. "Cold blood doesn't fit either the physical evidence or the accounts of the witnesses."

"Then we agree the premeditation theory sucks?" I asked.

"We agree, up to a point."

"And what is that point?" I asked.

"The point," Sweeney said, "is that if it was premeditated, it wasn't Anka who did it."

I looked at it for a moment. Twisting it in different directions. Looking for loopholes. And not finding any worth mentioning.

"Yes sir, I do believe we got us some reasonable doubt," I said. "Reasonable doubt at a reasonable price."

Sweeney nodded, started the car and began to sing along with a tune on the radio. Which is a sign that Sweeney is pleased with the world. Because Sweeney does not have what you'd call a sweet voice. Sweeney has a voice that sounds like a bear farting in soft mud.

Then suddenly he stopped singing. He leaned forward and turned off the radio.

"Wait a minute," he said.

I closed my eyes. "What am I waiting for?" I asked. I knew I wasn't going to want to hear the answer.

He didn't say anything until I opened my eyes again. "Do we agree that Anka probably didn't do this?" he asked.

"Maybe probably," I said. "She *could* have done it."

"But probably she didn't do it," Sweeney insisted.

"Maybe," I said. "Possibly. Conceivably."

"Probably," he said.

I didn't like the direction this seemed to be headed in. But what the hell, he was right. She probably didn't do it. "Okay, then. Probably."

Then Sweeney asked the question he'd been wanting to ask. The one I'd been trying to keep him from asking.

"Then who did?" he asked.

I shrugged. "I don't know. Does it matter? To us, I mean. As long as it wasn't Anka. Or as long as the police can't *prove* it was Anka."

"It would be nice to know," he said.

I shook my head. "You can't stop being a cop, can you? Damn it, Sweeney. It's not our job to find out who really did it. All we have to do is get Anka off the hook. Let the police find out who really belongs on the hook. That's what they pay the police for. Putting people on hooks."

Sweeney tapped out a drum riff on the steering wheel. "If Anka didn't do it, I'd just like to know who did. It would help Kathleen if we knew."

"Well, you and Kathleen will just have to get used to disappointment," I said.

Sweeney switched the radio back on. "Let's go check out the husband," he said.

Kevin Sweeney

Thursday Night

"Happy now?" Joop asked. "Pass the chips. Please."

I handed him the bag of potato chips. We were sitting in the office, drinking beer and eating junk food. It was almost midnight. I wasn't happy and Joop knew it. He was just trying to irritate me.

We'd spent the day checking out Charles Lowell, Amanda Owen's estranged husband. Since I was more mobile, I'd done the roadwork. Joop had stayed in the office and worked the phone.

Joop's exasperation was only partly the result of spending the day cooped up in the office. Mainly he was irritated because, despite all our efforts, we'd come up blank. Worse than blank. We'd shown that Charles Lowell might be a jerk of the highest order, but he almost certainly hadn't hit his wife in the head with a stone figurine.

He had no obvious motive. Amanda had a will, but she had nothing of any value to leave, and none of what she had was left to him. In addition, Charles's financial arrangement with her parents had been formalized as a legal contract. Joop was able to wheedle the terms of the contract out of a secretary who worked for Lowell's attorney. The contract said he'd collect the money as long as he remained married to Amanda. If there was a divorce, regardless of who initiated it, the money stopped. The same was true if Amanda died.

Charles Lowell not only didn't have a motive, he didn't even have much opportunity. Sweeney had learned that old Chuck had been at a Republican Party fund-raiser the night his wife was getting whacked in the head.

"I declare, we've gone and ruined a perfectly good suspect, thanks to your obstinacy," Joop said. "Kath can't point her finger at the husband when she *knows* the man didn't do it."

I drank some beer and signaled Joop to pass me back the chips. When Joop is being obnoxious, all you can do is wait for the episode to run its course.

"And something else, thanks to your obstinacy—is that a real word, by the way, 'obstinacy'?" he asked. "Or did I make it up?"

I told him I didn't know.

"Well, the point I'm trying to make is this. We could have left it alone," Joop said. "But no, you had to be a cop. You just had to know."

"Are you about done yet?" I asked.

Joop put on a thoughtful expression. "Yeah, I think so. Just about."

"Good."

"I could still do some personal insults," he said. "There's a whole range of—"

He was interrupted by a knock on the door. We looked at each other.

"I don't believe we're expecting company," Joop said. He took the six-cell Maglite out of a desk drawer and handed it to me. "I'd answer the door," he said. "But I'm a cripple."

I accepted the heavy steel flashlight and went to the door. We rarely have clients come to the office. Never at midnight.

"Who is it?" I asked.

"Open this door, Kevin Sweeney," Mary Margaret said. "It's powerful spooky out here."

I let her in. She gave me a hug and a kiss, told me I smelled like a brewery, and walked over to Joop. "Now what do you think you're doing, keeping my poor husband here at work at this hour?" she demanded.

"I thought it was the other way around," Joop said. "I thought he was keeping me here."

"Are you saying he'd rather be here working than at his own home with his adoring wife?" she asked.

Joop raised his hands. "You're right," he said. "It *is* my fault. I *am* keeping him here. Did I mention it was my fault?"

"Is there another beer?" Mary Margaret asked.

"Sweeney, fetch your charming wife a beer," Joop said.

While Mary Margaret drank the beer, Joop and I explained how we'd spent our day and night. Sometimes it helps to explain a situation to a third person. It makes you cover all the details, including those that you're so used to that you don't actually see them anymore.

"So all we've managed to do today," Joop said, "is to toss our best suspect down the toilet."

"Oh, that's not true," Mary Margaret said. "You also showed that your client is innocent."

"Probably innocent," I said.

"Maybe innocent," Joop said. "For all we know, Mrs. Dobson is lying right through her suburban teeth."

"What reason would she have to lie?" I asked. "To protect Anka? I doubt it. I don't think she was very fond of Anka. In fact, I don't think she liked Anka at all."

Joop picked up a potato chip and stared at it. "Maybe she was lying to cover for somebody else," he said. "You ever think of that?"

"Who?" I asked.

"Well, hell, I don't know." Joop ate the potato chip. "Okay. I admit it doesn't make any sense for her to lie about not hearing a car in the driveway."

"Why, you two are hopeless," Mary Margaret said. "And you call yourselves detectives. I doubt if you can find the noses on your own faces."

"We don't have to find the noses on our faces," Joop said. "I can see Sweeney's nose, he can see mine. We help each other find them. It's called the buddy system. We're buddies."

"What are you saying?" I asked Mary Margaret. "Have we missed something?"

Mary Margaret nodded. She held out one hand. "Here you have a man who is married to a lesbian. That poses some obvious problems, doesn't it? Their sex life can't have been very good, now could it?"

We agreed it probably hadn't been very good.

Mary Margaret held out her other hand. "And over here's his neighbor, a lonely woman whose husband is seemingly always away on business."

"Are you suggesting Charles Lowell and Callie Dobson had an affair?" I asked.

"You know, that about half makes sense," Joop said. "They could have been trashing around. The only problem is, so what? Ain't nobody accused of adultery. What does this have to do with Amanda getting her head caved in?"

"Maybe nothing," said Mary Margaret. "But if the neighbor is lying to protect somebody, maybe he's the one. She could have seen him pull into the drive."

Joop shook his head. "Sorry, that dog won't hunt. Sweeney said the husband was bending elbows with Republicans all night."

"Actually, he *could* have done it," I said. "We know what time the fund-raiser ended. But we don't know what time he got back to his apartment. He may have had time to drive all the way across town to his old house and attack his ex-wife. The question is, why would he do it?"

Mary Margaret shook her head. "The question is whether the neighbor is lying or not. If she is, who is she covering for? If she's not . . ."

"Yes?" Joop asked.

"If she's not lying," Mary Margaret said, "then I don't know what."

"We'd best go back again," Joop said.

"We have to go back," I said.

"In the morning," Mary Margaret said. "Now you have to come home."

J o o p   W h e e l e r

Friday Morning

We parked directly in front of the Dobson house. While Sweeney checked the batteries on the mini-recorder, I looked at the house. The curtains opened and Mrs. Dobson looked out.

"Five bucks," I said.

Sweeney swiveled his head far enough to see Mrs. Dobson at the window. And reached for his wallet. I'd bet him that if we parked in front of her house she'd look out the window. To check on who was out there. It's a thing that nosy neighbors do.

I didn't really know if she'd look out or not. But Sweeney was in a foul mood that morning and I was looking to find some way to distract him.

The problem was that Sweeney is an ex-cop. And the problem with ex-cops—and active cops, for that matter—is that they're idealists. In a way. They're cynical and idealistic all at the same time. They're cynical because they *expect* that certain folks will lie to them. But they're idealistic because they also believe there are folks who *won't* lie to them. Which is just nonsense, of course. Everybody lies. Some of the time.

And when cops and ex-cops think that the second group of folks *has* lied to them, the cops and ex-cops get radically angry.

Sweeney was thinking that Mrs. Callie Dobson had lied to him. And he was angry. Partly, I think, because she'd violated his understanding of the world. And partly because he liked her. Or felt sorry for her. Or something. I'd seen the way he'd smiled when she'd recalled his name the day before.

He handed me five bucks and said, "Batteries are fine."

We'd stopped at the office and picked up the mini-recorder. Just in case. You never know when a tape-recorded conversation will come in handy.

"Let's go to work," he said.

I wanted to tell Sweeney to calm down. We didn't really *know* Mrs. Dobson had lied to us. We only suspected it. And I wanted to remind Sweeney not to let his vexation screw up the interview. But that reminder would either be irrelevant, on account of he's a pro and doesn't need reminding, or it would make matters worse, on account of it would only make him angrier. I wanted to tell Sweeney to grow up.

But, since I couldn't say anything helpful, I kept my mouth shut. My old momma would have been proud.

I levered my crippled self out of the car, stuck the little tape recorder in my pocket, and limped after Sweeney.

He didn't even have to ring the doorbell. It just opened up as we walked up the steps. Like one of those doors in *Star Trek*. And Mrs. Dobson stuck her head out.

"You're back again?" she asked. She was wearing another outfit like my momma used to wear. Complete with apron.

But what she wasn't wearing was a smile. The day before, she'd been all teeth. On this day, worry lines had etched themselves into her face. She was obviously nervous. And probably a little frightened.

That seemed to calm Sweeney down. And he smiled. It wasn't pleasant to see.

"Is anything wrong?" Mrs. Dobson asked.

"I don't know." Sweeney kept smiling. "But we have a few more questions to ask. You don't mind, do you?"

She shook her head. "No, of course not," she said. But it was obvious she did. She looked at Sweeney with open concern.

I was having severely mixed emotions. Sweeney is my buddy. But I sort of felt like I should hand Mrs. Dobson a whip and a chair. On the other hand, she was plainly uncomfortable about something. And Sweeney is the best at digging out uncomfortable bits of information.

"May we come in?" I asked. There wasn't any point in doing this on the stoop.

Mrs. Dobson hesitated. But I could see what was going to happen. A few years back, my uncle Altus got himself in trouble with the law. A buddy of his had sold him a mint-condition 1948 flathead Harley-Davidson motorcycle. Sold it to him for $245 and said he'd get him the title "real soon." I was visiting Uncle Altus a few days later when the police showed up, asking if he'd mind if they looked around. Uncle Altus hesitated just like Mrs. Dobson. Then he just gave up, shook his head, led the police out to the barn, and showed them the motorcycle.

And that's what Mrs. Dobson did. She just closed her eyes, nodded, and opened the door.

Kevin Sweeney

Friday Morning

Mrs. Dobson opened the door. Joop thanked her and stepped into the foyer like he belonged there. Without another word, he limped straight down the hall. I made an "after you" gesture and we both followed Joop back to the family room. She removed her apron, and we all resumed our positions.

I took my time getting out a legal tablet. I wanted her to sweat for a bit. And she did. There was silence only for a moment, but it was a moment too long for Mrs. Dobson.

She stood and smoothed out her dress. "Can I offer you a cup of coffee?"

"No, thank you," we both said.

"I'm afraid I've become something of a caffeine addict." She smiled tensely. "You know, I've tried cutting down—I've even tried decaf, which just tastes horrible—but I can't seem to get away from it. I just have to have my coffee."

She excused herself and went into the kitchen, where we could hear her opening cupboards and drawers, rummaging around. After a moment, I stood up and signaled Joop to stay where he was. Then I followed Mrs. Dobson into the kitchen.

She was standing at the counter, carefully measuring the amount of coffee before spooning it into the filter. I leaned against the doorway. She turned to fill the pot with water, saw me out of the corner of her eye, and jumped. The glass pot dropped from her hand and bounced on the floor. I picked it up and handed it to her.

"Sorry," I said.

She looked the pot over carefully, then smiled. "Look at that," she said. "It didn't break. Not even a crack."

"I didn't mean to startle you," I said.

"Oh, no, it's quite all right. I just—well, I've always had a fear of somebody sneaking up behind me." She blushed a little. "It's silly, I know. But I'm just a woman. I'm allowed to be a little silly, aren't I."

I just looked at her.

"At least that's what my husband says. He calls me his little fluffhead."

"But you're not, are you. A fluffhead."

She looked at the pot. "No," she said. "I suppose I'm not." She turned to the sink, filled the pot with enough water for five cups of coffee, then poured it into the top of the coffee maker.

I decided it was time for a gentle form of pressure. "Would you like to tell me about it?" I asked.

"About what?"

"About what you saw that night. What you really saw."

She moved to the kitchen table and sat, her hands fidgeting with a pair of bird-shaped salt and pepper shakers.

I took the chair directly across from her and waited. She played with the salt shaker. We stayed that way until the coffee was brewed. She didn't seem to notice.

It was time to graduate to less subtle pressure. "When did the two of you become involved?" I asked. I wasn't at all sure she and Charles Lowell were involved. I wasn't even sure that she'd seen him the night Amanda was assaulted. But there are times when it's best to make a bald assertion. Even a wrong assertion can get things moving.

She put the salt shaker down abruptly and looked at me. "What?" she asked. "What?"

I repeated the question. "When did the two of you become involved?"

"Involved? What do you mean, involved?"

I shook my head. "Mrs. Dobson, please. This will be a lot easier if you don't try to play stupid."

"I wasn't involved with Amanda," she said, a thrill of

anger just audible in her voice. "I was never *involved* with her."

Amanda? "Okay," I said. "We can call it whatever you want. How would you describe it?"

She stared at me for a moment, then stood and looked out her kitchen window. I remembered she watched the birds at the feeder window while she washed her breakfast dishes.

"Mrs. Dobson?"

She turned an ear in my direction. "Yes?"

"Tell me about it," I said.

Her shoulders slumped. "I woke up when I heard a car in Amanda's drive," she said. "I got up. I don't know why. Just to make sure who it was, I guess. It's a habit. I would have gone right back to sleep, except Amanda didn't get out of the car. She just sat there."

"What did you do?" I asked.

"Well, I thought something might be wrong. So I put on a dress, a sundress"—she touched the hem of her dress— "and went outside. I was worried. I wanted to see if anything was wrong."

But nothing was wrong. At least none of the things she'd been worried about—heart attack, drunken stupor, drug overdose. Amanda had shut off the engine but not the head-lamps, and she was sitting in the driver's seat of the car, crying.

"It was because of that woman, her Jewish friend," Callie Dobson said. "I knew it right away, even though she didn't say so. So I told her she was better off without her. And you know what? She stopped crying and said, 'You're right, I am.'"

"Then what happened?" I asked.

"Then she cheered right up. She said we ought to have a drink. To celebrate her independence."

"And did you?" I asked.

She nodded. "I didn't really think I should, it was awfully

late. But she insisted. She said we were two women alone in the world and if we couldn't have a drink when we wanted one, we ought to be ashamed of ourselves."

Mrs. Dobson returned to the table and resumed toying with the salt and pepper shakers.

Amanda had insisted they go to her house because she had a couple of bottles of champagne in the refrigerator and it was a night for celebration. Despite her reluctance, Mrs. Dobson let herself be persuaded. She and Amanda spent the next ninety minutes drinking champagne, talking, listening to music, and giggling. They giggled their way through both bottles.

"It was as if I were back in college," Mrs. Dobson said. "We used to have . . . I guess you'd call them pajama parties. It was that same feeling. Just us girls."

The coffee was done. She continued to sit there, so I went to the cupboards and searched until I found the cups. I filled two of them. One for her, one for me.

"Do you take it black?" I asked.

She seemed to come slowly out of a trance. "A little milk," she said. "I'll get it."

"Please, let me."

She hesitated, then nodded. There was a quart of skim milk in the refrigerator. I poured a little into her coffee and set the cup beside her.

"You were saying it was just like in college," I said. "The first time we spoke, you mentioned knowing some lesbians in college."

"People *said* they were lesbians," she said. "But you know how people gossip. I certainly didn't know anything about it."

It was a mistake to bring it up. The feeling in the room changed instantly and I thought I might have blown it. I tried to ease my way back in.

"Still, it's the sort of thing a person thinks about," I said. "You wonder what it would be like."

She nodded. "I suppose you do. Maybe that was it. That and the champagne. I don't know. It just seemed to happen." She blew on her coffee and took a small, prim sip. "I let her do it to me. I knew it was wrong, but I let her do it." She shook her head and stared into her coffee cup. "I couldn't find it in me to say no."

She said she'd spent the rest of the night with Amanda. She didn't say what they'd done together, but it didn't take much imagination to figure it out.

"At some point I fell asleep," she said. "When I woke up, I couldn't believe where I was, what I'd done. It was still dark out. I was . . . I was so ashamed. Giving in to her like that. I wanted to get dressed and go right home."

She wanted to. "But?" I asked.

"But Amanda insisted on making me a cup of chamomile tea before I left. She could tell I was upset. She was sensitive that way. She wanted to bring me the tea in . . . in the bed. But I couldn't. I had to get out of that bed. I put on my dress and sat in a chair on the sun porch."

Amanda, she said, was wearing nothing but a long Oriental robe, which she refused to tie closed. She'd sat on the floor next to Mrs. Dobson's feet.

"She kept touching me," Callie Dobson said, "telling me it was okay, that what had happened between us was natural and okay, that I shouldn't get upset." Mrs. Dobson ran her finger along the rim of the cup. "She said she'd felt the same way the first time, dirty like that. She said that we were alike."

I doubted that was a smart thing for Amanda to say. I don't think Callie Dobson wanted to be like Amanda Owen.

"I didn't want her to touch me," she continued. "But I didn't know how to make her stop."

I made some sort of understanding noise.

"And then she put . . . she put her head, you know, down there. She kept teasing me, saying 'Tell me what you want.' She made me say dirty things, disgusting things."

Mrs. Dobson said she'd wanted to push Amanda's head away, and at the same time she'd wanted to pull her closer. She couldn't bring herself to do either. Instead, she put her arms behind her head and grabbed the windowsill. On the windowsill, directly behind the chair, was a stone statue.

"Tell me about the statue," I said. "What did you do with it?"

She stared at her coffee cup. "I felt . . . like something was about to happen to me. I felt this . . . this *heat*. This *rushing*. And I had to make it stop."

"How did you do that?" I asked.

"I hit her with the statue," she said.

I discovered I'd been holding my breath. I let it out as quietly as possible. "What happened when you did that?"

Amanda Owen collapsed to the floor and curled up in a ball. She rolled over, put her hands to her head and groaned. Slowly and with great effort, she managed to stagger to her feet. Her head was bleeding.

"When she got to her feet, I jumped up too," Mrs. Dobson said. "I was horrified by what had happened. I knew I'd done it. But it didn't seem as if I had. It was as if I were watching somebody else."

She watched as Amanda stumbled against the door to the sun porch and opened it. Amanda staggered, clutched for the rail, missed, and fell down the steps.

"I don't know how long I stood there," she said. "Probably not very long." She frowned and shook her head slowly. "I realized I was still holding the statue. I dropped it and looked out at Amanda."

Mrs. Dobson sipped her coffee prissily. "It was very odd," she said. "It was almost as if I'd been waiting for something like that to happen all my life. In just a few hours

I'd ruined everything, my entire life, just as I always knew I would."

She went home and took a shower. While in the shower, she thought of a plan. She went back to Amanda's house, threw the champagne bottles into the bushes on her side of the fence, washed the glasses, put them away, then dialed 911.

I heard a sharp click. Joop was in the doorway, leaning against the jamb, the office tape recorder in his hand.

"What was that?" Mrs. Dobson asked. "What's going on?"

"Sorry," Joop said. "Ran out of tape." He held up the recorder. "We have to tape all this," he said. "You understand."

I expected her to get angry or frightened, but she didn't. It didn't seem to matter to her. Joop stuck another tape in the recorder.

"What's going to happen to me?" she asked.

"I don't know," I said.

"You know, I'm glad I told you," she said, with something like a smile. "It's been bothering me. I couldn't even tell my therapist about it." She finished her coffee. "Can I get you another cup?"

"No, thank you," I said. "I'm afraid we have to go."

She walked us to the door. "Thank you so much for coming," she said.

I took out one of my business cards and wrote a name and telephone number on the back. "I want you to call this man," I said, giving it to her. "He's a lawyer, a good one. I want you to call him and tell him what you've told me. Okay?"

"My husband has a lawyer," she said.

"Probably not a criminal lawyer. This man is one of the best. Tell him I was here. Tell him I told you to call. And then you do whatever he tells you to do. Okay?"

She nodded. But I had the feeling she didn't really understand what I was saying.

"Do you want us to wait while you call him?" I asked.

She looked at the card and didn't speak.

Joop reached out and touched her shoulder. "Would you like me to call him for you?" he asked.

She nodded. "Would you?"

"Sure."

"I'm sorry to be such a bother," she said. "I guess my husband is right. I need a man to tell me what to do."

Joop Wheeler

All but one of the charges against Anka were dropped a few days after I taped Callie Dobson's confession over coffee. Kath had turned over a copy of the tape to the prosecutor. Who was a spiteful, low-rent son of a bitch who lacked the grace to just let go. He still wanted to press the disturbing the peace charge from the Roadhouse Motel. And he probably would have, if his boss hadn't sat on him.

Having the charges dropped didn't make a whole hell of a lot of difference for Anka. At least not at first. The psych unit at St. Albans kept her another seven weeks before deciding she was no longer a threat to anybody. Including herself. Which meant they'd drugged the poetry voice into silence.

The biggest difference was that she had friends again. All the folks who had shunned Anka when she was arrested reappeared grinning like Cheshire cats as soon as she was cleared. Fickle, is what I'd call her friends.

Still, they threw a party for her at Schotzie's the first weekend after she was released. Cotton called and invited me. And Sweeney and Mary Margaret and Kath O'Mara, of course.

I told Cotton I'd come if I could bring a baseball bat. Which she found funny. Strange woman.

I hadn't planned on going originally. But Mary Margaret was hot for it. And Sweeney said he'd go. And when Kath called and said she'd like to see Schotzie's, I'd changed my mind quick as a wink. I also suggested we try the new Ethiopian restaurant afterward. Which pleased Kath and Mary Margaret. Sweeney wanted to know if he could get a decent cheeseburger there.

I hadn't seen much of either Kath or Stevie since the case ended. The fall semester started at the university, and Stevie was busy teaching. Kath had a big personal-injury trial to prepare for. And Sweeney and I had our snooping to do.

I'd asked Kath out to dinner almost immediately after the case ended, and she'd agreed. Unfortunately, I had to cancel at the last minute. A client thought her semisuicidal son had driven up to New Hampshire and was going to drown himself. She wanted me to go after him and stop him. So I went after him. Turned out he'd just gone up there for the fishing.

I missed a date with Kath O'Mara to find a boy who was looking for lake salmon. I thought about killing him my ownself.

We'd made other attempts to get together, but something had always come up. I was beginning to believe it just wasn't going to happen. Until she called about Anka's party.

Schotzie's was a lot more quiet than the Saturday night I'd walked in and got my silly ass whupped. Stevie was there when we arrived. She gave me a kiss on the cheek. And Deirdre, the TS, was there. Who also gave me a kiss on the cheek. And so was Sweeney's homely shrink, Leah Rifkin.

He was right about her, I have to admit. The woman was downright unsightly. No way to get around it. Except for when she opened her mouth and spoke. When we were introduced and she told me it was a pleasure to finally meet me, it was all I could do to keep from crawling up next to her and putting my head puppylike in her lap.

Anka was at a table near the bar, smiling shyly. And maybe a little crazily. Surrounded by women. All of whom probably wanted to sleep with her, just like she'd said.

Cotton slapped me on the shoulder. "Where's your baseball bat?" she asked. "Didn't have the balls to bring it?"

"I got the balls," I said. "But yours are bigger."

She seemed to think that was funny and slapped me on the shoulder again. She bought me a beer and we started a game of nine-ball on that great pool table. Hannah stood nearby, sipping on a club soda and keeping an eye on me. In case I took it into my unfathomable heterosexual mind to commit some unspeakable heterosexual act, I guess.

Mary Margaret and Stevie were laughing off in a corner. And Sweeney—I swear to God—Sweeney was flirting with Deirdre. Kath was chatting quietly with Anka and the shrink.

I began to relax. And I felt this huge smile come over my face. Everything was going to be okay.

Cotton beat me two out of three. Of course, she knew the table better, being it was her bar. But I'm a good loser, most times. So I bought her a beer.

After the game, I saw Kath and Stevie having a little chat, so I wandered over and joined them. They were talking about Callie Dobson.

"Is she going to go to prison?" Stevie asked.

Kath shook her head. "I doubt it. She probably won't even have to go to trial. The State has offered to let her plead to an aggravated misdemeanor, but I'd be surprised if she took it."

"Why?" Stevie asked. "She'd be getting off easy."

"That's because you know she's guilty," Kath said.

"But so do they," Stevie said. "They heard her confession, didn't they? The one Joop taped?"

"Ah, but that may not be enough," I smiled. "They may *know* she's guilty. But they still have to *prove* it in court."

Kath explained that the only real evidence the prosecutor had against Callie was the confession she made to us. "And there are legal problems with the confession," she said.

"Legal problems?"

Kath nodded. "Statements made against the interest of the declarant and which tend to expose the declarant to criminal liability and exculpate the accused aren't generally admissible in court," she said. "Unless they're supported by corroborating evidence, and Callie's isn't. Callie's lawyer has an excellent chance of getting the confession suppressed."

Stevie looked confused.

"It's lawyer talk," I said. "What it means is this—no confession, no case. Callie Dobson walks."

Stevie looked shocked. "Doesn't that bother you?"

I shook my head. "It isn't going to help anybody if Callie Dobson goes to prison. Certainly won't help Amanda. Won't help Mrs. Dobson deal with her problems. Whatever they are."

"But she could have killed Amanda," Stevie said. "It's just a fluke that she didn't."

"Stevie's got a point," Kath said. "The real problem with the way you guys handled this is that now there's no way Callie Dobson can be required to get treatment."

"I suspect her husband will stick her into treatment real quick," I said. "But bottom line—she's not a dangerous woman. Not really. Not as long as you're not a woman performing oral sex on her."

Stevie shook her head. "Justice," she said with a sigh. "Well, I suppose I'd better get used to it."

"Why?" Kath asked.

She gave us a shy smile. "Because I've decided to apply for a private detective's license."

Kath gave her a hug. "Good for you," she said.

I got in on the hugging and congratulating. No point in missing out on the good stuff.

"You're not going to give up teaching, are you?" I asked. Teaching paid well and had better hours. And cleaner clients.

Stevie said she'd do it part-time. Evenings and summers. "I don't know if I'm cut out for it or not. Part of it is pretty sleazy. . . . No offense," she said to me.

I waved it off. How could I be offended by that?

"But I've never felt so *engaged* before. When we were out there, talking to people, it was so *real*. Even though none of it helped in the end, it felt important at the time."

I nodded and grinned. Being "engaged" is one of the reasons Sweeney and I do the work. But it's also what makes the work so painful. Which is why I didn't mind if Callie Dobson walked. There's no excuse for banging somebody in the head with a dybbuk, but when she told us what happened, I could hear the pain in her voice. So could Sweeney. Which was why he'd immediately set her up with a lawyer who'd keep her from making a legally admissable confession to the police. All that because we'd gotten "engaged" in her life.

I didn't say any of that. This was a party, after all. And the whole point of a party is that you're supposed to have fun.

"What's strange is the polarity," Stevie said. "I was happy when Anka was cleared, and at the same time I was depressed. That poor woman was so afraid of her sexuality that she had to try to destroy the person who brought it out. Stupid," she said. "Stupid and sad."

Welcome to the world, I wanted to say. But the mood was already getting a little too somber for a celebration. I was about to suggest turning up the tunes, moving the tables back and dancing like heathens. But Kath had to ask one more question. It's a thing she should have learned in law school; it's a mistake to ask a question you don't know the answer to.

"Is there any word about Amanda?" she asked.

There was, Stevie told us. And, of course, it wasn't good. Which I could have predicted. Which was why I hadn't asked.

"She's alive, but I guess she's brain-dead," Stevie said. "She can't breathe on her own anymore and they've put her on some sort of life-support system. The rumor is her husband and her parents are going to ask the courts to let them turn the machines off. At least that's the rumor. We don't really know. Her parents won't let any of her gay or lesbian friends visit."

"Jesus," Kath said.

Well, you had to ask, I thought. "What do her parents have to do with it?" I asked. "Seems like the decision ought to be her husband's."

"He may have the say," Stevie said, "but her parents have the purse."

"Oh. It's that way, is it?" I asked.

"That's the rumor," Stevie said. She waved at somebody who came in, and excused herself.

Kath looked at her drink, then put it sadly on the bar. No point in turning up the tunes and moving back the tables now. She wasn't in a dancing mood.

But I told myself we still had the Ethiopian restaurant in front of us. Things could pick up if we broke out of Schotzie's soon and got ourselves around some good Ethiopian food. All was not lost. Yet.

I looked for Sweeney, to see if he and Mary Margaret were about ready to go. They were standing in the middle of a little knot of women, laughing. And holding hands. And just seeing them made a quantum improvement in my mood.

"Joop?" Kath said. She sounded a little sad.

"Yeah?"

"I'm not sure I'm in the mood for Ethiopian food tonight."

I nodded. I was disappointed, but I understood. I like to think I'm a sensitive sort of guy. Or a sort of sensitive guy. Learning that Amanda Owen was brain-dead—and got that way simply because she picked the wrong person to go down on—it could put a person off their feed. Even a tough woman like Kath O'Mara. Of course, she wouldn't feel like going out to dinner.

Or maybe she just didn't want to have dinner with me.

"It's all right," I said. "Not to worry. Maybe some other time. The restaurant would probably be crowded at this hour anyway."

And then Kath smiled. And she touched me on the wrist. "How about Chinese instead?"

And red lightning lightened through my blood.